NEVER SAY NEVER

Elizabeth Waite

This first world edition published in Great Britain 2007 by
SEVERN HOUSE PUBLISHERS LTD of
9–15 High Street, Sutton, Surrey SM1 1DF.
This first world edition published in the USA 2007 by
SEVERN HOUSE PUBLISHERS INC of
595 Madison Avenue, New York, N.Y. 10022.

British Library Cataloguing in Publication Data

Waite, Elizabeth,
    Never say never
    1. World War, 1939-1945 - England - Fiction
    2. Hampshire (England) - Social conditions - 20th century - Fiction
    I. Title
    823.9'14 [F]

    ISBN-13: 978-0-7278-6505-2   (cased)
    ISBN-13: 978-1-84751-013-6   (trade paper)

All Severn House titles are printed on acid-free paper.

Typeset by Palimpsest Book Production Ltd.,
Grangemouth, Stirlingshire, Scotland.
Printed and bound in Great Britain by
MPG Books Ltd., Bodmin, Cornwall.

Part One

North Waltham, Hampshire, 1930

One

'That's it then, ladies. Please think hard about what you have seen and been told this afternoon. I think Mrs Joan Miles has certainly opened our eyes to the fact that we are very privileged to live here and that our children are far more fortunate than the boys and girls that don't have a family and have spent their young lives living in institutions.'

Kate Simmons, chairwoman of the Women's Guild, which met in the village hall every Wednesday afternoon, closed the meeting with an urgent appeal to all the members.

In her early fifties, Kate was a remarkable lady, sprightly with dark wavy hair, and an enormous ability to make folk laugh. Widowed early in her married life she devoted her time and great energy to helping others and ensuring that communication and comradeship was kept alive in their village. In short, because of Kate's efforts and her willing band of helpers no person need be lonely. Should there be a problem that Kate couldn't solve or at least offer advice on, she always knew someone who could.

Emma Pearson walked with several of her friends towards the village shop, the time was a quarter to four and their children wouldn't be coming out of school until four o'clock. She didn't think she would ever forget everyone's emotional tears when pictures of those young children had been shown to them. There wasn't one mother that hadn't been touched by what they had learnt this afternoon. Although they lived in what strangers might say was a quiet backwater there was not one amongst them that wasn't aware of the sheer misery that unemployment and poverty were causing nationwide. Only last night an announcer on the wireless had reported that there was now over two million unemployed in Britain.

This afternoon they had been shown picture slides of the

demonstrations held in major cities, where food was being handed out to patient queues of jobless men. In fact the speaker, Mrs Joan Miles, had said that for the first time the queues had included women each carrying a banner stating that they were asking for food and jobs, not charity.

The state that the country was in was unbelievable.

Mrs Miles had emphasized that the Wall Street Crash that had occurred in America in October of the previous year had been the greatest disaster ever to strike the financial world, wiping out millions of dollars of investments at a stroke. The consequences had been worldwide, the beginning of the Great Depression, causing hunger and poverty on both sides of the Atlantic.

'And we thought we were hard done by!' Aggie Brownlow broke the silence.

Aggie was hardly ever heard to complain though most would agree that she had cause enough. Her husband had died two years ago in 1928 in a farming accident. She had been left with three children, two boys who at the time had been aged four and six and a wee baby girl of eighteen months. There wasn't a day that passed that Aggie didn't thank God for her brother, John Chapman and his wife Mary.

John was a farm labourer and Mary worked in the dairy on the same farm, they had no children of their own, living in a tied cottage on the biggest farm in Waltham. These two kind hard-working relations were life savers to Aggie and her brood, keeping them supplied with fresh vegetables, rabbits and the odd chicken, not forgetting the fact they that also shared their ration of free milk with Aggie.

Emma Pearson took up the challenge. She had a plain no-nonsense look on her face as she quickly said, 'I've never thought we were hard done by. Born an' bred here, I've felt privileged all me life. I don't think this village is the back of beyond, quite the reverse actually. Bit of God's own country North Waltham is an' always will be. It's only twelve miles north of Winchester an' seven miles to Basingstoke if you want to do a big shop. As Kate said, what this Mrs Miles has told us this afternoon has brought home to us just how lucky we all are. It has made us aware of those poor little mites that have spent years shut away in homes. I think my two children have a lot to be grateful for. They've never known what it is to have to go without a good meal. They've always been surrounded by folk that love them dearly.'

Emma's husband Sam, the local blacksmith, was a burly man who looked tough enough to rip a man's head from his shoulders yet was as gentle as a lamb when dealing with their two daughters, Emily, aged nine, and Bella, who had been born just eleven months earlier. They were like twins because wherever you saw one girl the other was sure to be within a very short distance. Emily had been given her grandma's Christian name but God alone knew where Sam had come up with the name of Arabella for their second child. Though the only time her name had been used as a whole was at her christening.

Emma smiled with pleasure when she thought of her two girls. They were as alike as two peas in a pod; slim and pretty with thick glossy chestnut-coloured hair that hung well below their shoulders and the kind of skin that was only acquired from living in good country air. One of her greatest delights was brushing, combing and plaiting their hair as she got them both ready to go to school. She was sorry that she had never been able to give Sam a son, she knew full well that he yearned for one, but on the other hand she was eternally grateful that neither Emily nor Bella had inherited their father's brawny limbs or thick-set features.

Sam made time for the village boys and never turned one of them away from his forge if they wanted to watch him heating his irons in the furnace then hammering and beating the metal to form many farm implements. He also gave of his time to the Boys' Brigade, marching with the band on occasions when there was something for the village to commemorate.

'That's as maybe,' said Janet Swimford. She was just a few weeks short of forty-five and had a plain sort of face and mousy-coloured hair yet she stood out in a crowd because of her ability to always look smartly dressed. Probably because her husband Claude worked in a solicitor's office and she felt she had to keep up appearances. Janet acted as the tea lady and organized various outings for the members for the Women's Guild. 'But we haven't got a lot to brag about when you get down to the basic bits of life,' she added.

'If you're talking about the fact that we haven't got water on tap in the house you want to remember that although we

have to draw it up from a well in the garden using a bucket
on a rope it's pure, not polluted anyway, an' I certainly don't
mind having the lavatory at the end of the garden. Much
healthier I'd say than having it fixed inside of your house.'
Emma's tone was sharp.

Emma was short and plump with cheeks like rosy apples,
a true countrywoman with a heart of gold but when making
a point she could be very forthright. Yet, if Kate Simmons
was not around it was Emma that folk in trouble mainly turned
too.

'What about electricity?' Aggie wasn't going to be left out
of this discussion. 'Seems every other place is getting it.
Replacing gas lighting.'

'We'll get it eventually,' Emma assured her. 'Then I'd like
to see the look on your face when you have to start putting
money into slot meters. By then it won't only be for electricity it might be for gas as well. Come the day when we
haven't got a shilling, or whatever it is these meters will take,
what are we going to do then?'

'Same as we do now. Light the lamps or use candles,' several
voices chorused together.

The thought of having to find a shilling every time the
light went out shook Aggie Brownlow. She had a hard enough
job as it was to make ends meet, even though friends had
rallied round when her Joe had died, still did, especially
Emma Pearson. She'd share her last penny with anyone that
needed it.

The films slides they had watched this afternoon, showing
showed the plight of the youngsters who were in homes in
the poorest parts of London, had certainly had her counting
her blessings. Even before they had left the hall she had made
the decision to put her name on the list of folk who were
willing to take one or more of these children in order that
they might have a holiday. God love them, it was more than
likely that some of them had never even seen a tree.

According to this afternoon's speaker more than half the
children that were in their care had been institutionalized from
the day they were born. Or perhaps a more appropriate word
might be abandoned because some babies had been found on
the steps of churches or in shop doorways, without a soul
coming forward to claim them. The young girls who had given

birth to these babies had probably felt they had no choice but to relinquish all responsibility for their offspring. There was such a huge divide between rich and poor.

This group of kindly countrywomen looked thoughtfully at each other. They had reached the village shop. It was mainly a newsagent's but it also sold sweets and many essential grocery items.

Owned by Joe Cadman and his wife Lucy, who lived in the flat above the shop, it was the hub of village life. Mr Cadman was a tall dark-haired man who seldom seemed to smile. Children treated him with respect mainly because they were slightly afraid of him. Joe Cadman was used to this group of woman visiting his shop on a regular basis on Wednesday afternoons.

He greeted each lady and asked if they had had an interesting meeting. Many voices answered him.

'We're all being asked to consider taking one or two underprivileged children into our homes for two weeks in order to give them a holiday.'

'And where are these children coming from and is anybody going to be responsible for the group as a whole?' Joe Cadman asked. He was a practical man.

'A lady named Mrs Joan Miles showed us slides on a kind of magic lantern. They showed where and how the children were housed in London. One would have to have a heart of stone not to have felt we needed to help,' Janet Swimford said.

Dorothy James, a quiet middle-aged woman, mother of four children, put a restraining hand on Janet's arm.

'We've talked about how we live and we all know we don't go short of much. Most of us grow our own vegetables, Aggie's brother makes sure we get a rabbit now and again and Emma's husband is a great one for bringing down a pheasant or two, yet we haven't touched on the subject that we have just been lectured on.'

The whole group fell silent.

'Well?' Dorothy waited a minute. No reply was forthcoming so she asked 'This Children's Country Holiday Project, are we going to cooperate?'

The women looked at each other, no one wanted to be the first to make the decision. Then in complete unison they said, 'Of course we are.'

'It wasn't only kiddies from London that Mrs Miles was on about. What about those children that were in a home in Portsmouth?' Aggie said. 'Those two little lads whose father had been drowned at sea when he was out with a fishing fleet? They in particular made my heart ache. Their poor mother, what a decision she had to make. Couldn't afford to keep them so she didn't have much choice but to place them in a home. I wanted to shout out there and then that I would take them.'

The circle of friends all turned to face Aggie who had just made this emotional outburst. She already had three children of her own and no husband. Aggie made ends meet by working in the local pub and relying on the generosity of her brother and his wife. Not that her children went short of much, her brother and the locals saw to that. That was another good point about living in a quiet village, folk looked out for each other.

'You're right there, I think we all felt the same,' Emma said sighing. 'You could almost convince yourself that Mrs Miles was talking about children from another country, some of those young kiddies looked as if they hadn't had a good meal for ages. Not one child was plump and bonnie like our own children.'

'What got to me was that the streets and the surrounding areas where all the homes appear to be. Narrow, dark and dirty was the only description that would fit.' Kate Simmons spoke for the first time since leaving the hall.

'When we look around us at the fields, trees, bushes and even the village pond I don't think we have any option other than to say yes. Surely each and every household in the village can take a child or two into their home for a couple of weeks.'

Janet Swimford cleared her throat, thereby getting the ladies' attention.

'Since it has always been my job to organize various entertainments and outings for members of the Guild I will check the diary and the first evening that the village hall is free I will call a meeting. Meanwhile, please give a lot of thought to the idea of cooperating with this Children's Country Holiday Project and decide if you can take just one child or more. Just remember that Mrs Miles stressed that if you do take children into your home it will be for a period of two weeks.'

That reminder gave all the women food for thought. Having bought their bits and bobs and handed over their money to Mr Cadman, the group then spent five minutes explaining to Lucy Cadman, who had just put in an appearance, the idea of the Country Holiday Project.

'We aim to hold a meeting in the village hall to discuss the whys and wherefores,' Janet explained to Lucy. 'You will come, won't you?'

'Of course, so will Joe, I'm sure, and if you are able to get some pamphlets printed advertising the meeting we shall be more than happy to display them in our shop. The more people we can get involved the more worthwhile the scheme will be. By the way who exactly is sponsoring this Country Holiday Project? Folk will need to be assured that not only is it a worthwhile thing to do but that there will be a trustworthy organization co-ordinating the plan.'

'Mrs Miles did say that if we should agree to take any of these children a body of men from the Toc H Society will come to the village and not only outline their plans but will readily answer any questions that each of you probably want answers too.' Janet nodded head to emphasize her words. After all, she under stood a little about legal matters since her Claude worked in a solicitor's office.

Each and every one of the women were asking themselves, would they be able to cope with children who were not used to family life, let alone country life?

United they were determined to do their best.

The band of friends made their way to the school gates. Soon after the church clock struck four, the afternoon quietness was shattered as the children ran across the playground. Emma's two were the first to reach her. Usually Emily was only a few yards ahead of her sister but this afternoon she had a concerned look on her face. She loudly called out, 'Mum, our Bella's had a nasty fall.'

Emma's heart was thumping as she looked at her youngest daughter.

Bella's curly, reddish-brown hair was a mass of tangles, one side of her face had a deep scratch covered with dry blood and one knee was grazed, ingrained with dirt. Her pinafore was so tattered it looked only fit for the rag bag. Yet despite these clear signs that she had taken a tumble, Bella looked robustly healthy. She also had a remarkable air of happy self-assurance as she threw herself into her mother's arms.

'What on earth has happened to you?' her mother cried out as she hastily drew a white handkerchief from her handbag, knelt down and tied it around Bella's knee.

'We've been playing netball and my side won,' Bella said gleefully. Then more quietly she added, 'I was just about to pass the ball for a bigger girl to shoot because I'm not tall enough to reach the goal net when I tripped over. It would have to be in the goal area where the ground is all gravely but honestly, Mum, it's not as bad as it looks. Only the side of my face hurts a little bit. Miss Kingston was going to clean me up but as it was almost time to come home I said you would do it, Mum.'

Emma tut-tutted, took Bella's face between both of her hands and looked good and hard at the scratches.

'We'll call in to Mr Packard's chemist shop on the way home, he'll sort you out. I've got a big bottle of witch hazel indoors that will take the soreness away.'

Everybody called out goodbye to each other and as Emma walked on, one daughter on each side of her, both holding her hands, she thought she must be one of the luckiest women in the world to have two such lovely girls and a good man like Sam as her husband.

Two

The whole village was completely absorbed with the idea of having children from the poorer parts of London to come and have a holiday in the country. Individual families were being asked to take two or more children into their homes and care for them for a period of fourteen days.

Most were more than willing, yet it was only natural that the women were anxious about whether they would be capable of coping with children coming from what to them would seem a virtually different world. Mrs Miles had pointed out that quite a number of the children had never known family life. Living in an institution every day was monotonous and subject to strict control.

How would they react to freedom?

There was one other point that was slightly off-putting. Each woman who had put her name forward as willing to take a child into her home had to agree that a member of the local council should be allowed to visit their house and be assured that the accommodation that was being offered would be up to a certain standard. At first there had been a right old argument at the meeting of the Women's Guild. An intrusion! was the general feeling amongst the women.

As always it was Kate Simmons that had calmed the troubled waters.

'We aren't ashamed of our homes, are we?' she had asked quietly. 'Let's bear in mind that these will be young children being brought into our midst and it is only right that every precaution is taken to see that their stay will be not only an enjoyable one but a safe and happy one.'

Of course there was not one amongst them that could disagree with that.

Even so all the women set to work and did an extra bit of dusting and polishing.

The Pearsons's home was at the end of a terrace, which meant that they had the benefit of more ground. Not only did they have a large back garden but also a large plot along the side of the house. The front street was cobbled and across the cobbles were a row of identical houses all with wooden sash windows. Emma had been born in one of the houses opposite, number fourteen – her mother and father's house when they'd been alive. Both of her own children had been born at home in the house that she and Sam had rented from the day they had got married.

Like her mother had, Emma kept the front of her house looking smart. The walls of the house were solid yellow stone and the front door was professionally wood-grained and looked very smart. She was also very proud of the fact that she possessed a brass door knocker and a wide letter box. She had to be really busy to disrupt her weekly routine of applying Brasso to these every Wednesday morning, completing the job by vigorous rubbing with a soft yellow duster so callers were able to see their reflection. Local friends and neighbours never came to the front door. They always walked along the side path that led to the back door, it opened directly into the scullery, which followed through to the kitchen.

The council wouldn't find fault because the lavatory was outside in the back garden. Everybody's was. Of course it meant going outside in all weathers but it would be June when the children from London arrived. The cubicle had a brick interior, the walls of which were whitewashed, the seat was wooden and scrubbed by Emma every Saturday morning. A paraffin lantern stood on the sill of the small window and Sam always lit this lamp as darkness fell which made night-time visits a little less dodgy. The door to this lavatory had a four-inch gap, top and bottom, and the wind, rain and snow certainly made sure no one lingered in there longer than was necessary. The greengrocer supplied their toilet paper for free. That might sound weird to some but it was true. Oranges came packed in wooden crates, each single orange was wrapped in tissue paper which bore the grower's name. Sam collected these empty boxes, into which all the tissue paper had been pushed, from the weekly market at closing time. He chopped the wood and stacked it ready for lighting the fires and the tissue paper was given to Emma. A precious commodity. Each wrapper was carefully smoothed out and strung up for use in the lavatory. Much softer than newspaper!

Sam returned this favour by making sure that the greengrocer's cart-horse was kept well shod.

Household baths were taken in a large tin bath, which was placed in front of a roaring fire when the weather was cold. Her girl's hair was well washed by their mother using a soft brown jelly-like soap which came in a large round tin and was said to keep hair free from nits.

Emma had discussed with her husband the idea of having a couple of children to stay. He was wholeheartedly for the scheme yet he hardly knew what to say that would help to quell Emma's fears. This uncertainty was so unlike her.

With her own two girls she was never panicky. When Bella had had a really bad chesty cough it was her mother that had coped with it. No doctor's advice was sought.

Yes, his Emma had opinions of her own. 'Self assured' was how he would describe her and the women in the village had come to depend on Emma's sound judgement. If they did agree to take a couple of children into their home he had no fears that his Emma would be a good influence on them, patient, caring, loving, yes, but at the same time she'd stand no nonsense.

'Are we crazy?' Dorothy James whispered to Emma as they slid along the bench seat to make room for two more women to sit down.

It was a lovely warm June evening, the windows in the village hall were wide open and the hall was already packed although there was still ten minutes to go before the meeting was scheduled to start.

'No, I don't think we're crazy,' Emma answered quickly. 'I rather fancy that what we've learnt over the last two weeks has made us count our blessings and realize just how lucky we are. I am a bit fearful though, looking after one's own children is fine but will I be able to cope with other little mites?'

'Course you will,' Dorothy assured her. 'You're a born mother.'

There was no more time for small talk.

The Reverend Michael Coyle was standing centre stage and

calling the meeting to order. Looking around the hall he inclined his head slightly before saying, 'Good evening, ladies and gentlemen.'

There were only a handful of men in the audience. In the main the men in the village had no objection to young children from institutions being brought down to the country to have a holiday. It was a charitable thing to do, but the brunt of looking after them was down to the women folk and therefore the men saw no need to attend these meetings set up by the church.

Reverend Coyle had little to say on the matter, he knew no more than most of the local women had already learnt from Mrs Miles. It was sufficient. Mrs Miles had taken a lot of trouble to visit folks in their own homes, not only to ask for help but to give advice and there wasn't one woman who did not agree that she was a great organizer. Once or twice she had taken advice from an inspector and had endeavoured to persuade a family that there just was not enough room in their cottage to take in more children and that no one would think badly of them should they explain that they would not be able to cope.

Michael Coyle was leaning back against the far wall of the platform, telling himself that he couldn't think straight because of all the chattering that was going on. He would leave them a while longer, better that all doubts were voiced now rather than later.

Emma Pearson had made her decision. She had discussed it at great length with Sam and they'd agreed to take two children. She wasn't too bothered whether they were boys or girls but Sam was all for having boys.

He had said it would liven up their house to have boys out in their yard kicking a football about. Emma knew who would be out there with them should such a situation come about. Sam was still a lad at heart.

Finally the reverend tapped the table three times with a wooden gavel. There was much scraping of feet, nodding of heads and last minute comments before order was restored and the hall became quiet.

'In order to shorten the time there will be three sheets being distributed amongst you,' he called out loudly. 'Please print your name and address clearly and the number of children that you feel you are able to offer accommodation to. There is also a column where you may state whether you would prefer to have boys or girls but there is no guarantee.'

The reverend stepped back and the papers began to be distributed. It was an unusual silence that descended on the assembly and while Emma waited for the paper to reach her she looked up at Michael Coyle and was unable to stifle a heavy sigh. If ever a man had cause to lose his faith in God then it was this man. As she stared into his kind, attractive face, and noticed the wide smiling mouth, the deep dark brown eyes, the thick brown hair, she felt angry. Why had his life been so tragic?

A lorry had taken a sharp bend in the road far too quickly, mounted the pavement and Ivy, Michael's wife, and his two young sons – Eddie, five years old, and Peter, just three – were all crushed against the side of the village pub.

Ivy and Eddie had been killed outright. Little Peter had lived for four days after the accident. Michael was such a good man. What had he ever done wrong to have to suffer such a loss? He had left the village to stay at a retreat for six months, but he had returned to the village saying this was where his family was buried and this was where his life's work was. That had happened two years ago. You never ever heard him complain either, indeed the reverend was always ready to advise or comfort those that were sick or in need but there were times when Emma would see him and catch a glance of such sadness on his face that her own heart ached for him.

The papers began to circulate and soon Dorothy was passing a sheet to Emma. As she read down one side of the list and halfway down the other her lips were set in a tight line . . . plenty had pencilled in two, a few three. . . but there was only one four and that was Mr and Mrs Ford, who had a big house with six bedrooms. That very fact gave Emma food for thought. The Fords were an elderly couple, their two grown-up sons had long since left home to live and work in London. An extremely lively couple, they participated in all the activities of the village and gave generously to all good causes. All the same, to open up their home to four young children did not seem very practical. It was not the time to ponder on what the Fords were going to do, Emma

rebuked herself, and she turned her attention back to the
sheet that she still was holding.

The preference for boys or girls seemed to be in equal propor-
tion. She gave a sigh, and with a feeling of determination she
wrote the figure two in the first column, crossed her fingers
and printed boys in the second space. Another quick glance
told Emma that most of her friends had offered to take two
children. Another name stood out on the list – Aggie Brownlow.
Dear God, the poor woman had three children of her own and
having lost her husband she didn't have an easy life at the best
of times.

Why had she offered to take two children, Emma wondered.
For the best of reasons she supposed. No woman wanted to
feel that they hadn't offered to share their homes with these
needy children.

Passing the sheet to Kate Simmons, Emma pondered on
what Kate might write. Widowed so early in her married life
she had never had any children of her own. Fate was so cruel
sometimes. Emma sighed. Over the years she had learnt that
life could be very hard sometimes, but for every sad or terrible
thing which happened she realized that people grew a little
stronger.

Dorothy nudged Emma, lifted her eyebrows and nodded
towards the papers that were still being circulated. 'If all these
children do come to stay in the village it will certainly make
a difference to our quiet way of living.'

Emma's thoughts had been running along the same lines.

It had taken three weeks to complete the arrangements for
the Children's Country Holiday Project to go ahead. Now,
on the last Monday in June, most of the inhabitants of the
village were gathered around the green. One saloon car and
two single-decker buses were drawn up outside the church
hall. The occupants of the car were two gentlemen and two
middle-aged ladies. The older of the two men made the intro-
ductions to the Reverend Coyle.

'I am John Farrington,' he said, holding out his hand. 'I
feel we know each other having spoken on the telephone and
we have exchanged quite a bit of correspondence.'

Michael smiled, shook the offered hand, nodded to the two
men standing at his side. 'These two gentlemen are Robert

Chapman and Maurice Johnson, members of the North Waltham Council.'

Mr Farrington shook their hands before introducing his three colleagues.

'Miss Anne Hammond, Mrs Olive Collins and Mr Charles Ratcliffe. We are the forerunners for the Toc H Society. Charles and I will only be staying for the day but our two ladies will be on hand throughout the two weeks that the children will be staying with you good folk.'

The appearance of these social workers certainly made them stand out from the crowd. The two gents were obviously city types, dark suits, white shirts, smart ties and well-polished leather shoes. Both aged between thirty-five and forty.

The ladies, though dressed in expensive tailored clothes, both looked the matronly type. This fact was emphasized by the fact they were wearing close-fitting hats, gloves on their hands and sensible low-heeled shoes.

The children began to alight from the buses and as the drivers instructed them they formed two orderly queues, one of boys and one of girls.

There was no going back now. The children from the institutions had arrived.

Before the Country Holiday Project had been approved, an enquiry had been made by the charity commissioners in London and their report had given the scheme one hundred per cent approval. The characters of the families to whom the boys and girls were being sent had been researched. Since most had been born and bred in the village it had not been difficult to obtain references from the two local doctors, the Reverend Coyle and also Father Jonathan, the Catholic priest.

Miss Hammond stood in front of the line of small girls checking her list. Mrs Collins who was in charge of the boys was doing likewise.

The local women and the few men who had been spared from their work for a couple of hours watched in silence. It was unbelievable. The very look of these small boys and girls was appalling. Each child clung to a brown paper bag but other than that they had arrived with nothing more than the poor quality clothes they had on their backs. The girls were dealt with first and as she waited, Emma's fears grew.

Sam had been delighted when the official form had arrived

stating that two young lads, Tom Yates, aged nine, and John Kirby, who was ten, were being assigned to their care for fourteen days. Now it was reality time!

As the two boys walked towards her, Emma felt blind panic. This was far, far worse than she had ever imagined. Their hair had been cut so close it was almost as if their heads had been shaved. They each wore short trousers, which at their age just was not right. On top of which they were wearing nothing more than a man's ragged shirt, the sleeves of which were rolled up above their elbows showing skinny arms. She did her best to smile, but all she could think of was that she was grateful that Emily and Bella were not with her.

Pulling herself together, she resolved to get away from here as quickly as possible. She beckoned to them and smiling broadly said, 'Come on, tell me your names, which one of you is Tom and which is John?'

The tallest lad said, 'I'm Tom Yates an' this is John Kirby. Mrs Collins has told us we're supposed t'be staying with you?'

'Yes, yes you are,' Emma reassured them. 'I'm Mrs Pearson. Shall we get off? I'm sure you are both dying for a drink an' something to eat.'

Tom stared at her silently for what seemed like forever, then lifting his head higher he nodded.

Emma didn't know whether to take hold of their hands, offer to carry their bags, or what. Oh God, please help me to act normally and let these young lads know that she *did* want to look after them.

Suddenly she looked across to the other side of the green and breathed a heartfelt sigh of relief to see her Sam standing there. Her eyes prickled and she hoped she wasn't going to disgrace herself by crying.

Sam came running over. Taking in the situation at a glance he knew exactly what was needed. 'Hallo, boys,' he greeted the two lads. 'Are we looking forward to having you stay with us, I'll say we are. I've a list as long as yer arm of the things we're going to do an' our two girls can't believe we really are going to have boys to stay in our house. Now,' he said, placing a huge great arm around each of the skinny lad's shoulders, 'let's get you home an' I'm sure my good lady has a smashing meal ready for you.'

'God bless you, Sam,' Emma said beneath her breath. He

had never set eyes on these two boys until five minutes ago, but just the warmth flowing between the three of them, his kind words and the knowledge that they were truly welcome were enough to dispel their fears and bring a hint of a smile to their lips. He had also managed to drive away most of the doubts that had been lingering in Emma's mind.

'Sit yourselves down,' Emma ordered, pointing to two chairs by the stove as they entered the living room. 'We'll have a nice drink before we eat, you must be fair parched having sat so long on that coach. What would you like? A cup of tea or a nice glass of my home-made lemonade?'

The two lads were tongue-tied. Their faces showed that they couldn't really believe this was happening to them. They were used to eating and drinking whatever was put in front of them. Choices were unheard of.

'Lemonade,' Tom said, his face wreathed in smiles.

John quickly said, 'Lemonade, please.' Although John was the older of the two by one year, he was of smaller build and shorter than Tom, even at this early stage of their relationship it was obvious to both Emma and Sam that Tom would be the most forward of the two and probably more able to take care of himself.

'I'll get it,' Sam offered.

As he left the room Emma shuddered to think what kind of place these children had lived in all their life. Right now they were sitting in her large warm kitchen, the sun was streaming through the window, and on the table were two fresh loaves and a plate of fruit scones that she had baked early that morning. The kitchen range was enormous, black-leaded until it shone, and from the oven came the delicious smell of rabbit stew. The whole room was bright, clean and very homely, yet at this moment it was strangely quiet, as if the two lads were in some kind of a trance.

Sam gave a glass of lemonade to each boy and told his wife that he had put the kettle on. 'You an' me we'll have a cup of tea before we eat, shall we?'

Emma nodded and laughed as Sam planted a hearty kiss on her cheek. He knew full well what was worrying her. She had taken a quick peep into the paper bags that had arrived with the boys. They each had a clean pair of underpants, a spare pair of socks, a jersey, a flannel and a toothbrush but that seemed to be all that they did have. No pyjamas, no coat. It might be June but the evenings could still be a bit chilly and what about Sunday when they went to church? Surely they weren't expected to wear the threadbare clothes they had on now for the whole fourteen days!

'Bless me, I haven't shown you where you're going to sleep or told you why our Emily or our Bella aren't here to meet you.' Emma spoke quickly to cover her embarrassment. 'We'll all go together to meet them when they come out from school.'

'In the meantime we'll feed you bits and bobs cos we have our dinner at six in the evening,' Sam said. 'On the way to the school you can come an' see my smithery, most of the local lads love to come an' watch me work. It is great if you don't mind the heat. Also I've had another thought, I've got a case full of lad's clothing up in my loft we're sure to find a few things in there that will be of use to you lads, bet you'd just die to pull on a pair of long trousers. Shorts are all right when you're mucking about by the river or in the duck pond but come Sunday I bet you'd like to dress up a bit an' show off.'

Emma could not believe what her Sam was blurting out. She didn't for one moment think that either Tom or John had ever heard of a smithery and where on earth was he going to get the clothes he was talking about? She didn't think he wouldn't come up with them. He would! Even if he had to go to the local market himself, he'd find something that would do for the boys.

'What's a smithery? And what d'you mean when you said if we could stand the heat?' Tom asked suspiciously as he wriggled nearer to his mate.

Sam assured the pair of them that the heat was only full force when he was shoeing horses.

Horses! They looked at each other in dismay.

Ten minutes later and they were eating as if food hadn't passed their lips for a month. Thick slices of new bread spread with dairy butter and eaten with a hunk of cheese. A large fruit scone cut through and each half liberally spread with Emma's home-made strawberry jam and later washed down with a large glass of fresh milk.

Emma breathed a heartfelt sigh of relief when the boys

came downstairs having been shown the small room that they would be sharing at least Sam had made sure that they had washed their hands and faces. For the moment there was nothing that she could do about their clothing. Walking to the school her thoughts were all mixed up. These lads came from the city of London where shops were supposedly stuffed with every kind of food imaginable and clothes enough to cover the whole population. Yet children were abandoned to live in institutions, without even the most basic necessities. Were the great men who ran our country unaware that such poverty and misery existed? Was it only charitable organizations such as the Toc H society that strove to make their lives that little bit better?

Three

E mma listened to her daughter's description of the dramatic events of their day with a fixed half-smile. They were all seated around the large kitchen table but Emma couldn't bring herself to eat anything. It was a tense atmosphere. The girls kept trying to make conversation but the boys remained withdrawn, showing signs of thinking deeply but not saying much.

Both Tom and John's eyes had almost popped out of their heads when she had placed their dinner in front of them. A leg of rabbit, mashed potato, swede, green peas and thick onion gravy. Both of them were skinny as sparrows but they ate ravenously. Emma's heart ached as she watched them clearing their plates.

By the time they had polished off a bowl of spotted dick and custard the atmosphere was less restricted. Emily and Bella pounded the lads with numerous questions though both boys still had hardly uttered more than a few words.

Emily turned to her father and whispered, 'Why don't they want to tell us about themselves?'

'Curiosity killed the cat,' her father quietly told her, but all the same he was smiling as he spoke. He was very pleased that neither of the girls had complained or caused the slightest fuss when told they would sleep top to toe in Emily's bed and let the two boys have Bella's room for two weeks.

The sun had long since set and Emma got up to draw the curtains. The room looked so cosy, warmth still coming from the kitchen range though the fire had been banked down for the night. June or not, they still kept the fire going most days. It was the only means of cooking in the cottage and also it gave a constant supply of hot water.

It was good to see the four children sitting comfortably on the floor playing Snakes and Ladders. Suddenly the two girls roared with laughter and after a minute or two the lads joined in. It appeared the dice had rolled beneath the kitchen table and as it had been Tom's throw he had retrieved it. Straight-faced he swore the dice had shown a six!

Sam who had been acting as adjudicator since the start of the game, laughingly said, 'Watch it, son, you're sailing close to the wind.' Which made all four children laugh even more and the very sound had Emma's heart singing.

Emma sat by the fire sewing, watching the children out of the corner of her eye. Her girls were behaving quite normally, moving the counters along the board, every now and then reaching out to stroke Blackie their cat. She sensed the boys were not quite so relaxed, when they did speak their voices were subdued and when they laughed it sounded false. She guessed it was the first time that they had ever been away from the Home and being amongst a normal family was going to be an emotional time for them.

'Tom,' she said in a commanding voice, 'you seem to have your wits about you so you'll know this is the very first time that this holiday project has been put into practise. This fort-night will be a make or break time. We want you to have a holiday of a lifetime and you will if you give us half a chance. If these two weeks go well it could be the start of a regular holiday for several boys and girls, you do realize that, don't you?'

He nodded.

Emma was trying to conjure up a mental picture of the home in which these young boys lived. There were a hundred and one questions she would have like to put to them but was wise enough to know that now was not the time. She had to have patience, watching and listening were the only ways she was going to learn anything, at least for the time being. She was also worried about what the boys should call her and Sam.

She considered suggesting Auntie and Uncle but didn't think that would sit well with them, a bit sissy they'd prob-ably think. Ah well leave it for the moment see how the other families were acting.

'What time do you usually go to bed?' Emma had seen that John was looking up at her and she directed the question to him.

'Dead on seven o'clock most nights, no difference unless

the Master decides it has got to be earlier,' he said, staring at her with big, sad eyes.

Knowing she wasn't going to get any further with either of the lads tonight, she murmured, 'I'll talk it over with Sam.' She started to clear away her sewing and then, smiling broadly, she asked, 'What would you boys like to drink? Emma and Bella, do you want hot milk or cocoa?'

'Cocoa, please, Mum,' the two girls answered in unison.

From the boys all she got were blank stares. 'Well,' she urged, 'what is it to be?'

Tom shrugged his shoulders. 'Dunno.' That seemed to be his usual answer.

'Whatever you are making would be fine.' John spoke so quietly Emma had to bend nearer to the group to be able to hear him.

'So I'll make it cocoa all round, shall I?'

'If that includes me, great,' Sam said, letting out a great roar of a laugh. 'There's nothing in the world better than a mug of my Emma's cocoa to ensure that within minutes of yer head hitting the pillow you are sending the cows home.'

'Right then, you can come and help me to make it.'

Once out in the scullery Emma turned to her husband, her face drawn with anxiety. 'Maybe tomorrow will be a bit easier,' she said sighing. 'I'm going to pray for a fine day cos if it rains God alone knows what I'll do with them.'

'Oh, come on, love, it's not all been doom and gloom. Look at the way they scoffed the dinner you put in front of them.' He leaned closer to her, his eyes shining with excitement. 'It's going to be a great fortnight, you'll see. Didn't you notice they were scared stiff of the Reverend Coyle? I guess he represents all clergymen an' the church probably has a lot to do with the running of the home they're in.'

Emma sighed again. 'I suppose I am rushing things a bit but I do so want this scheme to be an outstanding success. Tell you what, Sam, while I'm making the cocoa will you run the boys a bath? I have had the plunger to the back boiler pulled out so I know there is plenty of hot water.'

'No problem pet, you go in and make a fuss of our girls, let them know that they are not going to be missing out on anything just because we have two boys in the house and I'll see the lads are clean before we all sit down to our cocoa.'

Emma told Tom and Johnny that Sam was getting a bath ready for them and a lump the size of a walnut came up in her throat as she watched the look that came over their faces. Neither of them had been prepared for this, they stood there looking despairingly at one another.

Sam had everything ready in the scullery but he could not believe how moved he felt as he gazed at these two waifs. He didn't know where to look or what to say. Both the boys were a sorry sight. Skinny wasn't half of it! Their limbs were so thin it was difficult to imagine how they could walk, never mind run around and play. Their collar bones stood sharply out showing how scrawny their necks were and the look on each of their faces, could it be fear? Sam felt he had to turn away, the very sight of them had shaken him and it took a minute or two to get him self under control. He had never seen anything like it before in his whole life. Suffer little children to come unto me, the Lord Jesus Christ had said. Had he really meant that little children should suffer?

No one in the whole village would have believed it if they if they'd been able to witness their brawny blacksmith so moved that tears were trickling down his cheeks.

The family gasped in surprise when the boys entered the room afterwards. They looked like two different boys, each wrapped in a blanket, as they sat up at the table. Even their hair looked a different colour now that all the dirt had been washed out and their faces glowed. As Emma hurried forward to place a mug of hot cocoa in front of each boy, she was rewarded by timid smiles.

All four children seemed sleepy as Sam marshalled them up the stairs. Emma brought up the rear. Having given the lads the clean vest and pair of pants from their bags, telling them that it quite all right to use them for sleeping in, she leant against the doorframe, her face wrinkled with smiles as she watched them snuggle down in their beds. I know Sam told you to wee into the bathwater after you had finished washing, but if you do need to go during the night there is a poe under the bed that you may use.'

She had hardly got the words out of her mouth when John whispered, 'What's a poe?'

Giggling, Emma bent low and dragged out from under the bed a very decorative china pot which had a large handle.

'It's probably better known as a chamber pot,' she told them and was happy to see that having glanced at each they too began to giggle. 'It beats walking down the garden in the middle of the night,' she assured them, before saying, 'sleep tight, I'll see you in the morning.'

The following morning Emily and Bella were very quiet as they got ready to go to school after a breakfast of boiled eggs.

Mrs Collins came breezing around the side of the house to inform Emma that for the period of their stay she was to be in charge of all the boys in the party and her colleague, Miss Anne Hammond was in charge of the girls. 'This morning we are proceeding as a group on a country ramble, to give the children a chance to look around and get a feel of their surroundings.' Her voice was full of good cheer. Evidently all had been plain sailing, so far.

As Mrs Collins finished speaking a second visitor arrived at Emma's back door. Maurice Johnson, one of the local councillors, greeted the boys with a hearty 'Good morning, lads, all set, are we? Then let's be making a move, everyone is waiting for us.' Turning to face Emma, he asked, 'Any complaints?'

'Not so far,' she said, giving him a half-hearted smile.

'Great, you ladies are doing a fine job.'

'Thank the Lord for that,' Emma muttered to herself.

Four

The day had flown by, there seemed so much to do. It was a quarter past four before any of the children had come home and Emma was relieved to hear that the boys had been given lunch. However, the last hour and a half had stretched her patience to the limit. First off the boys were tired and dirty and when she had suggested they had a wash Tom had been cheeky to her. 'Yer 'aving a larf, ain't you?' he'd said sarcastically. Apparently he did not think all this washing was doing him any good.

Emma heaved back her shoulders and sighed deeply. This was only the first day and already she felt that she was in beyond her depth. She suddenly noticed that John was standing on one foot. 'John, is there something wrong with your leg?' she asked, showing concern.

John quickly stood to attention before he answered. 'No, missus, it's my foot that's sore.'

Oh dear, she thought. I really must sort out with Sam what these boys are to call us. I can't have them calling me 'missus' for a whole fortnight.

'Sit down John,' she told him. 'Take your boot off and let me have a look.'

He wrinkled his face up in pain as he eased the boot off.

'Here give it to me,' Emma said, holding out her hand to take his boot. 'Goodness me,' she murmured as she moved her hand around inside. With a bit of effort she managed to straighten whatever it was that was all wrinkled up on the inner sole and eventually she was able to draw it out. Cardboard! That's what it was. Cardboard which had been cut in the shape of an inner sock and placed in the boot. As the lad's feet had got warm the rigid cardboard had shifted and become all rucked up. It was enough to cripple the boy for life. These lads didn't even have a decent pair of boots to their name. She'd have to tell Sam. He'd sort something out. Meanwhile she said, 'Stay there, John, I won't be a minute, just take the other boot off,'

Stooped on her knees in front of him, Emma smoothed yellow ointment on to the part of his heel that looked red raw and also smoothed some of the ointment across his toes, then she gently bound a piece of clean white rag under and over his foot and around his ankle. 'Here, put these on, they are an old pair of slippers, I know they will be too big but they'll have to do for now.'

'Cor, thanks,' John managed to mutter, but it was obvious he wasn't used to being made such a fuss of.

'Does it feel any easier now?'

'Yeah, it does, much better. Thanks, missus.'

There was that awful title again – it was embarrassing but for the life of her she couldn't think of what else to suggest.

Dinner was ready to dish up, the table was laid and the clock on the mantelshelf showed it was twenty minutes past six.

'You're very late!' Emma exclaimed when Sam came through the back door. 'What with one thing an' another I've been so worried, you said you weren't going to work this afternoon. It seems ages since the four of them came home just after four o'clock and I was hoping you were going to be here.' She was red in the face from repeatedly opening the oven door to check that the shepherd's pie hadn't dried up.

'It took longer to get all the things we needed than I thought it would.' Sam said, tapping the side of his nose and grinning widely as he opened the top of a cardboard box and gave her a glimpse of what he had collected.

'Sam, can we leave all of this until later? There is so much I have to sort out with you and if we start on it now the whole dinner is going to get spoilt.'

'That's all right,' he said, lifting the box down and placing it on the floor well out of sight. 'I'll just wash my hands in the scullery while you get the children to the table, and I'll be there to help you dish up.'

Later as Sam washed the dishes and Emma wiped them dry they maintained a silence. The hands of the clock seemed to be moving slowly but at last they showed the time to be half past seven.

'All right, pack the cards and the games away, that's enough for tonight,' Emma said, with great relief. 'Then you each can pay a call to the lavatory, have a wash and then the cocoa will be ready.'

'Wash again!' Tom said in amazement, his eyes nearly popping out of his head.

'Yes,' she said laughing. 'Or there won't be any cocoa.'

Half an hour later Emma felt her burdens lighten as she sat herself down in an armchair opposite to her husband. Oh, how she would have loved to give the boys a cuddle, kiss them goodnight as she did her two girls, but it was too soon for such displays of feeling. Yet how could she not wonder what kind of life the pair of them led in London. Had they ever known the comfort of a mother's arms wrapped around them or the joy of being told daily that they were loved? She had no doubt that they received the basic needs in the institution, but she was sure there were no personal touches.

'First off, shall I show you what clothes I managed to get hold of?' Sam asked with a note of triumph in his voice.

Emma had to laugh and that in itself was enough to relieve the tension that had been bottling up inside her. 'Yes, please. Where did you find it all?'

'In the end it was a lot easier than I thought it was going to be. I tried the second-hand stalls and managed to get socks an' a couple of jerseys but not much else. Then I tried Mrs Hope's shop, she was so good. Apparently I wasn't the only one on the scrounge today, but Mrs Hope still came up with flannelette pyjamas an' cotton vests and pants. I was on my way home when I met Aggie Brownlow, she'd just come from the vicarage. Seems everyone in the village had turned out their cupboards, drawers and old tin trunks an' had given a lot of clothing to Michael Coyle. Aggie was disappointed because it was mostly clothing for young boys an' she's taken in two girls so I told her about Mrs Hope and I went on up to the vicarage. Look,' he added, holding up two pairs of long trousers, 'can you do anything with these?'

Emma quickly lent forward to finger the dark grey flannel and her beaming smile was answer enough for Sam. 'I'll let them try them on first thing in the morning then I'll set to an' alter them, they'll be ready by the time they come home from school.' She fell silent for a moment and when she spoke again it was almost a plea. 'Sam, I don't suppose you came across any boots or shoes, did you?'

Sam sighed heavily as he listened to her tell him about the cardboard in John's boot. 'No, my love, no footwear of any kind but I'm sure we can run to buying the boys a pair each.'

'You're a good man, Sam Pearson. Did Aggie say how she was getting on with her two?'

'No, but she did say to tell you that there will be a coffee morning in the church hall at ten o'clock tomorrow.' He grinned broadly. 'Me an' every other bloke in the village would give a lot to be a fly on the wall an' able to listen in to what's going on. You women will have a field day!'

'Sam, last evening I heard you tell our girls that curiosity killed the cat, try telling yourself the same.'

He was saved from having to find an answer by a rap on their back door and a coarse voice calling out, 'It's only me, can I come in?'

Sam got to his feet and he grinned as he said to Emma, 'It's Jack Briggs from Corner Farm. Come in Jack,' he called and strode toward the door to greet their visitor. 'Have a seat and before we get going on to the subject of why you're here, how about a beer or a cider?'

Before Jack Briggs answered he went to Emma who was about to get up; pressing her back down in her chair he took her hand and held it between both of his own. 'Didn't quite know what we were letting ourselves in for, did we?' he said.

It was said so jovially that Emma wasn't too worried as she questioned this big, ruddy faced farmer. 'Did you and Joyce take in any of the children?'

'Yes, we did, but before we get down to the whys and the wherefores I will take a draught of cider, please, Sam. I've been in the mill this evening and my mouth is so dry I couldn't spit a sixpence.'

When all three were settled with a drink in their hand, it was Jack who started the ball rolling. Looking at Emma, he said, 'At least you had a peaceful morning while the children were taken on what was supposed to be a country ramble.' He paused, his big frame shaking with laughter. 'My dad was a bit put out though, he came yelling at me to come and see what was happening. What did I find? Seven or eight of the young lads hadn't been satisfied walking the lanes and the meadows –

they'd tried to outdo each other, ended up jumping fences, climbing walls and clambering over stiles, acting Jack the lad. That was all right until a couple of our dogs decided to give chase, then the boot was on the other foot.' He let out another great belly laugh. 'The dogs drove the boys into a field which held a herd of my cows, you never saw lads come to such a sudden halt as that lot did. I'd lay money they'd never before set eyes on such big animals.'

'Did you lay into them?' Sam quickly asked.

'Course not, poor little buggers. Been shut up behind walls practically from the day they were born, never had the privileges that our young mites have had. No I told them t'follow me but to make sure that they walked slowly.' He chuckled. 'God above, they didn't really need any telling. To let them know I wasn't all that angry with them I gave them a tour of the farm. Last place I took them to was the dairy sheds. Yer should 'ave seen their eyes almost pop out of their sockets when Dolly Ackworth told them the milk she was squeezing from the cow's udders into the bucket which she held between her knees was the same kind the milkman delivers in bottles.'

'Do you think we'll be having trouble all the time they're here?' Emma asked cautiously. 'I don't think any of thought about what problems could occur.'

'It's early days,' Jack assured her, 'and it must all seem like a different world to these children. My Joyce said the little girls were well made up at seeing the almond and apple blossom, though it's past its best.'

'Given time they'll all settle down,' Sam promised. 'You can't expect children, especially boys, who've never known a day that wasn't ruled by strict discipline to suddenly realize that they can run in fields, kick a ball around or just read a book.'

'That brings me to another couple of points,' Emma said sternly. 'It's bad enough that John stands to attention almost every time you speak you him, but there's the question of how do they address us? I've been called missus several times today and I don't think that is suitable.'

Jack Briggs seemed to find humour in most things. He swung his big frame around to face Emma, ran his hand through his thick wiry head of hair that was already bleached almost white by the sun and laughingly said, 'My Joyce has told the two billeted with us to call us uncle and auntie, mind you we have got girls so maybe it's easier for them.'

Now it was Sam's turn to grin. 'So for the next two weeks I'll become Uncle Sam and you, my dear, will be Aunt Emma.'

'Seems as good a solution as any,' Jack ventured. Then noticing the look on Emma's face, he said, 'It won't harm you, love, and it will sound a whole lot better.'

Emma felt she couldn't argue with that.

Five

Women smiled and hugged each other as if they hadn't met for ages, pleased to be having coffee together in the village hall. Each felt relief to be able to unburden themselves by telling each other of minor mishaps. There wasn't one woman in the gathering, if asked, who would not have freely admitted that since the London children had stepped down from the coach their days had been filled with taut anxiety.

Dorothy James and Janet Swimford had taken up their usual role of being the tea and coffee makers. Several other women had popped their heads around the door, calling out, 'Any help wanted in here?'

Janet came forward, wiping her hands on her apron, 'Be good if you could set the cups and plates out. We need to find the caretaker, when we arrived at the hall nothing was done, no hot water and no tables set out.'

'That's not like John Brown, he's usually so good, takes everything to do with this village hall quite seriously. I'll see if I can find him, if not I'm sure I'll be able to rustle up some help.' As usual sprightly Kate Simmons was on the ball.

Mary Chapman gave a knowing smile. 'You don't think a couple of the boys have bunked off and John has been given the task of finding them, do you?'

'Nothing would surprise me after what I've had to put up with this last couple of days.' Aggie Brownlow was all hot and fluttered as she expressed her opinion.

A few quick strides and Emma was at Aggie's side. 'Sorry I haven't been over to see you, luv, how many children did you get allocated?'

'Only one,' she said thankfully. 'A twelve-year-old girl. At the time I thought that a girl wouldn't be any bother but, my God, I've found out how wrong one can be. A right little madam she is, twelve going on twenty. You'll never believe what took place last night.' Aggie was in full flow now and nothing was going to stop her telling her woes to the group of ladies that had gathered round her. 'I'd seen my two boys into bed and I'd put the baby's cot in their room so that if the baby woke up they could see to her. Vicky, that's her name, was downstairs in the front room reading a magazine when I left to go to the Fox for my evening shift. She promised me faithfully that she'd go to bed by half past eight. We were busy in the pub, but I couldn't shake off the feeling that all wasn't right back at my house, I dunno why. So at nine thirty when Ted told me to take a break for half an hour, I ran all the way home. I hadn't even turned into my road when I saw Vicky with another girl and a couple of boys, smoking they were, and making such a racket it's a wonder no one had come out of their houses and tackled them.'

'Good gracious, what did you do?' Several voices asked the same question.

'First off I asked the lads where the cigarettes had come from but all I got was a load of old cheek. Then I told Vicky she had to come back to the house with me there an' then.'

'An' did she?' Emma asked, her hackles bristling.

'After giving me a load of backchat she did. As I said she is a very impertinent young girl. What surprised me most was this other girl that was with Vicky looked much older than her. Both of them had their faces plastered with make-up an' they smelt of cheap scent. I couldn't help wondering where they had got it all from. I don't think Vicky had it in my house, not that I've gone through the few things that she brought with her. When I made her bed and put the duster around there was no sign of any make-up, though now I come to think of it I did think I'd smelt smoke, but the bedroom window was open and I'd just put it down to someone burning rubbish.'

All the ladies were stunned and for a moment they stared at Aggie in disbelief.

'What happened when you got her back inside the house?' Emma asked, determined to get to the bottom of it and help her friend in any way she could.

'I just told her to get to bed, because I couldn't think of anything that could be done at that time of night. I did go back to the pub but only to tell them that I couldn't finish the shift. Didn't think I should leave the house again – I was worried in case she brought the boys and that other girl into my house.'

'Were Ted and Alice all right about you knocking off early?' Janet Swimford asked, her voice full of sympathy.

'Oh, yes.' Aggie smiled for the first time. 'I couldn't work for a nicer couple than Ted and Alice Andrews. They run a great pub. It's just that at the Fox, Ted doesn't call time until eleven o'clock and it would have been at least half past by the time we'd cleared up and I thought I'd better get back, make sure that Vicky hadn't gone out again.'

'You'd better see Kate after we've had our coffee, she'll go with you to see the organizers, they need to have a word with that young girl,' was the advice given to Aggie from all sides.

'Mrs Joan Miles is the actual chief organizer.' This information came from the quietly spoken Dorothy James who quickly added, 'Where is your baby daughter today, Aggie?'

'My next door neighbour minds Mary for me whenever I need her to and I am so grateful. Mrs Ford loves Mary and right from the day she was born Mary has been content to stay with her. Elsa Ford had two children of her own and I think that makes a difference.' There was a touch of pride in Aggie's voice as she spoke of her daughter and Emma knew there was also a deep regret that her husband had been killed before her third child had been born. A little girl who would never know her father. Such a sweet bonny child born with her dad's big blue eyes and blonde curly hair, which had darkened over time to a pale sandy brown but was still thick and shiny.

'It's good to have friends and kind neighbours, isn't it?' Dorothy smiled

Before Aggie had a chance to answer heavy footsteps were heard and the women who were grouped in the doorway moved to allow John Brown to come into the hall. 'Sorry, ladies, had t'go up t'the big house, one lad has gone missing.'

A look passed between the ladies and the shallow laughter that followed showed that their feelings were bordering on hysteria.

'Come on now, let's get some coffee made,' Kate urged the women as she came striding down the hall before turning to John and offering to help him put up the folding tables.

John Brown was the paid caretaker of the hall but he was also the odd-job man for the village. According to the Reverend Michael Coyle he was a 'gem' who could do anything from repairing a broken sash-cord when a window wouldn't shut properly to a bit of bricklaying. He was even said to have a sixth sense, when an elderly person was ill or in need of help John always appeared on the scene.

It wasn't too long before the ladies were seated and hot coffee was being served.

'I didn't ask if anyone preferred their coffee black,' Kate said. 'I've brought six white. Is that OK?'

'It's fine,' the women answered.

A slightly uneasy silence fell. Everyone was concerned for Aggie. How would those in charge deal with a girl of twelve who was acting up the way Vicky was?

'I wish I'd never put my name down to take a child,' Aggie admitted.

Dorothy James smiled sympathetically. 'No one would have blamed you if you hadn't. On your own with no man to turn to and three children already.'

'Yes.' Janet was quick to add her reassurance. 'You hold down two jobs and we all greatly admire you. So, why did you volunteer?'

'Because I thought it was the right thing to do,' she confessed. 'Does that sound awful?'

'No, it doesn't,' Janet said. 'We all understand and you are just the first one to find out that the child you have taken on is going to misbehave, defy and disobey you, but I think we shall all agree you won't be the last to have to suffer this experience.'

'There was bound to be a few bad apples in the barrel,' Mary Chapman offered. 'When you think about it, these children have just been let of the leash, freedom to them must be a wonderful thing. You, Aggie, have just been unlucky, it might not have happened if this Vicky had been boarded with a couple or someone with more time on their hands. Stop blaming yourself and let's see how the days to come progress, it might get easier.'

There was a deal of half-hearted laughter but Emma was thinking of Tom and the way she was handling him. She leaned towards Dorothy and said, 'Of course it could get worse.'

'Don't be such a pessimist, we have to keep each other going, it's early days and the last thing we need is a wet blanket being thrown on our efforts.'

This was a straightforward answer that had Emma thinking hard.

'Let me know how you get on, remember you can always come and get Sam if things get out of hand.' Emma was doing her best to comfort Aggie as they walked arm in arm towards home.

'Kate has very kindly offered to come with me this afternoon to see Reverend Coyle, surely he'll know how to deal with this situation. Though Vicky was a bit more subdued over breakfast this morning, so keep your fingers crossed for me.'

'I will, Aggie, and remember what I've said, you know where we are, come anytime. You know we can help if it's needed.'

They parted and Emma was relieved to see that her friend was smiling.

The annual fair was visiting North Waltham, an event which would provide plenty to keep the children interested. After much persuasion the school governors had given in and the local children had been given the day off.

Which as Emily and Bella had firmly told their parents, 'Seems only fair.'

'Well, are we ready for the off?' Stan said on Wednesday, his loud voice booming all through the house.

Even a couple of days seemed to have made a difference to both Tom and John, Emma thought as she walked behind the four children. Emily was carrying a wicker basket that was mainly used to carry groceries while Bella was swinging her mother's patchwork shopping bag. All four of them were well turned out. Sam had been as good as his word and a new pair of strong shoes had been bought for each of the boys. They weren't yet wearing their long trousers although Emma was more than pleased with the alterations she had made. She was saving them for when they attended church on Sunday. They each wore a new shirt, pullover and a decent pair of socks.

Her girls looked as pretty as a picture. Bella was looking clean and sharp in a blue and white cotton gingham dress with a plain white collar and white cuffs on the short sleeves. Emily always insisted she was too old for that type of dress which made Emma smile, eleven months couldn't make that much difference but it did to Emily. Therefore the dress she had made for her was entirely different. A pale green cotton dress, patterned with tiny pink rosebuds with a wide full skirt that swirled as she walked. Both girls had the most beautiful hair, while Bella's was reddish brown, thick and curly, Emily's was more auburn coloured than her young sister's, but her thick long tresses tended to be straighter.

As they neared their destination the market sounded noisy and music blared out from an adjoining field, the fair was in full swing but it seemed not to bother the flock of black-faced lambs that were grazing in another nearby field.

'Stay close to us while we do the shopping, then we'll all go to the fair,' Sam said to all four of them. Both Emma and Sam were pleased to see the excitement showing on the boys' faces. Cockerels were crowing, baby pigs penned up in a wire enclosure were grunting, dogs were barking and the stall-holders were shouting their heads off.

'Probably never before been anywhere near a country fair,' Sam remarked.

Guided by Emma they moved over to the dairy section. Each and every stall was covered in crisp white linen cloths and selling pats of yellow butter, cheeses of all shapes and sizes, lovely dark brown eggs laying in a bed of straw, pots of thick clotted cream and jars of home-made pickles and jam. Emma bought several items including a dozen eggs before moving on to the home produce stall.

'Gorgeous!' she exclaimed as her eyes came to rest on the small kidney-shaped new potatoes.

'Ours aren't quite ready to dig up,' she told Bert Hobson as he tipped them from the weighing scoop into her basket.

'Would you like a bit of mint?' Bert asked, his ruddy face grinning as he nodded towards the two boys. 'Double the children for two weeks, eh, how they doing?'

'All right, well nothing that Sam can't set them straight about,' Emma said, laughing along with him.

The girls were keeping up a constant stream of chat as they

pointed to the strawberries. 'You're going to buy some, aren't you, Mum?' Emily pleaded.

'What d'you think, boys?' Sam cheerfully asked. 'Strawberries and cream for afters tonight, would they go down well?'

The boys looked confused and Emma wondered if it were the first time they had ever been offered such a treat.

It was Sam that paid for two punnets and holding one of the punnets out to John he said, 'Go on, lad, try one.'

John's cheeks flushed bright red. He hesitated, not sure if he was hearing right.

'I'll 'ave one,' Tom announced, and as everyone laughed he put his hand into the punnet and pinched one. The soft fruit squashed between his teeth and the sweet juice ran down his chin. 'Lovely,' was his verdict.

The girls were now one each side of their dad both tugging at his arm. 'Dad, can we go to the fair now?'

They were only saying what the boys were thinking, their eagerness was plain for all to see.

'Of course we can,' Sam said, giving in easily. 'I'll take you, let your mother head for the tea tent where she'll no doubt be able to hear the latest gossip.'

'Oi you!' Emma cried, slapping Sam's arm. 'Nobody likes to keep abreast of the local news more than you do, Sam Pearson.'

He held his hands up, laughing in surrender, before leading his brood of four past the field where the sheep were grazing. He noticed that both boys had moved to walk on his other side the farthest away from the animals. Had they been amongst the lads that had ended up in Jack Briggs field where the really big cattle were? Probably never seen live sheep before, he reflected.

They had reached the boundary of the fair where a line of swing boats had been positioned; painted all colours of the rainbow they were an immediate attractive to children. Bella made it quite clear that a ride in one of them was her first choice. She stared hard at her dad, raised her eyebrows and gave him the most cunning of smiles.

Although her request had been silent Sam had been won over, he never could resist his daughters when they turned their smiles on him. Sam nodded to a man who had a leather money pouch hanging from his shoulder and gave him a sixpence which was the amount required for two swings. The boys didn't hang about, no sooner had Sam signalled the OK than they were climbing the ladder settling themselves one each end of the swing. Although John immediately grabbed hold of the rope with both hands, he remained still until Sam had settled Bella at one end of the second boat and Emily had made herself comfortable on the other seat. Only when Sam had nodded to the man in charge did he release the tether on both swings.

Sam never took his eyes off his girls as Emily took hold of the rope and tugged as hard as she could. John pulled on his rope without much effort and both swings moved. Sam grinned but decided it would be better if he moved away. Oh, he'd keep a close watch but hopefully without Emily being aware that he was observing.

A sudden shout from the fairground worker made Sam hastily turned round to see Tom was standing up, attempting to get his hands on the rope that John was pulling.

'God help us,' he muttered, trust that little tyke to turn a harmless ride into a precarious one. He ran like the wind until he was within feet of the second swinging boat.

'Tom, sit down an' behave yourself!' he bellowed.

Tom was ready with a quick answer, he so dearly wanted to be the one in charge, but he was wise enough to realize that the tone of Sam's voice meant that he would brook no argument. He knew it would be safer to sit down and keep his tongue between his teeth.

Sam and the man in charge stood side by side until both swings were steady. 'Sorry about that,' Sam said, feeling guilty.

'Don't let it bother you,' the man said generously. 'It happens all the time, but those lads aren't locals, are they?'

'No, they're down from London, a sort of charity holiday.'

'Gotta make allowances then, shut up for weeks on end an' then let out. We who live free can't imagine what's going through their young one's mind, can we? Tell yer what mate, I'll let them have a while longer, no charge.'

The fairground man didn't wait for Sam to answer, he walked off, but Sam had a feeling that he felt in tune with the lads, his voice when offering a free ride had been full of sympathy.

Six

It was Thursday evening, halfway through the week, and they had managed to survive without any real disasters.

Emma felt quite contented. It was a quarter past four in the afternoon on a beautiful June day. She was sitting out in her back garden and her heart was full of joy as she jogged Aggie's baby up and down on her knees, talking to her as if she were grown up and not just eighteen months old.

'See, Mary, we got four boys and two girls, besides you, for tea tonight. Don't you think we're lucky?'

Mary bounced backwards, her head hitting Emma in the chest. She was full of high spirits as she strained at Emma's strong arms that were holding her. 'All right, my lovely,' Emma said as she lowered the child down on the blanket which she had spread out over the grass. The late afternoon sun was slanting through the leaves of their apple tree, casting a coppery tinge on the baby's sandy curls as Mary attempted to get to her feet and walk to where the six children were. Just released from school they were boisterous, making the most of their liberty.

'Emily, Emily!' Her mother had to call twice to be heard above the racket they were making. 'Keep an eye on the baby for a few minutes while I just go and check on the supper.'

Emily came running up the garden. 'I'll take her down with us, she'll be fine, won't you, pet?' she cooed to the baby as she scooped her up into her arms and trotted away.

Inside the house Emma stood a while looking at the spread she had laid out for the evening meal. There was a large piece of boiling bacon, which Sam would carve as soon as he got home. It looked a lovely joint, skinned, smeared with honey and smothered with brown sugar. There was also a pork pie with hard boiled eggs set through the centre which she had made yesterday, a bowl of green salad, a dish of home-cooked beetroots and their own home-grown tomatoes. On top of the range a huge saucepan full of new potatoes was simmering, sending forth a glorious smell of fresh mint. Pudding hadn't been forgotten either. There was fruit in jelly and pink blancmange for the children, for Sam and herself there was freshly baked bread and strong cheddar cheese.

This morning, two carts loaded with women and men were drawn into the village by massive shire horses. The pea-pickers had arrived!

What difference does that make? some might ask. For Aggie it meant a much longer shift behind the bar of the Fox tonight and that meant extra money in her hand at the end of the week. These casual pickers worked hard and long hours but come the evening the men and their wives would prove that they had worked up a thirst. Emma never had to be asked twice as to whether she would mind Aggie's children when they needed to sleep over. It would be a tight squeeze this time but there were two single beds in the room that Tom and John were occupying and it wouldn't hurt the boys to sleep top to tail for just one night.

As to Vicky, since the Reverend Coyle and Mrs Miles had had a long talk with this young lady, Aggie had reported that the girl was settling down. Tonight Vicky was being taken care of by Mrs Ford. Elsa Ford was a good kind-hearted neighbour but Vicky had better mind her P's and Q's. Mrs Ford was a formidable lady; she wouldn't stand for any old nonsense.

Aggie wouldn't finish her shift at the Fox until nigh on midnight but Ted Andrews had promised he would walk her home.

It was only just on five o'clock when Sam walked round the side path and came up behind Emma who was standing at the sink washing a handful of spring onions that she had just pulled up out of the garden. He put his arms around her and pulled her close; nudging the thick bun of her hair aside he kissed the back of her neck several times. His grasp was so tight that Emma was unable to turn round; instead she relaxed, letting her back lay against his broad chest.

'I can hear that we have our full quota of lodgers for the night,' he said as he kissed her again before releasing her. 'And how about the other two boys, anything to report?'

'No, not at the moment, everything on that front seems to be in order, not that I've had much time to talk to them yet, too busy making sure we've enough to feed them all.'

'You said this morning before I left that my first job when I got home I was to carve the ham. Is it cold enough?'

'Course it is, all nicely glazed and a pile of plates are there beside it. You get slicing an' I'll call the children to the table.'

'We've got ever such a lot to tell you, Uncle Sam.' Tommy was breathless as he made the statement, his eyes stretched wide as plates of food were set in front of each child.

'I'm sure you have, lad, and me an' your Aunt Emma will be glad to listen but not until we have all done justice to this lovely food, so eat up all of you an' let's save the talking until after we've finished our meal.'

It was a good hour later before they had eaten their fill and each child had been given a glass of milk. 'Off you go out into the garden while it's still nice,' Emma told them.

'What about the wiping up? Bella and I usually have to help you,' Emily protested but not very enthusiastically.

Emma stopped wiping Mary's hands with a soapy flannel and looked at her eldest daughter, proud of her. 'It's all right, luv, we're letting you off tonight seeing as how your dad was home early and we've got more time, so off you go but stay in the garden and come in the minute I call you.'

At six thirty Emma fetched Mary in, bathed her and got her ready for bed. She had told the other children that they could have another half an hour. Meanwhile Sam had put a chenille cloth over the kitchen table and had set out two games, Ludo and Housey-housey. 'It'll make a change from cards,' he said as he noticed that Emma was grinning.

It was great to see four boys and two girls all concentrating on the games in hand with Sam making sure that they knew he was in charge. Emma sat away from the table and for once her hands were idle, held loosely in her lap she was enjoying a lazy hour, just lost in thought. It was Tommy's loud laughter that brought her up sharply.

'What's tickled you, Tom?' Emily asked, laughing with him.

'It's those great big horses that came into the village this morning, they dropped great big dollops of mess in the road and before it had even stopped steaming ladies were out there with a bucket and shovel scraping it up, dunno what they wanted that stuff for.' He wrinkled his nose and made an awful face, which in turn had Bella giggling.

'Tom, that "stuff" as you call it is worth its weight in gold around here. Ladies like to grow roses and there nothing that makes them roses grow better than horse dung.' Sam was grinning as he offered this information.

'It was soon after the pea-pickers arrived,' John volunteered and then quietly took up the telling as they all remained seated around the table. 'Once the workers were settled Miss Hammond and Mrs Collins took us to the farm to watch what they did. They didn't 'alf work quick,' he added in wonderment, almost as if he couldn't grasp what he had seen. 'There was rows an' rows of them snatching those fat green pods from the vines an' tossing them into huge baskets. Their fingers all seemed as if they were flying.'

'The farmer was nice,' Tom cut in. 'He brought cold drinks for all the workers and then he came and told Mrs Collins to take all of us over to the barn and when we got there all of us were given a big sugary bun and a choice of lemonade or ginger beer, all 'ome-made he said it was.'

'These pea-pickers, what do they do when all the peas are picked?' John queried looking at Sam and bringing the subject back on target.

Sam took his question seriously. 'Well, those folk are known as season workers. They go around different parts of the country according to the season.'

'You mean they pick other things, not only peas,' Tom butted in again.

Sam was a patient man. 'Yes, lad, many things. For the last three weeks they've probably been on strawberries, soon it will be raspberries, then loganberries, all the soft fruits. Then will come runner beans, broad beans even the new potatoes have to be got out of the ground an' sieved. Come autumn there will be all kinds of eating apples in the orchards and the famous Bramley cooking apples. Moving on towards Christmas these workers will go to the poultry farms, plucking all sorts of birds. Where there are farms there are always jobs that need doing.'

'Are you going to play another game or are you going to bed?' Emma asked, interrupting the conversation.

That put a stop to the questions and answers. It was still a lovely evening, the back door was wide open and the birds were still singing.

It was far too early for bed was the unanimous decision.

Seven

Earlier in the week a note had been put through letter boxes informing people that the Saturday hop, normally held in the village hall, would this week be hosted by Mr and Mrs Trenfield and the assurance had been given that everyone would be welcome up at the Big House. This news had been greeted by a great deal of excitement. Everyone was interested in what went on in the Big House, which was only natural as it had a larger amount of living accommodation than any other building for miles around.

As far back as Emma's memory went it had always been the family home of Mr and Mrs Trenfield and their three sons, two of whom lived and worked abroad, the third a barrister in London. He must think a lot of his parents, Emma mused, because he never failed to make his monthly weekend visit. He always had time to stop and exchange a few words with the locals and he never failed to attend the Sunday morning service in St Michael's Church.

This wouldn't be the first time that she and her family had been to the Big House. During the summer months the grounds were thrown open to all good causes to hold their summer fêtes or even a garden party. On such occasions the toilets which were available to the public were reached by walking down a long narrow passageway, passing through several doors and out into the courtyard.

Mr and Mrs Trenfield were a very popular couple, regularly seen walking the lanes with their two dogs and often holding hands as they walked. Marion Trenfield was a small elderly lady with tortoise-framed glasses and grey straggling hair.

That was at first glance. Second look would show her bright blue eyes that twinkled with merriment and her movements belied the fact that she was elderly. Full of fun and having a great store of energy would be a good description.

Lionel Trenfield was also a chirpy character, with a full head of white hair which he kept cut short, a weather-beaten face and a thin moustache. He hardly ever appeared in public not wearing a suit and a fancy waistcoat, was very partial to a cigar and jollity could easily be his middle name. They were indeed a happy couple and well liked by all who lived in North Waltham.

It was almost midday on Saturday morning before Emma finished putting away her shopping. She decided it was time to put the kettle on. Usually the girls would have gone to the market with her but there was no way they were leaving the house that morning, according to both of them they had things to do! Emma had thought that meant turning out their small wardrobes and rummaging through their chest of drawers. What they were going to wear to this do tonight was of the utmost importance. She smiled to herself, at eight and nine years old and they were concerned as to what they would wear! God help us when they are fourteen and fifteen. Suddenly a thought struck her, it was very quiet, neither sight nor sound of the children had she heard since she got back from shopping. Her feet flew across the kitchen but as she stood at the open back door she could see that they were not in the garden. Emily and Bella had pleaded and cajoled and she had given way and let the girls stay in the house and she had presumed that the boys would amuse them themselves out in the garden.

I suppose they could have gone for a walk, she thought, but then they would have had to go through the village and I would have caught sight of them. Emma felt herself getting angry and she knew that was not a good idea. She had to stay calm.

She heard voices ringing out, loud laughter was coming from the far end of the garden and Emma breathed a sigh of relief as she walked the length of the path. Then she hesitated, this was not on. John and Emily were in the garden both safe and sound by the look of things but Tom and Bella were sitting astride the high wall. It was obvious that Bella was frightened and Tom was doing his best to encourage her to jump.

'Bella, I'm here. Please, darling, sit still,' she called up, doing her best to keep her voice steady.

The look she gave Tom would have been enough to have frightened the daylights out of any other youngster but not Tom. He merely smiled and said, 'It's not far to jump, Aunt Emma, and there's only grass if Bella does fall.'

I'll give him only grass, the little blighter.

'Tom, just help Bella to turn around an' sit so that her legs are dandling over the front of the wall, then sit beside her an' stay still until I come back with a pair of steps.' She didn't wait to catch his answer, instead she shouted to John and Emily, 'Don't either of you move, just talk quietly an' calm Bella. I'll only be a couple of minutes.'

Out of breath Emma was coming back down the garden, an old pair of paint-encrusted steps tucked beneath one arm. John came running and relieved her of the steps, then quickly he covered the distance to where the wall was, put the steps up making sure that they were open the full width and that the were standing firm and steady.

Without any fuss he climbed until he was on the top rung and only then did he hold out a hand saying to Bella, 'Don't look down, wriggle yer bottom round until you can plonk it on the shelf at the top of these steps an' then put one foot at a time on to the rungs. That's it, good girl, yer doing fine, wriggle just a little bit more. No don't look down, that's it, yer there. Sit still for half a minute an' then you can come down.'

'Right, all four of you sit down and listen very carefully to what I'm going to say. First off I am not going to ask any questions.' This was said as she stared straight at Tom feeling that he had to be the instigator of this dangerous escapade. Then transferring her gaze to her daughters, she told them, 'The reason I am not going to mention any of this to your father is because he might just say that we all have to stay home tonight and not go to the hop.'

Loud groans came from each of the children but it was Emily who saw through her mother's wisdom. 'Thanks, Mum, we're all sorry, honest we are. We didn't mean to frighten Bella, she was all right climbing over it, was only when . . .'

Emma had raised her hand and no words were needed. The look on her face stilled Emily in her tracks. 'I've said all that's going to be said. The subject is closed. Now you two girls set to an' lay the table, we'll eat as soon as yer dad gets in,

just a light meal cos they'll be loads of food on offer tonight.'
Turning to John she said, 'You were good the way you helped
Bella down from that wall, thank you. Now you an' Tom get
upstairs an' wash yourselves. By the way you will both be
having a bath about tea time. You can wear your long trousers
an' your new shoes tonight.'

'We won't 'ave any skin left time we get back t'London,
if we wash an' bath much more. Still we've got off lightly,
ain't we?'

Emma distinctly heard Tom mutter these comments to John
and she couldn't stop herself from retaliating.

'Hold on a minute, Tom, you haven't got away with
anything, I've just decided to bide my time. Trouble with you,
my boy, is you not only think you can charm the birds out of
the trees, you convince yourself you could sell a pair of glasses
to a blind man.'

Tom tried hard to hide the smile that Emma's words had
brought to his lips. But it was no good – he looked at John
and they both burst out laughing. Naturally Emma could now
see the funny side and she was laughing with them. Laughter
is always infectious and now was no exception.

As she cut and buttered slices of bread she was still grinning. They were typical young lads, into everything, blooming
nuisances often, but deep down she'd admit they were both
adorable . . . well most of the time. Just like two boys their
age should be except that they had never known the joy of
being part of a loving family.

It was a lovely evening as Emma held Sam's arm and the
children walked along the lane in front of them. Brushing the
bushes as they passed they heard the screech of a fox and
then the hoot of an owl.

The whole evening lay stretched out before them and she
was determined that she and her extended family were all
going to have a great time. She turned her head sideways and
glanced up at her big brawny husband. He was an excep-
tionally handsome man, at least in her eyes. His hair may be
greying but it was still thick and tonight he had combed it
back from his high forehead. He was wearing his special suit,
indeed it was his only suit, worn only on special occasions.
A grey pinstripe, a freshly ironed white shirt and a sliver grey

tie. Emma was bursting with pride. She wondered if her girls had any real idea how truly lovely they looked. Emily looked prim and proper in her blue dress that flared and flounced well below her knees. Bella's dress was a creamy yellow with two rows of tiny pearl buttons running down the bodice. Separating the top from the swinging skirt was a wide sash which was tied at the back, showing a beautiful big bow.

Seeing Sam looking at Tom and John, Emma found herself saying, 'They're both a credit to us tonight, don't you think?'

'Yes, yes I do, though most of the credit has to go to you, Emma, my love. The wonders you work with a sewing machine and a needle and cotton have always been a marvel to me.'

Emma was about to protest but they had reached the boundary of the Big House and needed no telling that a party was in full swing. The trees that bordered the long driveway looked lovely with their branches now fully covered with new leaves, the front lawns had been newly mowed and the sweet smell of cut grass filled the air. She thanked God, as she had done many times in the past, that she and Sam had both been born in this village where nobody had to starve. Vegetables were grown all the year round, there were rabbits, hares and chickens everywhere and local farmers kept pigs that produced piglets regularly. The larger farms stocked cows and bred calves, others had fields of sheep. Come harvest time there was extra work for those that wanted it and when the harvest was safely gathered in and the fodder sealed safe for animal winter feed there was always the harvest barn dance to celebrate.

They had reached the steps that led to the main entrance, the doors were flung wide open and Lionel Trenfield hurried over to Stan, his hand outstretched.

'Good evening, Sam, Mrs Pearson, and what a lovely brood of children you have.' He looked over at John and Tom with interest. 'Have you lads enjoyed your first week in our village? Surely you've got up to some kind of mischief one way or another? I know I would have done if I'd been sent away when I was a boy.'

Emma actually felt sorry for the boys. They were totally tongue-tied. Secretly she was smiling to herself. The waist-coat that Mr Trenfield was wearing was elaborate to say the least and the entrance hall in which they were standing was daunting. There was a huge chandelier and the whole space was crammed with beautiful antiques. In two glass-fronted cabinets there were figurines so delicate it made Emma's mind boggle. There was a well polished bow-fronted chest of drawers with numerous brass handles on top of which stood an amazing doll's house, the doors of which were laid open allowing the beholder to see the miniature furniture and the very small occupants. Both Emily and Bella eyes had been drawn to this doll's house and Emma thought that at some future date perhaps Sam could make one for them.

Everywhere she looked Emma was aware of how tidy and neat the place was and she wondered who looked after the house as a whole.

'Go through, Mrs Pearson, there is plenty of activity going on out in the courtyard,' Mrs Trenfield urged as moved towards them to welcome them, and then turning to the children she lowered her voice and said, 'There is plenty to eat and later on there will be cakes and ice cream so save a place in your tummies for that.'

Poor Tom and John, Emma didn't think they could have formed an answer if they tried. She supposed that never before had they been in a house like this one and certainly not received such a gracious welcome. Emma told them to stand and wait a minute because Lionel Trenfield was discussing the shoeing of his horses with Sam.

Soon they were making their way through the dark cobbled alleyways, finally arriving in the courtyard, which the boys would probably have described as a wonderland. The court-yard was adorned with streamers, ribbons and bunches of balloons and was lit up by numerous coloured lanterns. Long trestle tables were placed the whole length of one wall, the surface of which was groaning with the weight of all the food. Each person was met by a member of staff, handed a dinner plate and serviette and told to help themselves.

Sam remarked, 'Good God, where does one start?'

'We'll eat outside,' Emma decided. 'There's room over there, where your Aunt Agnes is sitting.'

It seemed that everyone was discovering the attractive side of eating outdoors and sharing a meal with friends and neigh-bours. Music was playing, folk began to sing, in fact the occupants of the whole village were in high spirits, including a couple of councillors who at the beginning had looked as if they were only there because they were duty bound to accept the invitation. Games were organized for the children and as it grew dark a torch was put to a huge bonfire that had been built on a rough patch of grass some way from the courtyard. As the flames took hold it was an amazing sight. A three-piece band was set up on the cobbles and folk were tapping their feet, some even dancing jigs on the cobbles. One old gentleman had brought his fiddle; mostly he played old Irish songs, which were popular and he found his talent was very much in demand. For the London children it was unbelievable, more than just a party, people were all so friendly. Sam and Emma felt a sense of elation that they were showing the boys that folk did care and that the world was not such a hard place.

Very late that night the bats were flying low as dozens of families made their way through the lanes towards their homes. Everyone was dead tired but so happy. Emma had her arm safely linked through Sam's and she felt very emotional walking behind the children.

'Sam,' Emma murmured with a distinct sob in her voice.

Sam bent his head and asked, 'What's the matter, love?'

'Nothing really, just everything had been so good, almost too good to be true and I can't help wondering how we're all going to cope at the end of next week when all these children have to go back to the institution.'

'Oh, Emma, my love, you're putting the cart before the horse, all the worrying in the world won't alter the outcome. We all knew that this was only a trial holiday but as it has mainly turned out so well, who knows, the Toc H may decide to do it every year.'

'Well, you said yourself it has brought the best out in most of the kids. Take that Vicky who has been staying with Aggie, God knows she gave Aggie enough problems to start off with but look at her tonight. She was going round carrying plates of food, offering folk seconds and you couldn't fault her manners. All it needed was someone in authority to show her the error of her ways and she listened. Nobody had ever bothered to talk to her before is my guess.'

'Only one more week and then they all have to go back.'

'Yes, that's right, but a week ago we hadn't even set eyes

on John and Tom and now we still have them for another week so let's be grateful for that and help them to make the most of the next seven days.'

'All in all, would you say it was a successful night, Mrs Pearson?'

'In every way, Mr Pearson, it couldn't have been better and I think that will be the opinion of everybody that was there. But now I think it is time *we* went to bed.'

'That's a very smart idea,' Sam said, smiling down at his wife. 'And if you're very good I shall bring you tea in bed in the morning.'

They stood clutching each other's hands for a moment before Emma gave a contented sigh and made for the stairs.

Eight

After three days of arrangements were made and then altered Emma found herself filled with almost as much enthusiasm as the children. Tomorrow they were definitely going to Southsea for the day. The fact that not one of the London children had ever seen the sea was hard to believe and their excitement was hard to control. Yet despite the arguments as to travel arrangements, goodwill had prevailed. It hadn't helped that the two coaches which had been used to bring the children down from London had returned the same day. However the Local Council had received a remarkably generous offer from a coach company based in Portsmouth. Having heard of the need for transport in order that some fifty-odd children might enjoy a day at the seaside they had offered the use of two open-topped charabancs with drivers. The offer saved a lot more disagreements. It meant that most children of the host families were also able to go along on the trip.

A prayer of heartfelt thanks had been offered up by Emma when she'd learnt that her two girls had received an invite. She and Sam had readily agreed to be helpers for the day when the Reverend Coyle had asked for volunteers. Six private cars, their owners and a few passengers had also been called into service for the day because it didn't seem fair to leave so much responsibility to Miss Hammond and Mrs Collins.

With everything in readiness for the morning Emma had fallen asleep for a couple of hours, once the children were sleeping and Sam was gently snoring, but she kept waking with a start, afraid that they might all oversleep and miss the charabanc which was due to leave from outside the village hall at eight thirty.

I'm so glad that all the families that I know of have received invites for their own children, she thought, aware that it would have been very hurtful for the local children to have been left behind.

Last night she had overheard John asking questions about country life and wanting to know if it was difficult to obtain work in villages if a person were not born there. Sam had shown a great deal of patience, he knew exactly what the lad was getting at. Like herself, she knew Sam was dreading the time when they had to say goodbye to these two boys. How much worse must it be for Tom and John!

There was only four days left to go. *I just cannot bring myself to think that far ahead*, she thought sadly. The reality was that there was no alternative on offer.

Yet despite her fears sometimes she couldn't help but lapse into a little daydreaming, during which time she would imagine that both boys had become a permanent part of her and Sam's life. It would be such a good family, two daughters and two sons. She imagined them all growing up into fine well mannered young people of whom they would be so proud. It was of course an unrealistic and fanciful daydream, for she knew full well that within a matter of days the boys would be saying their goodbyes and heading back to London. The very thought brought tears to her eyes and a lump in her throat that threatened to choke her. Oh, they would promise to keep in touch and Sam had already said that he would make sure that they did. No doubt the reality would be an entirely different matter. Would the matron at the Home in which the boys lived encourage them to write letters? She could always enclose a stamped addressed envelope when she wrote so they would not have to pay postage.

Time will tell, she decided, they'd need a tremendous amount of perseverance to keep up an ongoing correspondence. If the girls wrote to them how would they relate all the nice things that were taking place in the country when the lads had only been given a brief encounter with this way of life and God alone knew what the letters from the boys might contain.

The weather couldn't have been better for the trip, the sun was shining brilliantly, the sky was blue and the few clouds above looked like fluffy white cotton wool.

The whole village had turned out. Two rows of orderly children were boarding the charabancs overseen by willing females.
The male population had been drawn in, those that were not
joining the excursion were busy filling the empty spaces both
at the side and the back end of the coaches with well stocked
hampers, blankets, rugs, crates holding large bottles of
lemonade and tap water. Amid a lot of laughter, the villagers
stowed a great number of brightly coloured buckets, spades
and balls of all shapes and sizes in the depth of the hold.

When everything had been checked and the Reverend Coyle
had declared all was shipshape and Bristol fashion the two
coach drivers stood back, each waving a Union Jack they
shouted, 'All aboard that's coming aboard.'

The cheers that went up from the children as the two coaches
moved off were deafening. After travelling for about an hour
the drivers decided to have what they called a comfort stop.
To the boys this meant freedom. The coach had been pulled
into a large area behind a petrol station and their curiosity
had to be satisfied. Down the stairs of one coach and up the
stairs of the one behind, they made sure that the second party
hadn't got more than they had. Whooping and hollering,
hanging over the sides of the top deck, calling to the lasses
that they were chicken because they wouldn't join them.

'Time to hit the road,' both drivers called whilst Sam and
several other men volunteers did a head count. Emma had
been talking to Dorothy James when Aggie butted in to say
that two lads were missing.

'I just knew it was too good to be true, everything has been
going so well,' Dorothy said, sighing impatiently.

It was at that moment that Emma looked up, to her great
relief she saw that both Tom and John were safely sitting in
their seats on the top deck. At least it wasn't her two that had
gone missing.

It was John Chapman, Aggie's brother, who finally discovered the two lads hiding in the gents toilet and the only
explanation they offered was that they didn't want to go back
to the Home. They thought that this was their one and only
chance to break free.

Sam and John had made it their business to sit with the
two runaways as the coaches moved off. Later, Sam had
confided to his wife that it had made his and John's heart

ache as they tried to tell the boys to enjoy the day and put off worrying about what was to come. 'Talk is so cheap,' he had said in sheer desperation, 'but neither John nor I could really find the right words.'

The drivers brought the coaches in as close to the beach as they could, by then it was useless to try to retain any sense of order. The sun was still high in the sky as the children tumbled off the coaches. In seconds shoes and socks were being tugged off and the children were racing along the beach. The boys ran, full of beans, shouting and laughing at the sheer joy of feeling sand beneath their feet and watching the sea stretching way out in front of them as far as the eye could see.

The girls giggled as the helpers showed them how to tuck their dresses into the waistband of their knickers and told them to go and have a paddle in the shallow water that was lapping the sand. Those in charge thought it best to let the children have their freedom whilst everything was unpacked from the coaches.

A little later Michael Coyle, who had been exploring, suddenly bellowed out that he had found a good spot. Everyone looked to where he was pointing and saw a small sandy cove shaded slightly by a high grassy bank. Sam walked closer and agreed it was ideal.

While half the men collected wood the other half set up a tent so that the food they had brought with them could be set out in the shade. While the women unwrapped the food John Brown and John Chapman lit a fire and within a short while they had placed a pan of fresh water on to boil and were asking the ladies if they would like a mug of tea.

Using a couple of the coloured spades, Emma and Aggie had dug and scraped a shallow hole in the sand, placed a towel into the bottom on which they had sat baby Mary, who was now surrounded by several coloured balls and was having a great time.

Boys and girls were running back and forth to the edge of the sea filling buckets with the salt water, bringing it back to where some of their mates were already building a sandcastle.

'Don't it do yer heart good to see them all so happy,' Aggie asked, smiling at Emma.

Emma nodded agreement, and then became very busy helping others to lay out vast amounts of food. For her the departure day was looming up far too quickly. Those two lads that had tried to hide away this morning had made their feelings known and brought the parting sharply to mind. They did not want to return to their previous existence and they wouldn't be the only two. It had set Emma pondering on whether the idea for this holiday had been such a good one after all. The saying goes that what you've never had, you never miss. The people of North Waltham had shown these underprivileged children that there was a very different way of life to the one they were used to.

Had that been a good idea? Or had the whole holiday merely served to make the boys and girls feel unsettled? Emma felt ashamed that she couldn't honestly answer her own question.

Two poles had been set in the sand and a net strung across them and Jack and Joyce Briggs from Corner Farm were teaching the girls how to play handball. The boys were far more rowdy, football was more their style but each time a kick at the ball was missed the players were showered in sand, causing a great deal of boisterous laughter.

Once the children showed signs of getting tired Dorothy James told them to wash their hands as best they could and to come and make a start on this mountain of food that they had brought with them.

The fourteen or so helpers stood back and just watched. It was a sight to gladden the heart of each and every one of them. Although it was a lovely warm day it was still great to see the fire glowing so brightly and the smell of burning wood outside in the open was something else. Suddenly the food was most important to the children, and instead of going to help themselves Emma and Aggie move away a little to sit down on a rock just to enjoy the quiet. Quiet times were something of a rare treat for Aggie and she rarely got the chance to be entirely alone with her best friend.

Looking up at the blue sky, with the sea lapping gently at the shore they were both dreaming. Aggie was imagining that her husband was here helping to care for the kiddies. Would he be pleased that their third child was a girl? She knew for a fact that he would think that no other baby was more lovely than their Mary.

Emma was still pretending that there might be a way whereby she could keep Tom and John with her and Sam. She could see in her mind's eye her family of four becoming six and all getting on so well together.

Later when the two friends walked towards the refreshment tent their eyes were dry but inside both were weeping. Aggie for the fact that her husband had died so young and had not lived to see his daughter born. Emma for the hopelessness of sending all these children back to live in an institution.

All good things have to come to an end. The sun was very low in the sky when the orders were given to start packing up and get aboard the coaches and there was a moment when rebellious mutiny was on the cards.

'Hold up all of you,' Reverend Coyle shouted at them. 'We're not going straight home, we're heading into Portsmouth where you will be able to get a brief look at the naval dockyards and then, wait for it, we're all going to have a high tea of fish and chips with ice cream to follow. How does that sound?'

'Fish as well as chips?' The question came from one of the younger lads.

'Yes, with bread and butter and a drink.' Michael Coyle was grinning as he helped to lift the smaller children up the high step and into the charabanc.

The kindness and patience that Michael Coyle continually showed to all children had most of the women shaking their heads in disbelief. This was a man who had lost his wife and two very young sons and yet he still gave thanks for all God's goodness.

Beneath a sky well sprinkled with stars, Sam had his arm around his wife's shoulders as they walked behind what they had come to regard as their four children. Grubby, tired out and a bit sore from being slightly sunburnt, it didn't matter. There was never a happier family.

'I'd say that was a very successful day, what do you think, Emma?'

'Couldn't have been better, the saints were certainly on our side,' Emma answered and her heart swelled with pride as her husband lowered his head and kissed the top of her head.

Seconds later she offered up a silent prayer, not just for Tom and John's future but for each and every one of the London children who had no family of their own.

Nine

The day they had all been dreading had come. Breakfast had been a very subdued time and now Emily was staring at her mother.

'Please, Mum, let Bella and me come to see the boys off. Our teacher won't mind if we're a bit late getting to school.'

'Oh, I don't know about that, school is very important,' Emma said, more abruptly than she'd meant to.

Suddenly Emily's bottom lip started to quiver and tears filled her eyes.

Emma looked across to where Sam was still seated at the table and he nodded his head. 'Maybe just this once won't hurt.'

'Oh, yes,' Emma murmured half to herself. 'I forgot you are making the journey with the boys, aren't you?'

'Well, it was only last night that the Reverend asked me to keep him company. Seems the Toc H Society wants to ask a few questions and get a gut reaction from local folk who have been involved in this holiday project.'

'Yes, well . . .' Emma sounded really doubtful. 'At least you'll be able to give us a first hand version of what this Home is like and just how well the children are cared for.'

'Hang on a minute, love, I'm only going to be there for a couple of hours at the most. I'm not taking up residence for a week or so.'

'I know that, but surely you'll get some kind of impression?'

'You'll know soon enough when I get back. Maurice Johnson and Robert Chapman from the council have been asked as well and the four of us are coming back on the train, but I've no idea what time the train will get in.'

'Dear God, I'll be glad when these coaches move off,' Aggie said despondently as they waited outside.

'So will I,' Emma agreed. 'It's only prolonging the agony

now. Look up, even the sky is grey this morning. But it just goes to show how these kiddies have touched our hearts, more than half the village has turned out to say their goodbyes.'

The children looked very much better than they had when they had arrived two weeks ago. John and Tom weren't the only two boys who were now wearing long trousers and different jumpers and as for the girls there wasn't one amongst them that hadn't been given a change of clothing. Pretty clean frocks, white socks and colourful cardigans were shown off to the full by the fact that the girls' hair had been washed several times during their stay, brushed and combed and held back from their faces by silk ribbons in all sorts of colours. The main factor that all the women agreed the organizers of the Home would notice first was their faces. Cheeks had filled out and now had some colour in them and arms and legs did not now appear to be so scrawny.

'All aboard, please.' There was no flag waving or voices cheering today.

It was Agnes who made the first move, she folded her arms around Vicky and urged her to be a good girl.

The poor girl could only say, 'Goodbye, Auntie Agnes. Can I come back again next year?'

'Of course you can, pet,' Aggie told her, her voice deep with emotion.

John stood beside Sam and solemnly held out his hand to Emma.

'Oh, no, you don't get away from me as easily as all that,' Emma told him, forcing herself to smile. She tugged him to her and enfolded him in her brawny arms, held him close for a full minute before she rested her cheek against the top of his head. Then pushing him towards Sam, she said, 'Don't for one moment think this is the last you will see of me. I will write to you an' you do your best to write to all of us, you will, won't you?'

The poor lad was choked to his high teeth, all he could do was nod as he turned his back to her and let Sam lift him up into the coach. Tom was a different kettle of fish. It was very difficult to imagine what he was thinking. Emma stretched her hand out and ruffled his hair. 'You're an artful one, you are, Tom. You don't let your right hand know what your left one is up to.'

Tom lent his head backwards and stared into Emma's face. There was no mistaking the fact that the big brown eyes of young Tom Yates were glistening with unshed tears. 'Come here, Tom,' she commanded, wrapping him close to her. 'You're not the hard nut you'd have us all believe, are you?' She got no answer and she did not expect one for she could feel that his tough little body was trembling from head to foot.

In the end it was Sam who came forward and signalled to Emma that she had to release her hold on Tom because everyone else was on board and the coach was ready to go.

It felt like it was the hardest thing she had ever had to do, more so when she loosened her arms and Tom still held on to her as he said, 'Goodbye Auntie Em, I'm going t'miss you.'

Not half as much as we'll miss you, is what she almost said, then out loud she quickly told him, 'We're going to be on your tail for the rest of your life, son. Both the girls an' your Uncle Sam an' me are all going to write to you. The week that you don't answer is the time that I shall want to know the reason why. Now get up into that coach and try behaving yourself.'

Emma was almost knocked off her feet as Tom planted a great wet kiss on her right cheek before turning and boarding the coach without so much as a backward glance. Sam also kissed her saying, 'Look after the girls. I'll see you all tonight, though it might be very late.'

As the coach moved off, folk were half-heartedly waving and Emma could quite plainly see John and Tom seated halfway down the coach. John smiled at her but Tom had his head buried in his hands.

'Come on, girls, let's get you off to school.' Emma turned to Aggie and asked, 'You keeping Sid and Lenny off for the day or are you coming to the school with us?'

'My boys are going straight into school, but then I suggest that you an' me take Mary into the nearest café an' get ourselves a nice cup of coffee. My house will feel real empty now that Vicky's gone. I don't want to go home.'

'You've never had a better idea,' Emma said, quickly adding, 'my place will seem like a morgue without those two boys. Funny, isn't it, two weeks ago we were dreading them coming and now we feel dreadful because they've gone?'

'Kids have a way of working themselves into your heart,'

Aggie said smiling. 'I've always thought that an' it's proved to be right with that lot.'

'Wonder what kind of a report Sam will have when he gets back. Half of me is glad that he's gone with Michael and that we'll find out a little of how those children are faring and what the Home is like but—' Emma stopped abruptly.

'I know exactly what you're thinking,' Aggie reassured her. 'The other half of you is frightened that we might not like what your Sam may have to tell us. That's it, isn't it?'

'You've got it right! What will we do about it if it's all bad news?'

'Come on, Emma, this is not like you. You're always telling me not to trouble trouble until trouble troubles me. So, we've reached the school gates but where are our kids?'

'We're right behind you, Mum,' Lenny said, 'but we're all wondering do we really have to go to school today?'

The two women looked at each other and burst out laughing. It took a minute or two before they said in unison, 'You most certainly do.'

They stood watching as the four children reluctantly made their way across the playground. Then Aggie said, 'They heard what I said to you and were hoping we'd take them to the café with us.'

They laughed again. 'No chance,' Emma said, taking control of Mary's pushchair. 'We've a bit of time to ourselves an' I'm buying this lovely little girl anything she fancies.' She bent over to playfully pinch Mary's plump cheek. 'We've all the time in the world to play with you this morning, you've been such a good little girl.'

'Hey, hold on, don't go putting ideas into her head. Little as she is she understands everything and I don't have all that much time. When we've had this cup of coffee there are beds that need stripping and a whole lot of washing to be put in the boiler.'

'Aggie, love, don't go all sober-sides on me, the washing and the work will still be there tomorrow. We'll have this coffee and maybe a sticky bun and then we'll sit in my garden for a while, Mary will like that.'

There was no arguing with Emma when her mind was made up, and suddenly Aggie decided she didn't want to. It was true the work would still be there tomorrow.

Ten

Sam exchanged glances with Michael Coyle and it was odds on that the same thoughts were running through each of their minds.

Neither of them had ever seen such a grim, forbidding building as the London Foundation For Needy Children. It looked more threatening than any of the grimy blocks of tenements that were scattered around the City of London. As they had journeyed along the sun had broken through the clouds and the June afternoon was quite pleasant. Even so this high double-fronted building looked very bleak.

The children were off the coach and without being told had formed two lines, one of boys and the other of girls. A wide flight of stone steps led up to a large wooden door, and there were six-foot high iron railings, with sharp spikes at the top, completely surrounding the building. The windows to the front were tall and narrow and were grimed with dirt. Looking down over the side of the steps Sam saw that the basements windows were much smaller and had bars fixed across them. A flagstone area skirted the front of the building but not a flower or a blade of grass was to be seen. Sam wondered if there was a garden at the back, surely there had to be a few trees and shrubs of some sort?

The front door had stood ajar whilst the coaches had been unloaded, suddenly it was thrown wide open and three ladies and one gentleman were now standing on the top step. The smallest of the ladies stepped out to stand in front of her three colleagues. It was as if an order had been rapped out, yet no command had been given.

Moving as one each boy and girl stood to attention and in unison they loudly chanted, 'Good afternoon, Mrs Curtis.'

'Good afternoon, children. Welcome back,' the slim well dressed lady replied.

The sound of Mrs Curtis's voice was a pleasant surprise to Sam. He knew from the letter that Michael had given him that Mrs Curtis was the matron of this home and that a Mr Malcolm Mortimer was the Manager. This positive feeling was wiped away as the gentleman stepped forward. The very size of this man was enough to frighten the socks off young kiddies. *And I think I am a big man*, Sam thought. Broad shoulders, at least six foot three inches tall and heavily built didn't really go halfway to describing this giant of a man.

'Boys and girls, you may go to the dormitory and leave your parcels, use the lavatory and wash your hands. No loitering! A meal is ready for you in the main hall and I expect to see you all seated there in fifteen minutes.'

Not a child moved as Mr Mortimer remained staring down at them.

'Dismiss!' he bellowed without warning and from then on it was a mad scramble to get up the stone steps.

Reverend Coyle was shaking his head as Sam remarked, 'Wonder if I'll get to say goodbye to John and Tom?'

The coaches drove off and Sam had a few minutes in which to get his bearings. His overall impression was dirty and noisy. There were many carts and carriages drawn by horses but also a few petrol driven cars and vans that he had heard so much about. Back home there were a few folk who owned a car, four of whom had generously offered their services when they had taken the children to Southsea for the day.

Sam grinned. He didn't think cars and such like were for the working man and he wasn't bothered that the need for a smithy in North Waltham would dry up. He was of the opinion that horses would help supply him with a good living for some years to come. From the signposts he gathered that he was in the district of Vauxhall on the south side of the River Thames in the borough of Lambeth. Staring across Vauxhall Bridge he could see a mass of boats in the distance and his brain went into overtime as he tried to imagine where the great ships had started out from and what kind of cargo these ships had brought to London.

The four men delegates remained standing on the pavement, unsure as to whether they were supposed to enter the building or not. When John Farrington and Charles Ratcliffe appeared in the doorway and indicated that they should come it was with great trepidation that they did so. These two gentlemen were not strangers, they had travelled down to North Waltham when arrangements were being made for the children's holiday and at the start of the holiday.

Michael Coyle found himself remembering the information he knew about the Toc H. It was a society that helped the sick and needy and it worked in secret. No publicity, no fanfares or items in the press. One foot inside the main hall of this institution and he gasped, it was the beginning of summer yet in here it was freezing cold and he knew that before they left they would be chilled to the bone.

Sam was thinking along the same lines and shuddered. The place was dark, damp and terrible, he thought with a sinking heart.

After handshakes all round John Farrington asked if they would like to join the children for tea or to have a quick guided tour of the building. The two councillors hastily showed their preference for a cup of tea

'I think that Mr Pearson and I should take the opportunity to see where the children are cared for,' Michael answered, doing his best to bring some enthusiasm into his voice.

'I'll show you around,' John Farrington quickly offered.

'And I'll see the councillors are fed and watered,' Charles Ratcliffe said jovially.

Having seen two dormitories, John told them that there were four in all. 'Would you like to see the other two?'

Sam and Michael shook their heads vigorously. The first two had been enough of a shock. The walls were just bare bricks and the floor might just as well have been bare boards because the covering of linoleum was very thin and in places badly cracked. The beds were placed as close as possible to each other and there was a lingering smell of urine.

'Where do the children wash and use the lavatory?' Michael forced himself to ask.

Taken in that direction both he and Sam withdrew their handkerchiefs from their pockets and covered their nose and mouth. This huge place was dreadful, spare and cold, the brick walls running with water. A line of metal basins stood in a long zinc-lined trough, with cold water taps placed at three-foot intervals and slabs of hard red Lifebuoy soap held in racks above. The smell that pervaded this wash-house was far worse than that in the dormitory, it was a filthy smell. Fixed against the far wall was a row of closets, more like one long trough with a wide wooden plank of wood placed on top through which a round hole had been cut and evenly spaced allowing several children to sit and use the lavatory at the same time.

The three men could not get out quick enough. They needed to breathe deeply once outside. The last area they visited held the classrooms and Michael was relieved. The three large rooms were by no means perfect but could certainly be graded better than the sleeping arrangements, a fact for which he gave thanks to God.

'At least we have to be grateful that the children are being given an education, albeit pretty sketchy.' John Farrington sounded sincere and apologetic. 'I expect the pair of you could do with a cup of coffee or tea, I know I could. Shall we make our way to the dining hall?'

Mrs Curtis was seated on her own at a small round table. On seeing the three men she beckoned them over. Within minutes of them being seated, a pot of tea and a pot of coffee was placed in the centre of the table. A white cup, saucer and a side place on which a laid a large slice of Victoria sponge cake had already been set for the three visitors.

'I'll be mother, shall I?' Mrs Curtis kindly asked.

Both Robert and Michael requested coffee, Sam made known his preference for tea, thinking to himself that this cup would need to be refilled at least six times if he were ever to be able to wash away the bad taste in his mouth left by the foul air and smell of those washrooms.

They had hardly begun to drink their beverages when the loud clanging of a bell rang though the long room. Immediately every child in the room was on their feet and solemn lines of quiet children filed out.

Mrs Curtis sighed gently seeing the look on Sam's face. 'Life here has to be very regimented and ordered for all the children, I'm afraid.'

Michael Coyle suddenly felt an overwhelming sense of pity for this genteel lady. She was placed in a very precarious position but what a wonderful kind woman she must be to take on such a position as matron in such an institution.

Mrs Curtis smiled, almost as those she were reading
Michael's thoughts. 'At any given time of the day each child
knows exactly what is expected of them. They have no decisions to make, they live by strict rules and they are bound by
a code of proper behaviour.'

The children had all gone, the silence now was ominous
and Sam was wondering if he would ever get to see John or
Tom again. He brushed his thoughts away. They didn't bear
consideration, not even for a moment.

Finally the visit was over. John Farrington was the first to
leave. Shaking hands with Sam, he quietly said, 'I won't lose
touch, that's a promise. I'll meet you in the near future.'

Michael and Sam did not immediately walk away. They
each had questions they needed answered. 'How much
funding per child does the Home receive?' Michael Coyle
asked.

'Reverend, you may find my answer difficult to believe but
the answer is I have no idea.'

'Do you not have to provide accounts at monthly meetings?'

'I am a matron, I care for the well-being of the children in
my care to the best of my ability. I am not asked to attend
meetings that are pertaining to money affairs or revenue.
Malcolm Mortimer deals with all.'

'Thank you, I didn't mean to offend.'

'I do assure you, reverend, that in no way have you offended
me. I and all my female staff do the best we can with what
we are sent if and when it arrives.'

'Thank you Mrs Curtis,' Michael patted her arm, 'I shall
pray that long may your good work continue.'

Feeling that they were about to be dismissed, Sam hurriedly
spoke, 'May I please ask a question?'

Having received a smile and a nod Sam rushed on. 'We,
that's my wife and my two girls, would dearly like to keep
in touch with the two lads that were staying with us. We don't
want it to end here. If we send letters will they be allowed to
write back to us?'

'Mr Pearson, you have gladdened my heart. It is great news
that these children will not be forgotten and I do hope that
more folk in your village will feel the same way that your
family does. By all means write to the boys and I will see that
paper, pen and ink is provided so that they may reply to you.'

Sam was tongue-tied. He just about managed to say, 'Thanks, madam.'

Mrs Curtis walked to the front entrance with them. Maurice Johnson and Robert Chapman were already there talking to the two female assistants. Goodbyes having been said and thanks given, the four men walked down the flight of steps and stood still for a full minute watching the three women re-enter that grim place.

It wasn't five o'clock, yet already the sun had disappeared and even outside it was difficult to breathe. The trains rattled over Vauxhall Bridge, men sat high on their carts causing havoc as they steered their horses' heads between the new-fangled motor cars that were so fashionable in this city.

They walked quickly along the uneven pavement, each thinking how lucky they were to live and work in Hampshire. Sam in particular was thinking of his wife and their own two beautiful healthy girls and he thanked God that their mode of living was so different to what he had been given a glimpse of today.

Eleven

Emma walked along without hurrying. She liked to get to the farm shop by nine thirty, that way she had first pick of what was on offer. It was ten weeks now since the children had gone back to London. There weren't many days that she didn't give a thought to Tom and to John, none of the family had realized exactly how much they would miss them. They had received one letter from each of the boys but it had been a cold unfeeling note. Merely saying thank-you for having given them such a happy holiday.

Probably the letter writing in the Home had been supervised or else the boys weren't used to putting words down on paper. The girls had written three times to both John and Tom but no longer watched out for the postman to call with as much enthusiasm. Sad, very sad, but not more than she had expected. She would persevere though, she wasn't going to willingly desert those boys.

As she was about to pass the top of the road where Agnes lived, she saw her friend manoeuvring the pushchair backwards down the path with Mary strapped in it. Emma waited to walk along with them. The two of them usually met up two or three mornings during the week.

'Morning, Aggie,' Emma called. 'You all right?'

Aggie bouncing the pushchair along the cobbles, hesitated before answering.

'Not at my best,' she admitted.

She did look washed out and tired, even though it was early in the day, Emma thought. And surely it was nearly time that Mary was walking.

'It's easier this way,' Aggie said, reading Emma's thoughts. 'Mary can be a little monkey sometimes, she hates me holding her hand and it's not safe when she runs off. She's only got to fall over in front of one of those big horses.'

Emma bent down and kissed Mary. 'You're gonna be a good girl today, aren't you, pet?' Then straightening up, she linked her arm through her friend's before voicing her worries. 'Aggie, are you going to tell me what is wrong? You haven't been yourself for sometime, you've even missed the Women's Guild two weeks running an' that is not a bit like you. So,' Emma asked again, 'what is wrong?'

'I'm pregnant,' Agnes said in a quiet, flat voice.

'Pregnant?' Nothing in this world had prepared her for this statement and she had almost shouted the word she was so shocked.

'Tell the whole village, why don't you?' Aggie said, in a stroppy voice.

'Sorry, luv,' Emma was quick to say, 'but you, pregnant, are you sure?'

'I wouldn't have been at my wits' end for these past weeks if I weren't,' Aggie said, sounding quarrelsome.

'I'm sorry,' Emma said. It had been a natural question, even if a silly one. But Aggie was a single parent, single since her husband had been crushed beneath a farm tractor.

She stopped walking and stared hard at her friend and what she saw cut her to the quick. It was plain to see Aggie was suffering unbearable grief. Gently she placed her arm across Aggie's shoulder and held her still. Words wouldn't come and if they did would they be the right words? All she could offer at this moment was the inevitable cup of tea.

Because they had stopped walking and her auntie was kind of cuddling her mum, Mary started to wriggle. Funny how even young children know when something is wrong.

'It's all right, pet, we're going to the corner café before we do our shopping, yer mum and I fancy a cup of tea, what about you, a milk shake?'

'A strawberry one?'

'Of course, and I'll see that you get a real strawberry on the top.'

Mary turned round, settled back against her cushion, pleased that nothing was wrong and that she was going to be given a treat.

There was quite a few tables occupied in the tea room but Mrs Rogers, the homely owner of the café, greeted them warmly and steered them into a window table where there was plenty of room for Mary's pushchair.

While Agnes put milk into each cup and poured the tea and Mary was occupied with her milk shake Emma allowed herself time to think.

Joe Brownlow had been a wonderful husband and a really good father, why oh why had disaster struck this ordinary loving family? She tried to imagine how it must have been for Agnes when he died. She'd been left with two boys and had been seven months pregnant. She had lost the man she'd thought she was going to spend the rest of her life with. It must have been an absolute nightmare.

Now what? If it were true, who on earth could be the father, and whoever it was, when had it happened? Aggie never went anywhere without her children except to the Women's Guild. She certainly never met men!

Taking a sip of her tea Emma glanced at Aggie and her heart felt as if someone was tearing it apart. Oh, how could she find a way to comfort her? She laid her arm across the small table and let her fingers stroke the back of Aggie's hand. She had to ask once again.

'Aggie, are you absolutely sure?'

This time Aggie never even looked up, she stirred her tea and kept her lips closed.

'I'm sorry, luv,' Emma said yet again.

'No, I'm sorry!' Aggie said. 'I shouldn't be snapping at you. I realize you have questions you want to put to me but I'm not ready with the answers, not yet. Can we just leave it for now? There is one thing I will tell you. There is no doubt. I've done the tests. I am definitely pregnant.'

Time had no meaning. Both Mother and Aunt mouthed baby talk to Mary, each pretending that they were about to steal her strawberry. Neither wanted to persist with their conversation.

'Would you like me to come round to see you tonight?' Emma asked cautiously. 'I could, after the girls are in bed.'

'Oh, Emma, will you?'

'Of course, is there anything I could . . . ?' She broke off knowing there wasn't much anyone could do.

'Not unless you've got a magic wand you could wave and turn the clock back.'

'Agnes, my dear friend, there is not a soul in this world who at some time or another hasn't wished that wish. Only sorry it doesn't work like that. But I'll be round tonight. We had better make a move or we won't get anything done today.'

Mrs Rogers strapped Mary back into her pushchair, all the while making a great fuss of the child. Emma went to the counter to pay their bill. Mrs Rogers looked at Agnes and said, 'You doing too much, luv? You look a bit washed out.'

Agnes softly sighed. 'It's just this hot weather, August is always a lovely month if you've got ought else to do but laze around. You must feel the same sometimes.'

'Funny lot, aren't we, always moaning about the weather? Another six weeks and the farmers will be praying that this weather holds long enough to get the harvest in,' she said, laughing a little.

'See you soon. Mary, say goodbye to Mrs Rogers,' Agnes said by way of an answer, but not laughing at all.

It had been harvest time when her Joe had been killed.

The two friends paused as they reached the lane that led to the farm shop. Aggie was going to the library. Emma and Aggie looked at each other. Warily, Emma flung her arms wide, 'Come here, let me give you a hug,' she said with a sob in her voice.

Agnes let go of the pushchair and allowed herself to be folded into those friendly comforting arms. 'I'll be there for you, no matter what, that is a promise. We'll talk more tonight. You OK for now?'

'Yes, I'll be all right, but I am glad I've been able to tell you. Thanks for listening, Emma, see you later.'

There didn't seem anything more that could be said at that moment. They parted company, Aggie and her daughter going towards the village, Emma up the lane to do her shopping. Her mind was in complete turmoil as she thought about Aggie. As she was so adamant that she was pregnant, then she must be. In her own experience women always knew. Most didn't need a doctor to tell them. But what a surprise! Shock would be a better word. Aggie had no life of her own, only devotion to her three children. She'd never been seen with or spoken about any other man since Joe had been killed. She had two jobs, God knows she needed the money, could she have met someone when working in the pub?' She didn't moan or ask for charity and her main aim was always to feed and clothe her children. Her brother John and his wife Mary helped her in every way they could, what would they have to say about this predicament?

Still thinking about Aggie, Emma walked up the wooden steps into the well-stocked barn shop. Here you were spoilt for choice. The customers flowed in and out all day and even at this early hour Emma had to wait a good fifteen minutes before it was her turn to be served. Stan Parker was behind the counter, boning and rolling a breast of lamb for Nellie Bristow. Nellie was an elderly lady, one of the oldest residents of the village.

Having wrapped the meat in two sheets of white paper, Stan held out the parcel, saying, 'There you are, Mrs Bristow.' Lowering his voice, he added, 'I've put in a couple of our pork and apple sausages, just to show you that we appreciate your custom.'

'Oh, Mr Parker, thank you so much,' Nellie said beaming.

What a great place North Waltham was to live, Emma told herself. Here folk had time for each other and the elderly were treated as if they were special. When it came to her turn, she bought a pound and a half of steak and kidney and asked Mr Bristow if she could have eight of his special sausages.

For a moment Stan Parker hesitated, then he grinned. 'I never got around to asking you what those two boys thought of our sausages. Like them, did they, Mrs Pearson?'

'Like them,' Emma repeated laughing, 'there was never a meal that I put in front of those lads that they turned their noses up at.'

'I think we'd all agree on that, those children ate food as if they had never before seen such meals.'

Emma turned to see Dorothy James standing behind her but before either of them had time to add to the comments the voice of Kate Simmonds came from the back of the shop.

'Who amongst us would have guessed that we would miss those children so much? We all found it hard work to start, but as the days went on I think we all were rewarded by the appreciation those girls and boys began to show.'

Emma and Dorothy stared at each other, their thoughts very

similar. If Kate had found it hard work having youngsters in her house then they shouldn't feel so bad.

It was a very thoughtful Emma who took her time to walk home.

Twelve

It was half past eight when Emma left the house. All she had said to Sam was that Aggie needed to discuss something with her.

Catching the obvious concern in his wife's voice he immediately said, 'I'll let the girls have another half an hour out in the garden and then I'll see that they get ready for bed. You get off, go on, we'll be fine.'

'Thanks Sam,' she said, before walking across the grass to where her girls were seated at the big wooden table. She kissed Bella first, then Emily. Ignoring their questions as to where she was going, she said, 'Just behave for yer dad.'

'We will, Mum,' they said laughing, looking as if butter wouldn't melt in their mouths.

As she went though the back gate she turned her head to look at her two girls. 'I won't be too long,' she called. It was a gorgeous summer evening, the schools were all closed for the summer holidays and they should be discussing where they were going to take the children during the coming week. Instead she was going to see her friend who was in deep trouble. The trouble was she hadn't any idea as to what help or advice she would be able to offer.

Agnes opened the door almost immediately on Emma's knock, as if she had seen her coming. Fingers to her lips, she led Emma into the living room.

'Mary won't wake up now and I've dared the boys to try to come downstairs. They protested loudly when I said they had to go to bed but they're settled now, both reading a book. Would you like some tea or coffee?'

'No thanks.' Emma smiled. 'I'm sorry I'm a bit late, I had to play the first game of dominoes with the girls. They're all right though, Sam is with them.'

Agnes pointed Emma to an armchair and set herself in another facing her.

Emma thought they would sit in silence for a while if she didn't open the conversation.

'Come on then, what about you?' she asked.

'Yeah, poor old me! Up to me eyes in a load of trouble, don't you think?'

'Do you want to tell me a bit more about it? Don't if you'd rather not.'

'Oh, but I do! If I don't get it off my chest I think I'll go mad an' you're the only one I feel I can talk to.'

'So talk away, Aggie, I want to help if I can an' I'm certainly not going to judge you.'

Agnes was a mother to three children. Where and when and with whom were questions she wanted to ask. Yet, on the other hand did she want to hear the answers? Somehow she couldn't get her head around the fact that this had happened to Aggie. Aggie was the last person you would think of.

'Where shall I begin?' Aggie asked, obviously distressed.

'At the beginning is always a good start.' Emma said, doing her best to keep her voice light.

'I suppose you're right,' Agnes agreed. 'Well, do you remember the first Saturday the children from London were here and the Trenfields hosted the Saturday hop up at the big house?'

'Only too well. I think everyone was so pleased and the Trenfields did the same the second weekend, it was a grand send-off for the children. You enjoyed both evenings, didn't you, Aggie?'

Aggie's eyes brimmed with tears. 'Only too well,' she murmured. 'I had my hair done in the village and I made myself a new dress in time for the second do.'

Emma knew if she wanted the facts she'd have to be patient and let Aggie tell her story all in her own good time.

Having taken a deep breath, Aggie continued. 'One of the men that was staying at the Fox paid me a lot of attention that first Saturday, kept bringing me glasses of cider to drink. He danced with me several times and as the evening was drawing to a close he insisted he took me and the boys home in his car. Sidney and Lenny thought he was the bee's knees. At the time I thought he was a real nice gentleman.'

Agnes's eyes glazed over, and suddenly she shivered.

'What happened? Did you see that man the following week?' Emma prompted.

'No, he had to go back to London, but he did say he would see me the next weekend.' Aggie still had that far-away look and her fingers were busy wringing her handkerchief into a tight ball. 'He did come down again on the Friday, he went out for a meal with three other men. Then all four of them came back to the Fox, spent the rest of the evening in the bar. He brought me a drink and when Ted called time he made a point of coming to the bar to say goodnight to me and to tell me he would see me tomorrow at the hop.'

Silence dragged on and Emma was worried about Aggie. Her lips were quivering and it seemed as if her whole body was trembling. Time we both had a drink, she thought. Having filled the kettle and lit the gas ring beneath it she took down two cups and saucers, found the sugar and poured milk into a small jug and set about making a pot of tea.

'I've changed my mind,' she said, coming back into the living room. 'There's nothing like the cup that cheers when trouble comes a calling. I've made it good and strong so here, take hold of this and drink it while it's hot and then you can finish telling me what you've started.'

Aggie used both her hands to hold the cup but at least she was smiling when she said, 'You really are a good friend, Emma. You don't let anything get on top of you.'

'Don't you believe it, my luv, I have my downs as well as my ups, that is what life is all about. Now drain that cup an' then you can carry on.'

Aggie did as she was told, and when the empty cup and its saucer were laid carefully on to the table she sat up straight in her armchair and finally said, 'The second do was even better. Mr Trenfield had booked a proper band and everyone thoroughly enjoyed themselves, though several of the kiddies got upset when it was time to leave. Only one more day, Sunday, and then they knew it was back to where they'd come from on the Monday morning.'

'Yeah, we all felt it,' Emma agreed remembering.

Aggie sighed. 'It was very late when this man took me and the boys home again, only this time he stayed whilst I saw Sid and Lenny into bed. Then I felt I had to offer him a coffee.'

This last sentence had been said with so much regret and to see Aggie suddenly shudder was almost too much for Emma. But to interfere or offer comfort at this point would not get either of them anywhere. So she waited.

'It was almost one o'clock an' I was getting worried,' Aggie finally admitted.

'*And?*' Emma did prompt this time. This was getting to the bone of the matter. This was unfinished business and it would never get sorted if Aggie didn't manage to tell the full story.

'He changed. Just like that, honestly Emma, it was so unexpected. I just never saw it coming. I told him it was about time that he was making tracks and I thanked him for another lovely evening, but when I stood up he pushed me back down and stood over me. I protested quietly at first because of the boys but when his hands were all over me and he tried to kiss me with his mouth wide open, I tried to scream. I thought he must have gone mad . . . I couldn't understand the change in him . . .' She buried her face in her hands.

Emma went to her, took her into her arms, stroking her hair as the sobs tore at her body.

'Are you telling me that he raped you?' Emma asked softly.

Aggie nodded. 'He said . . .' She struggled to get the words out. 'He said I had encouraged him all along, but I hadn't. True I liked him, it wasn't just that he was so good-looking, he had a wonderful sense of humour, he made me laugh, was so easy to be with. Truly, Emma, up until then I had thought him to be a kind gentleman. When he started to tear at my clothes I tried hard to stop him cos I'm not like that. I didn't want what he was doing. Honestly I didn't.' Suddenly the memory of it appeared too much for her to take. As she went to speak again her voice cracked and she gasped. Tears welled up in her eyes and ran down her cheeks.

'Of course you're not like that, Aggie,' Emma said, wanting to reassure her. She was shaking with anger, but that wouldn't help Aggie. Her need was for compassion and understanding, good solid friendship and someone to talk too, someone who would listen and not pass judgement.

Agnes sniffed and wiped her handkerchief around her tear-stained face. Then heaving herself more upright in her chair she made a great effort to pull herself together and to continue. 'Oh, Emma, I do so want you to believe me. He kept saying I was a lovely lady an' I deserved to be loved. He forced me flat on my back on the floor and I couldn't stop him.' Agnes had her head buried in her hands and the words that followed were muffled. 'I can't go into details, it was like a nightmare, he was on top of me, being brutal, worse than an animal an' it seemed ages before he rolled off of me. When he stood up an' pulled his trousers on he actually said, "That was good, wasn't it?' Then he had the cheek to ask if I was going to make the coffee.'

Emma was furious, asking herself over and over again, what can I do? There must be something. I could kill this bloke, she thought fuming, someone should, he must think he's had what he wanted and got away with it while poor Agnes is left with her life in ruins.

The room was silent now, the only sound being the ticking of the clock on the mantelpiece. She took a clean handkerchief from her handbag and nudged Agnes.

'Here, luv, have this dry one, yours is soaking wet.'

Agnes handed over the soggy handkerchief and murmured her thanks.

Emma took this chance to gently ask, 'How did you get rid of him?'

'I made the excuse that I had heard one of the boys call out and that I had to go upstairs otherwise he might come down. I thanked God that both Sidney and Lenny were dead to the world but I knew I had to go back down or he might shout for me or even come up the stairs. I was scared stiff, but I knew I had to. So I did.'

There was a long pause. Finally she said, 'He'd gone. I hadn't heard his car start, but I parted the curtains a little and looked out and it wasn't there. That was a great relief. I put a kettle and a saucepan of water on to boil. I had a good wash, scrubbed myself really hard. For days afterwards I tried hard to put it out of my mind. I thought I was able to cope, well, just about, then my monthly didn't appear, the nightmare was back and I went mad. It wasn't fair, it really wasn't. I hadn't done anything wrong. I had only met the man those two weekends, been in his company only on the two Saturday evenings at the Big House. I don't even know his surname. I could look it up in the booking register at the Fox but what good would that do me? His word against mine. I invited him into my home late at night.'

Having got it all off her chest, Agnes broke down completely. Emma could tell they were tears of relief this time as at last she'd been able to tell someone. They were tears of fatigue as if the burden of it all had been a physical weight on her shoulders.

Emma wrapped her arms around her, held her, let her cry, at the same time once again asking herself what in God's name could she do. This was such a big problem to take on. She wasn't capable of offering advice. Things like this didn't happen in such a quiet village. But it had happened and folk would gossip, then Aggie's life wouldn't be worth living. Oh God, what a mess!

'Emma, what am I going to do?' Aggie cried.

If only I had the answer, Emma thought.

Of course there was abortion, but that was a sin, almost murder, at least that was the view that she had always held. It was also illegal.

'Aggie, my love, you've got to make up your mind to take one step at a time,' Emma finally said, the concern showing on her face. 'You've done enough for now by just telling me, but you must make up your mind to go and see the doctor as soon as you can. He'd be the one to advise you an' he would respect your confidence. I'm sure he'd be able to help you.'

'Thanks, Emma, I know what yer saying is good advice but I'm dreading going. That would make it all official an' he would ask questions which would be embarrassing and compromising . . .' Her voice trailed off and her eyes filled with tears again.

Emma knew there was nothing more to be said for the moment, she'd talk to Aggie again when she was less distraught. Besides there was a strange silence between them now, was Aggie regretting having confided in her? I'd like to ask her if she'd mind if I spoke to Sam about this. A problem shared is a problem halved but that must have been what Aggie thought when she told me and for all the help I've been she might just as well kept quiet. But Sam and I never have secrets from each other he was bound to question her. She could hedge all she liked but Sam would know if she wasn't telling the truth.

'Aggie, love, I must go. Sam will be wondering why I've

stayed so long. So . . . tomorrow is another day, we'll talk then. Will you be all right?'

Daft question and they both knew it. They hugged each other and Aggie managed to say, 'Thanks for listening, Emma, an' for caring.'

'Only wish I could offer better advice but I will go to the doctor with you if you want me to.' Emma tried to sound reassuring as she gave Aggie's hand a last squeeze.

'We'll see, as you say, tomorrow is another day,' Agnes said with a faint smile.

What a difference that would make God only knows, thought Emma.

Thirteen

The evening sun was shining through the windows, the back door was propped open as far back as it would go and the low ceiling gave the house a lovely homely feeling. Emma was thrilled to bits as she stared down the garden, the flower-beds were a blaze of colour and the two apple trees were leafy green and although not yet quite ripe there was an abundance of fruit on the branches.

She took a deep breath and told herself how lucky she and Sam were. They didn't have a great many possessions, but their girls were healthy, Sam had regular work and they were never short of food. Yet the whole world seemed to have so many problems.

Last October the Americans had suffered what had become to be known as the Wall Street Crash. The greatest disaster to strike the financial world and it was this that had started the Great Depression. Sam regularly read the newspapers and together they listened daily to the news being broadcast on the wireless. Thousands of people had seen their entire life savings wiped out in a matter of days. Hunger and poverty were growing on both sides of the Atlantic.

The financial crash had touched every major city and London was no different. Two million men were put out of work throughout Britain. Three hundred and fifty marchers had converged on London from Scotland, Wales and all corners of the country for a great demonstration in Hyde Park. Such were the depth of despair that the owners of great manufacturing firms were committing suicide after their businesses collapsed.

Men who had worked in factories, iron-foundries or spent their lives hundred of feet down in the darkness, digging out the coal were all affected. They were all now on the scrap heap without the means to feed their families or keep a roof over their children's heads. It almost made her feel guilty. The whole world had been turned upside down and yet she and her family were still safe and secure. Sam's attitude was reassuring. He maintained that if folk did not have their horses shod his family still wouldn't starve, he would always find something to do at his forge. They had land around their house and farms within easy reach. They would survive. In fact he planned to buy some six-week-old chicks. Soon they would be collecting their own fresh eggs.

Emma was so surprised the depression seemed to be passing them by that her pressing problem with Agnes was temporarily forgotten.

Only last Wednesday Sam had been to London for the day with Reverend Coyle. The purpose of their visit had been to meet some members of the Toc H Society and to find out how the children that had visited North Waltham were doing. Sam had been a willing volunteer, he'd been yearning to know how their two boys were faring. There hadn't been any more letters despite the fact that Emma continued to write at least once a fortnight.

Sam had been close-lipped since he had returned from that trip. He was reluctant even to discuss the visit with her and every time she mentioned Tom Yates and John Kirby he held up his hand to silence her, always saying, 'Emma, will you please leave the matter alone for now, we'll sort it out when the opportunity arises.'

What was she supposed to make of that?

Sam wouldn't talk about the institution where the children were housed or even say if he and Michael had been inside the building this time, yet he would talk endlessly of the other places they had visited.

On their return both men had been carrying a very large, strong brown-paper bag containing bunches of bananas. They had presented them to Mrs Verity, the head mistress of the local school, who had promised that the children would be given one each to eat during playtime.

Sam had told her that the meeting with members of the Toc H had been very successful. They had been very encouraged by the fact that people from North Waltham had continued to keep in touch with the children and had expressed a wish to participate in any future holiday projects. They had eaten a good lunch and had then set off for the railway station only to find they had a wait of three and a half hours before they could start their journey home.

Michael had put forward the idea that they should take a launch trip on the Thames.

'That journey left me feeling absolutely amazed,' Sam had said many times.

'One could be forgiven for thinking we were in another country,' Sam had remarked as Emily and Bella had sat at his feet, staring up into his weather-beaten, smiling face, listening as he had told them of London. 'The Port of London is like no other place in the world. Michael and I got on the launch at Tower Pier and were given a tour of the busiest parts of the Thames. Beginning at the Royal Albert and King George V Dock. Everywhere we looked there were ships, tugs and barges. Their crews spoke so many different languages it was bewildering to listen to them.'

'How could you tell, Daddy, did you talk to them? Bella's curiosity had been roused.

'We did, as we came back on to the docks, that's how we came to be given the bananas. But before that we saw all the famous bridges. We passed warehouses, factories, gasworks, many more docks and jetties, piers, public houses, and heaps of rubbish dumps. Even on the water the noise was terrific, the constant sound of engines, ship's sirens and the rattle of cranes and anchor chains. It was never-ending.'

'Dad, why have we never been to London?' Emily had questioned her father.

'Do you know, pet, these last few days I've asked myself that question a few times.' Sam had turned to draw his wife into the conversation. 'We ought to make an effort an' take the girls, don't you think so, dear?'

'As long as we don't have to stay in the city.' Emma was unmoveable on that score. 'We could maybe stay near to Hampton court where my Aunt Ada used to live an' where I had a couple of lovely holidays with her and my uncle Frank. I was only young then but I still remember the River Thames and Hampton Court Palace.'

'Maybe all of us could stay with your aunt an' then see both places.'

'We'd have a hard job love.' Emma's smile had been full

of regret. 'My auntie and uncle both died the year you were born, Emily. 1921.'

'Never mind.' Sam had broken the silence. 'As soon as the country settles down again an' there is not so much unemployment we will take both of you to London for a holiday. I will make sure that we are standing on one of London's bridges at high tide.'

'Why is that?' both girls wanted to know.

Sam grinned. 'Because close to high tide the Thames becomes alive. Big ships, which have been moored or anchored, move off with pilots on board. It's a very busy time but a great sight to see.'

'Am I allowed to ask a question?' Emma sounded a bit put out.

Both girls turned their heads to stare at their mother while their father just said, 'Ask away.'

Emma drew herself up in the chair and heaved herself into a more comfortable position. 'I would like to know how suddenly you know so much about the working of the London dockyards?'

Sam threw back his head and let out a great roar of laughter.

Emma looked at her girls, they shrugged their shoulders and within seconds all of them were laughing.

Eventually Sam said, 'Michael and I hung about a bit when we got off the launch at the Royal Docks. There was a ship moored and the doors to its hold were lowered. We could see into the hold. Stacks of large containers were filled with bananas and these containers were being lowered on to the quayside.

'The dockers all seemed to be dressed alike, long dark overcoats which looked pretty much the worse for wear, thick dark trousers and black boots. Each man wore a flat cap and a white scarf was knotted around his neck. We got talking to them, proper Eastenders they were and Michael and I agreed we had never spent a more interesting or more informative hour than we did with these hard-working men.'

'And was it these men that gave you the bananas?' Bella was eager to know.

'Yes, it was, or strictly speaking it was to the reverend that they actually offered them. Suppose they thought he would share them amongst his flock. Either way it was a generous thing to do and the men would have been offended if we had refused. All that information that I've just passed on to you we learnt from the dockers. They really were great men.'

Intrigued, Emma shook her head. 'How come the dock-yards are still so busy when the news is so terrible? Didn't the men mention the hunger marches?'

'Indeed they did.' Sam looked at Emma for a long moment and when he spoke again his voice was sombre. 'I don't mind telling you that from what they told us matters are far worse than what the Government is leading us to believe. It isn't going to get settled overnight either. Millions are unemployed. Mostly family men with children to feed and clothe and it's going to be a long, hard struggle.'

Sam's conversation with the girls had reminded her of how hard the conditions in London must be. Now, her eyes screwed up in concentration, she worried. The more she listened, the more she learnt and every day she counted her blessings, but she wished that Sam would open up and tell her more about the institution where Tom and John were. If it were within her powers she would be up in London asking to be given the right to bring those to boys back to live with them.

She raised her eyes to heaven. 'Dear God, we have so much, why can't we be allowed to share it with others?'

Even her letters were never answered by the boys, it was like banging her head against a brick wall. One thing was for sure, she wouldn't give up, she'd have a word with Reverend Coyle, there was just a chance he might be a bit more forthcoming.

Her thoughts went to her girls, they had been enthralled with the tales that their father had to tell and it was only natural that they wanted to visit London. Not much chance of that, not if she and Sam were being realistic.

A lot of water would have to run under the bridges before the country was back on its feet. At that point in time Emma couldn't possibly have known just how right her prediction would turn out to be.

Fourteen

As far as Agnes Brownlow was concerned, night-time was far and away the worst part of each day. That had been the case ever since she'd realized she was pregnant. After she had put the boys to bed she felt so low and despised herself. Knowing she had no one to turn to about the predicament it was at this time that she felt the true weight of loneliness. She did have Emma though, but there were times when she felt she couldn't burden her any more than she already had.

Through no fault of her own she was carrying this baby and she just could not bring herself to do anything about it. Have an abortion? If she forced herself to face the truth that meant getting rid of it by killing it. Reluctantly she'd been to see a doctor. She had travelled seven miles to Basingstoke to keep an appointment with Doctor Williams, a female doctor. The visit had not been a waste of time, yet she was no nearer to making a decision.

She had hardly sat down in Doctor Williams's surgery before she had blurted out the whole story. The doctor had listened, asked a great many questions about Agnes's other children, and shown great sympathy and understanding.

Day and night Aggie went over and over that visit in her mind, and always ended up getting nowhere. She was now ten weeks pregnant, and was sick every morning before she dragged herself off to work. Her shifts at the pub weren't the same. She felt she could no longer laugh and chat with the customers because she always felt so tired. If she didn't watch out Alice or Ted would notice and ask what was wrong. She didn't want to lose her job at the pub, she enjoyed serving behind the bar. In fact she almost regarded it as her social life. Nowadays it was the only bit of life she did get to see.

All this thinking had got her nowhere.

She had to make up her mind today. There was no point

in keep going round and round in circles. Out loud she counted her options once more.

One, she kept the baby. Two, she decided to have a back-street abortion.

Which was it to be? Neither decision seemed to be right.

There was also the matter of her three children, by God the rumours would fly around the village. Even her best friend Emma had been totally shocked when she had first confided in her. 'How? When? Where? Who was the father?' Emma had screamed in disbelief. Good old Aggie, shabby, reliable Aggie, who never went anywhere without her three children, was pregnant. Unbelievable! Wouldn't that be the reaction of everyone who knew her? And the children at school, how would they react to Sidney and Lenny when they heard their parents talking. Children could be so cruel.

Leave all the whys and wherefores be, she decided. Having read the riot act to herself she got to her feet and drew herself up to her full height.

'I am going to keep this baby.' She had said the words out loud. It seemed to make them more convincing. There! She had made her decision and she would stick to it, come hell or high water.

First things first, she thought. I must go straight away and tell Emma.

Emma was working in the front garden when Aggie arrived.

'Hello, love. I'm glad to see you, good excuse to stop work,' Emma said as she pulled off her gardening gloves and laid them on the path together with the trowel which she had been using. 'Let's go round the back into the kitchen and I'll put the kettle on.'

Aggie didn't want to wait to sit down before she made her announcement, once inside the house she blurted out her news.

'Emma, I want you to know I've made up my mind to keep this baby.'

There was a pause before Emma could bring herself to answer. 'Are you sure?' It was not what she had expected to hear.

'Quite sure,' Aggie said firmly. 'Though to be truthful I'm still not sure if it is the right decision. I only know I just couldn't live with myself if I killed this baby. After all it is a living thing inside me now an' it didn't ask to be born, did it?' Without waiting for an answer she added, 'So, rightly or wrongly, I am going to have this baby.'

'I understand,' Emma said, doing her best to smile. 'It must have been a very hard decision . . . I mean . . . what with you being on your own with three small children an' all. Have you really come to terms with just how hard it is going to be?'

'Yes. Yes, I have. I've spent hours an' hours going over and over it in my mind. As I've already said it may not be the right decision but that's my problem now be cause I *am* going to stick with it.'

Poor Aggie, it was as if all the life had gone out of her and she sat herself down with a plonk.

'As long as that is what you want,' Emma said, 'then you know I'll be there for you, will give you all the support I can.'

'Oh, Emma, thank you,' Aggie replied tearfully. 'Yer the best friend anyone could wish for.'

'Well, it works both ways, you've always been a jolly good friend to me. There's just one thing though. Do you mind if I tell Sam? It would be difficult to keep it from him.'

'Of course not, he and everyone else is going to know before too long. Your Sam is a good man he won't look down on me or pass judgement. But can you tell me what I should say when folk want to know who the father is, cos I'm blowed if I know?'

'Take your time,' Emma advised. 'You're not under any obligation to answer anyone. Let things ride an' folk can form their own opinions. I promise you, Aggie, you'll find that not everyone will be against you.'

It was as if a weight had been lifted from Aggie's shoulders. She felt a wave of tiredness sweeping over her and she leaned back in the chair and closed her eyes. The perfume of flowers floating in from the garden was sweet and she could hear the birds singing. Sleep overtook her and she didn't resist.

Much later she saw Joe standing in front of her. Dear God, he looked so fit and well. He smiled and held out a hand to her. She opened her mouth to speak but nothing came out. He stretched his arm forward, pointing to her stomach. 'You will be all right, really you will. Stop blaming yourself.' It was her Joe's voice, strong as ever. He hadn't altered one bit. He leant even further forward and put out his hand and Agnes felt his strong grip on her shoulder. He was gently shaking her and she so badly wanted him to take her in his arms.

'Aggie, open your eyes. Come on dear, wake up.'

It took a minute or two for Aggie to realize that it was Emma who was gently shaking her shoulder.

'I've made a pot of tea,' Emma quietly said, pointing to a tea tray she had set down on a small table.

'You were sound asleep for about an hour, then you started mumbling so I thought it was time to wake you. Do you feel better for the rest?'

'Oh, yes.' Aggie gave a soft sigh. 'It's done me a world of good.'

Emma looked hard at her friend, Aggie was pulling herself up in the chair and her face looked different, she was beaming, and it was almost as if her face had been lit up. 'Ready for a cuppa now, are you?' she asked as she poured milk into both cups.

'Yes, please, and that fruit cake you've laid out looks really great, did you make it, Emma?'

'Of course, when did you or I ever have a shop-bought cake in the house?' Emma teased her laughingly.

There was suddenly something entirely different about Aggie. I'm not imaging it Emma told herself, she's brighter, certainly much calmer, let's hope this new attitude will continue. For far too long she has been weighed down with guilt. Then the reason for the change in Aggie suddenly struck Emma. She had made her decision to keep the baby. No more dilly-dallying. Well good luck to her, Emma thought, she deserves all the help and encouragement she can get and I hope good folk will rally round and not stand in judgement.

Simultaneously the friends really did feel that Aggie's future was no where near as black as they had feared it would be. They changed the subject, drank their tea and nibbled at Emma's rich fruitcake.

Aggie left the house shortly after feeling that her visit had been well worthwhile in more ways than one.

Emma was of the opinion there was now room for skilful tactics. She would begin to knit baby clothes and she would take her knitting with her to the meetings of the Women's Guild. When the truth came out it might encourage others to look more kindly on Aggie. There would still be wagging

tongues and derogatory remarks which would hurt Aggie
but if today was anything to go by she'd cope and cope
well.

Fifteen

Reverend Coyle knew exactly why Emma had approached him and asked whether it would it be convenient for her to have a few words with him. Each day since he had been to London with Sam Pearson he had been expecting Emma to turn up on his doorstep. In a way it would be a great relief when she had asked her questions even though he had no idea what he was going to say to her. He and Sam had been unable to find answers so there were none that he could give to Emma.

Opposite to the church hall there was a half-timbered building that the reverend used for all sorts of meetings that weren't necessarily connected with his work for the Church. Emma didn't have to tap on the door to announce her arrival because Michael had been standing at the window and had seen her crossing the grass. He had the door open wide and hand outstretched as he said, 'Come in, Emma, it's nice to see you, good meeting this afternoon, was it?'

'Nice to see you too, Michael, I began to think you were avoiding me as you haven't dropped into the house once since you and my Sam spent the day in London.'

'Guilty,' he murmured, throwing up his hands in mock surrender.

'Then you'll know why I need to ask you a few questions,' Emma said, thinking it was best to be straightforward. 'I wouldn't normally bother you because I know how busy you are but Sam just clams up the minute I broach the subject, For that reason alone I know something must be wrong an' I'm worried sick.'

'Come and sit down, Emma,' he said, pointing to a round polished table that had four high-backed chairs arranged around it.

Emma sat facing the window and immediately took her cardigan off. The afternoon sunshine was still very bright and inside this large shed-like building it was very warm.

'I'm sorry I can't offer you any refreshments,' Michael began but Emma waved his apology away.

'Please, Michael, we're both aware that I need to know what you found out about the children. For me that means John and young Tommy.'

'At this moment, Emma, I am regretting that Sam and I didn't come straight to you on our return. To be honest we were hoping against hope that the problem might have been solved by now to everyone's satisfaction.' He shrugged his shoulders and his eyes showed his concern.

'Well, that's one question answered,' Emma said sighing softly. 'You've admitted that there is a problem. So, are you going to tell me what it is?'

Michael hesitated for a long time and looked so uncomfortable that Emma felt bound to ask, 'Are the boys in trouble?'

'We honestly do not know.'

Emma suddenly felt very cold and her stomach lurched. 'For God's sake, Michael! Will you please stop talking to me as if I weren't able to cope with bad news, what with Sam not saying a single word an' now you beating about the bush all the time, don't you know the thoughts going round and round in my head are driving me mad?'

Michael could imagine the horrors that Emma was summing up and the pact that he and Sam had agreed on suddenly did seem daft. They had agreed to wait until someone in authority contacted them with news before they told Emma the full story. Nothing had been heard, and it was time to put a stop to all this misery. But, and it was a big but, would Emma be any happier when he'd put her in the picture?

'All right, Emma, I did agree with Sam that we should wait, but now I think you need to hear the full story.' He took a deep breath before starting. 'When we arrived at Vauxhall the institution was closed up. Every door was locked and every window was boarded up. Sam and I spent some time speaking to street traders, shopkeepers and we even tried the dockers but no one at all seemed to know why the place had closed down or what had happened to all of the children that had been living there. Our last resort was the police.'

Emma bit her lower lip and looked very scared.

'We got no joy from the local station so we returned to the offices of the Toc H. John Farrington was still there and we had our first stroke of luck. Mrs Curtis had been on to them. In case you didn't know, Mrs Curtis was the matron of the London Foundation for Needy Children, that's the proper name for the institution where the children were living at the time.'

'Did this Mrs Curtis know where the children had been moved to?' Emma felt she had to move things on a lot quicker if she were ever going to hear where the children were now.

'Yes, she did, apparently she is still in charge at the new home which is in Kent.'

'So, do you have the address? Are the children safe and well? Are they happy about this move away from London?'

'Hang on a minute, Emma, so many questions all at once are too much for me.'

Emma felt a shudder run down her spine. Something was terribly wrong here! If Sam had known all along that the children's home had closed down why had he and Michael been so secretive? God almighty, she just had to hope that the bad news hadn't been left until last.

'Michael, why was Mrs Curtis in touch with the London branch of the Toc H if the children were now housed somewhere in Kent?'

'I suppose you had to know sooner or later,' he answered, heaving a hefty great sigh. 'During the transporting of all the children from London down to Kent, John and Tommy went missing.'

Oh dear God! She'd known it was something like this but had been afraid to even admit it to herself. 'Where are they? Surely you've heard something from them?'

'No, nothing at all. I have been getting a daily report,' he added sheepishly

'What? A report that says nothing.'

'Something like that,' Michael admitted, feeling more uncomfortable by the minute.

'How long has it been?'

'Nearly three weeks. Eighteen days to be exact.'

'And not a word! Did they have any money between them?' Emma had to ask. It didn't bear thinking about. Where were they were sleeping and how were they managing to feed themselves?

He didn't reply, just looked at her with sorrow in his eyes, hoping he'd said enough to satisfy her for the moment yet his conscience was pricking him. The boys had been missing a long time and he'd prayed for news of them every day but nothing so far had been forthcoming. He couldn't let Emma go on such a sour note but what could he say?

'Every day I am in touch with the Toc H and they assure me that those children are being properly cared for down in Kent. It is a much better place for them to be living than London. It will be good for the boys once they return.'

'I know what you're saying is perfectly true, Michael. It has always been said that Kent is the garden of England, but we have to find them first before they can take up this wonderful new life.' Emma wiped away a tear that had trickled down her cheek. She was fast losing her patience.

'I know,' Michael agreed gloomily as he paced up and down.

'Have the authorities been notified that two young boys have gone missing?'

'Both Sam and I asked the same question over and over again. Each time we received the same answer. Everything is being done that can be done.'

'God help them,' Emma muttered, 'they must be terrified, nowhere to sleep and nothing to eat, how the hell did a large association come to mislay two of the children they were supposed to be responsible for?'

'People have been hauled over the coals, so Mrs Curtis has told me, because a head count wasn't taken during a break in the journey and it wasn't until they reached Kent that they found their numbers were short.'

'Eighteen days is a hell of a long time for those boys to be fending for themselves, isn't it?'

'Yes, Emma, it is, and I am constantly praying that the good Lord will keep them safe.'

For a long moment they looked despairingly at one another, while Emma was trying to work out whether she felt better for knowing that the two boys had gone off on their own or was ignorance really bliss? At least now she would be able to get Sam to talk to her even though they would both need to keep calm because she had a feeling that until they had news that John and Tom were safe they'd be truly living on the edge of despair.

*   *   *

Sam was feeling relief flood through him as he listened to Emma give her account of her meeting with Michael Coyle.

It wasn't an easy situation, but as Sam shovelled another scoop of coal into the grate, he knew that it was down to him to reassure Emma and try to stop her worrying quite so much. He put down the shovel and glanced out of the window. The weather had certainly taken a sudden turn for the worst. This last week had been great, days of clear blue skies and bright warm sunshine, but today a north-easterly wind was blowing a gale and there was no sign of the sun as it hid behind the thick banks of dark clouds that had caused the heavy downpour earlier this morning. It was a cold, wet, miserable day, yet there were still two weeks left in August.

Sam turned and stared at his wife, a day like today would make matters worse. She would let her imagination run riot, not knowing if the boys had any shelter. She looked ragged and worn-out.

'You could have saved me a heck of worrying if you'd been straight with me from the beginning,' Emma suddenly upbraided him.

'How do you work that out?' Sam snapped. 'Are you saying that if I'd come straight from London an' told you that the two boys had hopped off an' no one had the slightest idea where they had got to or how they were managing you would have been happier?'

'No, of course not, but has not talking to me made it any easier?'

'I never for a moment thought it was going to drag on for so long. I imagined that the pair of them would be tired, probably cold at night an' so hungry that they would have the sense to walk into a police station an' ask for help.'

Sam's words made sense and Emma was sorry that she had bitten his head off.

'Sorry, Sam,' she said. 'What do you think we should do now?'

'It's all right, luv, we're both nearing the end of our tether an' as to what shall we do, I was about to ask you the very same question.'

'I'm scared. Sam, nearly three weeks is a long time.'

'Yes, I know you are, but let's think back. In the short time

that the boys were with us I came to think that John was quite
an interesting character; if he ever gets the chance of an education that lad will take it an' quite quickly prove his worth.
There would be no stopping him. I just can't see him meeting
trouble halfway.'

'And Tom? I dread to think what he's getting up to.' Emma
couldn't resist a cheeky smile and Sam responded with a
hearty chuckle.

'Different kettle of fish altogether is that cocky fresh-faced
kid. Chuck him down a sewer an' he'll come up smelling of
roses. Don't get me wrong, luv, I think Tommy is a great lad
but there are times when he needs watching like a hawk. He's
grown up in a tough environment an' has taught himself to
believe that God helps those that help themselves. One thing
with him you will always be able to count on, plenty of
muscle, even if there's a shortage of brains. Growing up in
an institution means he's learnt about survival. At first, he
more than likely came in for a great deal of bullying but I
don't think Tom harbours bitterness, probably did him more
good than harm.'

'How d'you make that out?' Emma asked, wanting to believe
that Tom was capable of taking care of himself.

Sam looked again at his wife's unhappy face. 'I'm hoping
that over the years Tom has learned a lot about self-sufficiency.'

Clearly the situation was doing neither of them any good.
Something had to be done. And soon.

'Sam, about Tommy, you don't think he's a bad lad, not
really, do you?' Emma asked cautiously. She needed reassurance and she needed it now.

'No, of course I don't, given the same opportunities he'd
do just as well as John would, but now, well to be honest I
think it will be Tommy that is taking care of John. Having
said that, they'll survive, you'll see, they'll turn up soon, right
as ninepence.'

Sam had his fingers crossed behind his back as he made
this promise. He was also silently praying that his words
would be proved to be true before many more days had
passed.

Emma would have loved to be able to believe him. Much
as he made life easier for her in every way he could, that
didn't make her Sam a genius. He had said what he hoped

would turn out to be true because he knew that was what she needed to hear.

Except it wasn't a firm promise. She knew very well it wasn't. She'd just have to wait and hope that Sam was right.

Sixteen

The table was set and Emma was deep in thought as she stood in the kitchen stirring the rabbit stew. Steam filled the kitchen and Emma brushed a hand over her forehead. Two wet windy days had been the only break in the weather, now the heat-wave was back. This morning she had pulled her long hair into a bun and set it on top of her head, she needed some air around her neck. She was wearing a faded cotton dress with a bibbed white apron tied around her middle and on her feet were a pair of sandals which had seen several summers but they were so comfortable she was loath to get rid of them. She knew she looked scruffy but she was cross with her Sam and for the moment she didn't care.

It was Saturday afternoon and salmon with some new potatoes is what she had had in mind for their evening meal, but Sam had announced he wanted a proper dinner. To strengthen his case last night Sam had come back from visiting his friends with a freshly skinned rabbit.

Oh well, she sighed, as long as it keeps him happy.

She crumbled the margarine into the flour until it looked like breadcrumbs and ran it through her fingers. She'd tried so hard to make the school's summer holiday time a really happy few weeks, but her heart hadn't always been in it. Not wholeheartedly.

Emily and Bella had been told that Tom and John had gone missing but after the first flood of tears nobody seemed to want to talk about them. Sam had put forward the idea that because the weather had been so good it was highly probable that the two boys had obtained work on a farm. Emma wished over and over again that that might be true. A month had passed and still no news. How could two young lads without any visible means of support disappear without trace?

The boys were not her only worry. She also wished that

Aggie would take things a little easier. Nowadays when they went for a walk it was always Aggie who suggested that they sat down somewhere. The heat wasn't helping. Aggie was tired, sometimes short of breath and her ankles always looked swollen. She had given up her cleaning job, but still worked evening shifts at the Fox.

During the day she still had the three children to consider. Sidney and Lenny were typical boys, both good lads, but naturally boisterous. Aggie's brother John took them up to the farm with him whenever it was possible but you hardly ever saw Aggie without little Mary. Already Emma had the feeling that the strain was telling on her dear friend and couldn't help but wonder whether Aggie's decision to keep the baby had been the right one.

Emma made a decision. Sam had got his way today, she would even make him some parsley dumplings and pop them into his pan of stew but tomorrow she was going to have her way. No roast dinner. There wouldn't be many more hot Sundays left so she was going to make the most of this one. A right royal feast she would lay out; ham, hard boiled eggs, slices of cold roast pork, crusty new bread, new potatoes and salad. Tonight after the girls were in bed she would make a huge trifle, jelly and blancmange.

She planned the feast so she could invite Aggie and her children to come and spend the day with them. It would show Aggie that she and Sam did care and that they were not going to neglect her.

The Gods were on her side, Emma thought as she walked down the garden carrying a tray that held half a dozen glasses and a large jug of home-made lemonade.

It was a beautiful day, several degrees warmer than yesterday, and her decision not to cook a roast dinner had been right.

She was in yards of reaching the spot under the tree where Aggie was sitting when she realized that all was not well. Carefully she placed the tray down on the grass and slowly approached Aggie. She didn't want to panic but the way Aggie was bending forward and clutching at her stomach worried her.

For a while she sat next to Aggie, gently rubbing her back

between her shoulder blades. The pain seemed to ease a little and Aggie straightened herself up.

'Sorry to be a nuisance,' Aggie whispered, letting her deep breath out by puffing her cheeks out and blowing. 'I really don't know what happened. One minute I was fine, then I suddenly had cramp in my tummy.'

Emma was fearful but there was no way she was going to let Aggie know. 'You haven't been eating the crab apples, have you?' she asked, forcing herself to smile.

Aggie was about to answer when another wave of pain shot through her, she reached for Emma's hand and held on to it so tightly that she could feel Aggie's finger nails digging into the back of her hand.

The two friends sat side by side, the silence was comfortable yet each knew what the other was thinking. The minutes ticked by, the birds were singing and some were splashing in each of the two bird-baths that edged the lawn. The sounds of happy laughter coming from the bottom of the garden were proof that their five children had found something to amuse them.

'I think it's best if we get you indoors, it's probably cooler in the front room,' Emma suggested, her voice filled with concern.

Aggie struggled to her feet.

'Easy does it,' Emma said in a soothing voice as she held Aggie's arm and guided her along the garden path towards the house.

Sam, who had been sitting just outside the back door, reading the Sunday newspaper, sprang to his feet as they came nearer. For once he looked rattled.

'What's the matter?' he asked.

'Aggie's not feeling too well,' Emma quickly explained. 'I thought she should come in out of the sun. We were going to go for a walk with the children but they've gone off on their own. Our Emily is wheeling Mary in her pushchair.'

Sam turned to look at Aggie. 'I can see by the look on your face, luv, that you are in pain. Did it come on suddenly? Is there anything that I can get you?'

Aggie wasn't able to answer. Even the short walk had been too much. The colour had drained from her face and she was having great difficulty with her breathing.

At once Sam took charge. 'Get the other side of her, Emma, an' I'll take this side. The quicker we get her lying down the better.'

It was a slow, clumsy process trying to manoeuvre the bulk of Agnes through two doorways without letting go of her but they finally made it. Sam put his arms round the middle of Aggie and half lifted her until her bottom was on the settee.

Having taken a breather, Emma bent low and placed her hands behind Aggie's knees which enabled her to swing her legs up and so allow Aggie to stretch out full length.

Sam took two cushions from an armchair, placed both of them beneath Aggie's head before quietly asking, 'Is that more comfortable, luv?'

Aggie nodded her head and smiled her thanks before closing her eyes and letting her head fall backwards to rest on the cushions. She looked ghastly. Her forehead was clammy, showing beads of perspiration.

Sam turned to his wife. 'Shall I go for an ambulance?'

It was Aggie that moved her head in protest. 'No, no! Please don't. I'll be fine once this pain eases off.'

Emma nodded to Sam, he caught on and followed her outside. 'Where can you get an ambulance from? I think it's best that we do get Aggie to hospital,' Emma said, sounding very close to tears.

'So do I,' Sam quickly agreed. 'By the look of her she's really suffering. How about I pop up to the Fox, I'm sure Ted will phone for us?'

It was at that moment they heard Aggie give a sharp gasp of pain.

Sam moved quickly to the front door calling out as he went, 'I'll be as quick as I can.' With that he was gone.

Emma rushed back to be with Aggie. She didn't like what she saw, in fact she was really frightened. Aggie was doubled up in pain and her face looked even worse if that was possible.

'Are you bleeding?' she asked.

'I'm not sure,' Aggie said. 'I don't think so but I'm not sure. I feel dreadful! Oh, Emma, perhaps I should try to get home. I'm not sure if I could manage to walk there though.'

'You'll do no such thing,' Emma said firmly, 'Now lie back

and try not to worry, Sam has gone up to the Fox to ask Ted to telephone for an ambulance.'

'Oh, Emma, please, I don't want to go to the hospital. I'll be all right if I rest up for a bit.'

'I think you really need to see a doctor, luv, just to be on the safe side.'

'But what about me children? If the hospital were to keep me in they can't stay in the house all by themselves.'

'Agnes Brownlow! I don't think I want to know what you're going on about. You think for one moment that I'd leave your kiddies to fend for themselves? Doesn't say much for our years of friendship, does it?'

'I'm sorry, Emma. Course I should know better, guess I'm panicking.'

'Yeah, well, don't give another thought to the children. They will be here with me and Sam until you're better. Meanwhile, you stay here with your feet up an' I'm going to warm some milk for you. I think I'll fetch you a blanket as well, I know it's boiling hot outside but you're shivering.'

Agnes did as she was told and lay on the settee. What she desperately wanted was to be in her own home. It was embarrassing enough but to be taken ill in Emma's home and have Sam involved made her feel even more uncomfortable.

Emma was soon back carrying a small tray, holding a glass of warm milk, and a blanket drapped over her arm. 'Hang on a minute, luv,' she said, stetting the tray down, 'I'll fetch you another cushion. Would you like a hot-water bottle to cuddle?'

'No, but I will have that blanket over my legs. Thanks for the offer, Emma, in fact thank you for everything.' Aggie's eyes were brimming with unshed tears.

'Now then, Aggie, don't go all soft on me, you know I don't need any thanks. I just want you to lie still until we can get someone to help you.'

If only Sam would come back and tell me what is happening, Emma thought.

Aggie had raised her head and was sipping the warm milk when suddenly she let out a cry of anguish. She knew for certain now that she was bleeding. Tears spilled over and ran down her cheeks as she cried out, 'Oh, Emma, I think I am losing blood now.'

Emma felt fairly certain she knew what was happening. A miscarriage, she was sure of it, and she was truly sorry for her dear friend. 'Please Aggie, try to stay calm, let your head go back, relax if you can.' Emma knew she was talking for the sake of talking, nothing she said or did was going to make Aggie relax. *Oh dear God, what can I do? Time was passing so slowly. Where the hell was Sam?* Aggie had refused her offer of a hot-water bottle but it would give her something to do. Ten minutes later Emma was helping Aggie to raise her shoulders while she slipped the hot-water bottle on to her back and was rewarded by a soft sigh of relief.

'I'm sure Sam won't be much longer now,' Emma said, hoping her words would turn out to be true. She picked up the glass that stood beside the settee and raising Aggie's head with one hand she held the glass to her lips. 'Try a few more sips of this milk, it is still nice and warm.'

Thank God, Emma silently prayed as she heard Sam opening the front door and when he came rushing into the front room it was all she could do not to burst into a flood of tears.

'Ambulance is on its way,' he said thankfully as he squeezed his wife's hand. Ten minutes later, to their relief, the sound of sirens could be heard.

'What's yer name, pet?' a tall blond young man dressed in green asked as he leant over Aggie.

'Agnes Brownlow,' she murmured.

'Well, Agnes, yer coming for a ride with us, which can't be bad, it's a lovely Sunday afternoon an' we're going to take good care of you.'

Agnes appealed to him. 'I've got three children I can't just go off without seeing them . . .' Her voice trailed off but she seemed really agitated.

A nurse smoothed the hair from Aggie's damp forehead and looked to Emma for help. Emma stepped closer. 'Aggie, we've been through all of that, I've told you Sam and I will see to the children. They'll be fine, the least of your worries, you just concentrate on yourself.'

Wrapped in a bright red blanket Aggie was lifted with ease on to a trolley. The ambulance man joked, 'Here we go then, didn't think I'd be taking a lovely mum for a ride this afternoon.'

Sam stood by the open door of the ambulance and as the

trolley was lifted he bent low to speak to Aggie. 'Now, luv, promise me you'll not worry over Sid an' Lenny, we won't let them out of our sight an' our girls will be made up having Mary sleeping in their bedroom. We'll be in to see you as soon as the doctor says it's all right.'

Both Emma and Sam felt a bit guilty not going in the ambulance with Aggie but the children had not returned yet. Instead they got the lunch set out and when the children's voices were heard they went out into the lane to meet them. With a fixed smile on their faces they told the children that their mum wasn't feeling too well and that she had been taken to see a doctor.

The two boys thought it was a good lark to be staying with their Uncle Sam and Auntie Emma, Little Mary was at first a bit tearful saying she wanted to be with her mummy. However as the day went on everyone settled down, they played all sorts of games and when the Wall's ice-cream man was heard calling, 'Stop me and buy one.' Sam went out and bought a wafer for everyone.

The children had all behaved well and it had been a happy day, but that was not to say that both Sam and Emma didn't breathe a deep sigh of relief when they looked at the clock and realized it was nine o'clock. All the children were safely washed and in bed. The only bit of opposition Emma had met was when she had suggested that Sidney and Lenny should wear one of her girl's nightdresses to sleep in.

'Give over,' Sid had stormed, 'I'm not a sissy.'

Len had been equally annoyed and when Sam had taken their side and told them they were right to refuse, sleeping in their underpants would be fine, that Emma knew the laugh was on her and the boys wouldn't let her forget it for a long time.

Emma sunk down into her armchair and placed her feet on a low footstool, telling herself it had been quite a day!

'I think I'll take a walk up to the Fox,' Sam said, patting Emma's shoulder. 'I could murder a pint an' I'll bring you back a ginger wine, shall I?'

Emma's eyes had been half closed but they snapped wide open now. 'You're not just going to the pub for a drink, are you?'

'Well, no,' he said. 'I did think I'd ask Ted to phone the hospital, see if there is any news on Agnes.'

'Well, why didn't you say so? If it is bad news weren't you going to tell me?'

'I don't know, luv, I'm all at sixes an' sevens. We've got to find out one way or another. To tell you the truth I'm dreading hearing what they will say. The ambulance man did give me a slip of paper with the telephone number on it.'

'Does it say where they have taken her?'

'Yes, it does. The Basingstoke Cottage Hospital. I don't suppose they'll let anyone see her, not at this time of night, but I'll ask Ted to find out about visiting times. I'll stay with the children an' you can go, perhaps one of the ladies from the Women's Guild will go with you.'

'All right, Sam, thanks. You go an' have your pint, I'm going to make myself a cup of tea.'

It was two o'clock on the Monday afternoon when the Ward Sister removed the screen from the double doors and flung them wide open. Pulling herself up to her full height she smoothed her stiffly starched apron and glared at the number of folk who were patiently waiting to see their loved ones.

'Visiting will be allowed until four o'clock. A bell will be rung at five minutes to the hour warning you that visiting time is almost up. Two visitors only at any one time at the bedside and please keep your voices low, remember there are sick people on my ward.'

Emma glanced at Kate Simmons. 'I wouldn't want to get on the wrong side of her,' she whispered as they walked down the long ward. 'It's a wonder she didn't want to inspect our bags. I suppose it is all right to bring grapes.'

'Oh, I'm sure it is,' Kate said, grinning widely, 'but I don't know about this pot plant that I've brought. Sister might well find a reason for it not to stand on Aggie's locker.'

'Surely not, those chrysanthemums are such a beautiful colour they will brighten up the whole ward.'

'We'll see. Look, there's Agnes on the other side, about four beds down.'

Emma put her shopping bag down beside the bed and leaned across to kiss her friend. 'How are you feeling today?' she asked, as she pulled a sheaf of papers from her bag. 'Before you ask, the kids are doing well an' to prove it they've each made a card for you. One in that lot is from Mary, she's settled well and her drawing is very colourful even if it is not very specific.'

Kate Simmonds knew why Emma was rattling on so, she was afraid and she had every right to be so. Agnes Brownlow looked awful. Her face was the same colour as the pillow case on which her head was resting, almost as if the blood had been drained from her cheeks. A chair had been placed, one each side of the bed, Kate pulled the nearest one out and guided, almost pushed, Emma down on to it.

Aggie's hands lay flat on top of the white counterpane and Kate stooped and covered one hand with one of her own. 'Everyone is so sorry to hear that you have had to come into hospital, all the women from the Guild send their love and said to say they hope to see you home again real soon.'

'Oh, that's kind,' Aggie murmured. 'And Kate it is kind of you to come with Emma to see me.'

'Not at all, I was concerned when I was told you were ill. Have the doctors given you any idea as to what is wrong?' Emma had decided not to tell Kate about Aggie's pregnancy.

'All they have told me is that I am to have plenty of bed rest – ' she looked up at Kate and was clearly embarrassed, in a hushed voice she added – 'they won't even let me get out of bed to go to the lavatory.'

Kate smiled. 'We women are all the same, aren't we? We hate having our privacy taken away from us, but you must do as they say and then soon you will be able to come back home.'

Emma had calmed down and had taken the grapes out of her bag and placed them in a dish on top of the locker. The pot plant that Kate had brought was planted in a beautiful blue ceramic bowl and it had its own blue saucer for the pot to stand in and catch any excess water.

Aggie expressed her thanks to them both, then asked Emma if she would hold up the drawings that the children had done for her. This Emma did, stating who had done what and then laying all five out flat on the counterpane for Aggie to see.

Kate turned her head towards Emma and out of the corner of her mouth she muttered, 'Better not let Sister see you disturbing one of her tidy beds or she'll have you banned and you won't be allowed to visit again.'

Although Emma knew that Kate was joking she feared that there might be a great deal of truth in what she had just said. So with a quick glance up and down the ward she quickly began to gather up the drawings. 'Sam made you a stiff cover to keep them all in, nice bit of cardboard he had saved. I'll pop them on the top shelf of your locker, shall I?'

'Oh, yes please, or perhaps you ought to take them back home with you, I wouldn't want to lose them.'

'No, they'll be all right there, later on you can have a good look at them and I'll make sure you don't forget them when we come to bring you home.'

'Oh, Emma, I wonder how long they will keep me here.'

'Only just so long as you need to rest, so do as you're told. I'll tell the children that they will be seeing you soon, all right?'

'Yes all right, kiss them for me, will you, Emma?'

'Course I will.' Those three little words were almost drowned out by the clanging of the big bell that a hospital orderly, wearing a khaki-coloured overall, was swinging from side to side.

Kate and Emma said their goodbyes to Agnes and they each had the feeling that she wasn't sorry that visiting time was over. She was dead tired and they both hoped that she would be able to get a good night's sleep.

At the door the Sister stood flanked by two of her nurses. 'Next visiting day is on Wednesday, two until four, again on Sunday from two until four. Thank you all for coming. I should remind you that no children are allowed to visit at any time.'

Both Kate and Emma breathed a sigh of relief as they came out into the bright fresh air. 'Remind me never to be ill,' Kate said grinning. 'I should hate to be at the mercy of that dragon.'

'Me too,' Emma admitted. 'She certainly runs a tight ship.'

It was eleven thirty on Wednesday morning when Alice Andrews came round the back way to Emma's house and stood in the open doorway to her scullery.

The stone sink was half-filled with hot water and Emma was up to her elbows in suds. She had been moaning to herself as to how much more washing three children made, especially the extra pairs of socks. She looked up and saw Alice's face and needed no telling.

'It's Aggie, isn't it?' She gasped the question out.

'Yeah, the hospital rang about an hour ago but Ted was seeing a brewery order in so I had to wait until the cellar was safely closed before I could come here.'

Emma felt the colour drain from her face. 'How bad is she?' she managed to ask, all the while fearing the worst.

'Oh, Emma, I'm sorry, I didn't mean to frighten you. Ted took the call and he said the doctor was really sympathetic. Aggie is not too bad, she will recover given time, but she has lost the baby.'

'How long have you known about the baby?'

'For some time now. Don't forget Ted and I have got three grown-up children of our own. It suited Aggie not to tell us and we respected that. Sooner or later she would have confided in me, meanwhile we did all we could to lighten her jobs, she needed the money and she's always been a good worker as far as we were concerned.'

Emma dried her hands on the roller towel that hung behind the kitchen door. 'So it's over,' she said sighing, staring straight at Alice. 'You never know, Aggie might come round to the idea that it has happened for the best.'

'Well, I for one think so. My firm belief is that Agnes has been relieved of what could only have been a life-long burden.' Alice didn't mince her words and she didn't fight shy of giving a straight answer.

'Have you got time for a cuppa, Alice?'

'Not really, as I said it's Ted's day for cellar work so I'd better be getting back. I knew you would want to be told so I came as soon as I could get away. Now these next few weeks might be a bit sticky for Aggie, so if you think of anything I or my Ted could do, please promise you'll let us know.'

'Yes, of course I will, though we both know how independent Aggie can be.'

'Yeah, well, the offer is there and I shall be watching her to see how she's coping.'

When Alice had gone, Emma sat down at the kitchen table and rested her head in her hands. People in the village were good. There was no doubt about that. Alice knows full well that Aggie and I are best friends, she thought, and that there

is a very good chance that I know how she came to be in
this horrible situation. Yet she hadn't shown the slightest
curiosity. Never asking how or when it had happened or did
I know who the father was? She had accepted the fact that
she was pregnant but that the details were her own private
business.

One couldn't ask for more than that! Aggie finished her
washing and had it all pegged out on the two lines which ran
across the garden. Now she needed to talk to Sam. Having
combed her hair and tidied herself up, she put a thermos flask
of tea and a pack of cold meat sandwiches into her shopping
bag and set off across the fields to his smithy.

'It's all for the best, I think,' Sam stated, giving his opinion
and that was the end of the subject as far as he was concerned.
He did say he would cadge a lift from the postmen's van, they
usually went up to Basingstoke about six o'clock in the
evening, and call in at the hospital to find out how much
longer Aggie was likely to be kept in. If they could give him
a date then he could go and fetch her home.

'You're not saying you're tired of having her children stay
with us, are you, Sam?'

'I think you know me better than that,' he almost growled.
'I only want to know that I've done my best for Agnes an'
her children. She doesn't have a great life at the best of times
an' I for one think she's come through this patch of bad luck
with great spirit.'

Emma felt there wasn't a lot she could add to that, so she
decided to keep quiet.

The Sister wouldn't allow any rules to be broken and so it
wasn't until the following Sunday that Emma was allowed to
visit Agnes.

The change in Aggie the following Sunday was remarkable,
at least there was some colour back in her cheeks. Yet there
was a haunting look in her eyes and Emma regretfully told
herself that look would linger for some time to come. Her
endless questions were all about her children. She hadn't asked
about the sex of the baby which she had lost and no one had
told her. Given time Emma hoped Aggie would get over it.

They kept Agnes in hospital for three more days and she
was not only surprised but bewildered by the number of cards

wishing her well that were delivered to the ward. She did so appreciate them.

Then came the day she was allowed to go home. On her own insistence Sam took her to her own home where Emma and all the five children were waiting to welcome her. During the first hour the letter box on her front door rattled several times as mail fell on to the door-mat. What had she done to deserve so much kindness, she'd certainly not known that she had so many friends in the village.

'Dear God, thank you,' she murmured as she watched Emma prop more cards up on the sideboard and on the mantelshelf.

She still felt sad and lost about her unborn child. She looked through the back door to where her children were playing in the garden with the two daughters of her best friend and she knew she had a lot to be grateful for.

Seventeen

It was October, the summer truly gone, the nights were drawing in. Dinner was over, the girls had gone to the church hall for Brownies, Sam had eaten his fill and was now sleeping soundly and Emma felt it would be a shame to wake him. She glanced up at the clock on the mantelshelf and saw that it was almost time. Sam had said he wanted calling at seven thirty as he was due to meet a couple of friends in the Fox.

The knock on the back door made her jump. Who in heaven's name could that be? Folk usually pushed open the door and called out, 'It's only me.' She threw her sewing down on to the floor as she eased herself out of the chair. Sam had not stirred and she had to step over his feet to go through to the scullery, mumbling as she did so about him stretching out like that and taking up all the room.

'It's not! It can't be!' Her hand flew to cover her mouth as she stared at the two thin scruffy-looking lads standing in front of her.

''Ello, Aunt Em. I don't s'pose yer pleased t'see us but we don't know where else t'go.' It was John doing the talking.

Not able to find words to say Emma's eyes darted from one anxious face to the other. It looked like all the stuffing had been knocked out of Tom. This ragged, under-nourished dirty boy did not bear any resemblance to the cocky self-assured lad that had left here five months ago.

But what on earth was she doing keeping the boys standing out here? She now did what her instinct had told her to do from the moment she had set eyes on them. She took a step forward, pushed the lads together and wrapped her arms tightly around the pair of them. John was the tallest, her face was resting on his head and the tears that were running down her cheeks were falling on to his shoulders, wetting the thin shirt that he was wearing yet she continued to hold them close, saying over and over again, 'Thank God.'

'What's going on out here? Why is the door wide open letting the cold . . . ?'

Sam never got to finish his question. His head and broad shoulders were poked around the doorway and the exclamation he gave was like a roar from a lion.

Emma released her hold on Tom, but still kept one arm around John. Without saying so much as one word Sam scooped Tommy up into his arms and headed for inside the house.

For the first time since she had heard the knock on the door, Emma smiled. 'Come on, John, everything is going to be all right, you'll see.'

'Where's yer sense, woman, keeping them out there? Didn't you notice neither of them had a coat? John, come nearer to the fire and wrap this towel round you for now.'

'Thanks, Uncle Sam,' John said, grinning even though his teeth were chattering.

'Will we be able to stay with you, Aunt Emma?'

'You're certainly not going anywhere tonight,' Emma answered, looking at her husband.

From the look that passed between the two boys Sam knew they had picked up on Emma's hesitation. He pulled both lads nearer to him before he said, 'You've made it here at last an' yer aunt and myself are thankful that you have, believe me boys, we are. There hasn't been a day that we haven't prayed that you were safe. So, yer to stop worrying, you'll stay with us until something definite is sorted out. First off I know yer aunt is going to round up a feed for you, then it's a good wash an' so to bed for the pair of you.'

'We can both work, we've proved we can,' John said, sounding really sensible.

Tom had a grin on his face that spread from ear to ear. It made Emma turn to him and ask, 'What's tickled you, Tom?'

'How did I guess that you'd make us wash before you fed us?' he cheekily asked.

'Ah, so you haven't had all the stuffing knocked out of you then, you little beggar.' Sam tried to sound stern but laughter won the day.

After their faces and hands had been washed and a hot

flannel had been rubbed over their heads they were sat on the floor in front of the fire, each with a tray which held a bowl of thick soup, crusty bread, butter and cheese. Sam and Emma shut themselves in the scullery.

'You know we won't be allowed to keep them with us, don't you?' Sam sadly told his wife.

'So what do you suggest we do?' Emma asked with heavy sarcasm, 'just let them stay the one night and then turn them out to fend for themselves again?'

'Of course that's not my intention. I want to know where they've been all these months and then we shall have to notify the authorities.'

'You aren't going to tell the police, are you?' she asked in alarm.

'Not unless I have to,' he said quietly. 'First thing in the morning I'll go to see Michael Coyle, he should be able to deal with this situation.'

He didn't stop to see if Emma agreed or not, instead he went back to the kitchen and sat on the floor with the boys acting like a big kid who had just won first prize at a county event.

Once they had eaten their fill the boys had a wash in the tin bath. Once the grime was removed Tom's skin showed he had acquired a good suntan though there was not much flesh on his bones.

Sam had decided to leave the questioning until the morning but without thinking he said, 'Been out in the sun a lot, have you?'

'Yeah, we got took on at a farm, picking hops.'

'Did yer now! Got paid for the work?'

Tom thought for a moment. 'Well, not directly,' he hedged.

John thought it was time he did some explaining. 'There was this big family, the Watsons, they had four kids and all sorts of relations. They told the boss man we belonged to them as well, they did all right out of it. Got given two huts instead of only one and they collected our pay.'

'How long were you picking?'

'All of September and about twelve days into October, then one morning everyone was paid off. The Watsons went back to London but they gave us a quid each before they left.'

'Don't forget Ma Watson fed us real well every day and of

a night time, when everybody went down the pub, her old man always brought us a drink an' a packet of crisps an' sometimes a hot meat pie.' Tom spoke up in defence of his new found friends.

Sam smiled to himself, it was obvious that food was still of the utmost importance to Tom.

The girls went wild when they came home to find the two, now much cleaner, boys sitting at the table playing cards with their dad.

There was so much laughing and teasing going on that Emma hadn't the heart to break it up and it was eleven o'clock before she finally had the children safely tucked up in bed. It had been a happy evening, a great reunion, yet each hour had been taut with anxiety for herself and Sam. There were so many unanswered questions. What had the boys got up to during the months since they had absconded? She shuddered at the possibilities.

Were they wanted by the police? John seemed the more worried of the two. Two or three times he had gingerly tried to find out if they were going to be allowed to stay.

How could she and Sam say one way or another? They didn't know themselves.

One of the saddest aspects of the evening was that Emma realized that Tom was not well. He had a rasping cough and he was so thin. She could only guess at his physical condition but of one thing she was sure. He needed to see a doctor.

Over breakfast next morning they talked in general about why the boys had run away. It was easy to tell that Emily and Bella looked upon it all as a great adventure and were keen to hear everything down to the last detail. However Sam was eager to be gone, he needed advice as to whether or not he was breaking the law by keeping two runaway boys under his roof.

Two minutes after Sam had left the house Emma put her coat on and practically ran through the lanes to the doctor's surgery. She hadn't told the receptionist, Miss Sharpe, the whole truth but on the other hand she hadn't lied. She had merely stated that one of her children wasn't at all well and she needed the doctor to come out to the house as soon as possible.

If Dr Hamilton was shocked to find that the patient he had

been called out to attend was a young lad, knowing that Mr
and Mrs Pearson only had two daughters, he hadn't batted an
eyelid, and Emma respected him for his discretion.

'He's made of stern stuff is that one,' Dr Hamilton informed
Emma after he had taken Tom upstairs and given him a thor-
ough examination. 'I have to get him into hospital. What might
have started out as a summer cold has gone to his lungs, we'll
need an X-ray to see exactly what damage has been done.'

'The fact that he is so terribly thin is what is worrying me,'
Emma said fearfully.

Dr Hamilton took her hand and patted it, telling her not to
worry, he would see to everything.

By midday Emma felt that if one more person stepped into
her house she would scream. But there was another knock on
the door and she knew she had to answer it. She got up, her
legs felt heavy as she made her way through to the front of
the house.

'Come in,' she said to the three men who were standing
on her doorstep. One was Michael Coyle, the one in uniform
she knew to be Sergeant Blackwell, their local village bobby.
The third was an older man, introduced to her as Detective
Inspector Clarke, he was wearing a very heavy navy-blue
overcoat which was unbuttoned showing a dark pin-striped
suit underneath.

To have a policeman call at your house was bad enough
but a Detective Inspector as well was intimidating and when,
even before she had suggested that they all sat down, she
heard Sam come round the side of the house and through the
back door, she felt a flood of relief flow through her.

'Oh, Sam, thank God you've come home,' she cried, without
giving him time to even walk into the living room.

'Calm down, luv,' he begged. 'Michael an' I have already
had a long chat. It was himself that persuaded me that we had
no option but to let him notify the police. Let's all sit down
an' find out what is the best that can be done for the boys.
By the way, where are John and Tom?' he asked looking
through to the empty front room.

'Tom is upstairs in bed, I told you last night that he was
far from well. Anyway, I got the doctor out to him and he
gave him a dose of medicine an' said he'll be back later when

he's arranged for Tom to be taken to hospital. I sent Emily, Bella an' John round to Agnes, and I told Emily exactly what to tell her auntie, no more no less, and that they were to stay there until one of us came to fetch them. Aggie will give them some lunch, no worry on that score.' Sam looked at her in total disbelief. 'You didn't hang about, did you?' he said with a sigh, loosening his tie and undoing the top button of his shirt.

Emma wanted to get on with things, there were a dozen or more questions she wanted answered but thought she'd better tread carefully. 'What will happen to the boys now?' she asked, looking at Sergeant Blackwell.

It was the inspector that answered. 'Later on today they will be taken to a place of safety,' he said. 'You don't need to worry your head about them any more.'

Emma bristled. *Stuck up old so an' so,* she thought. 'What if Tommy is taken to hospital, why can't John stay with us, until you decide where they have to go? Much better if they can both go together surely?'

'Mrs Pearson,' the inspector began pompously, 'I'm sure both you and your husband are good kind people and I'm sure you both mean well, but you have no jurisdiction where these two boys are concerned.'

'And why shouldn't they be allowed to stay with a normal happy family?' Sam retorted sarcastically.

'I don't make the rules, sir, but since you and your wife have obviously formed a bond with the lads I suggest you make an effort to keep in touch with them.'

Good God! Emma wanted to spit. *What the hell did he know? Hadn't she and the girls tried their hardest to do just that?*

Michael sensed that Emma was uptight and he tried to pour oil on troubled waters. 'Try to look at it sensibly, Emma, the boys will be well cared for and they will be found suitable employment as soon as they are old enough and that day cannot be so far away.'

Emma was staggered by his response.

'Sam and I only want what is best for these two boys. We are comfortable. We could give them a good safe home and we'd care for them. I thought you of all people would appreciate that,' she said indignantly.

Michael's face flushed, he got to his feet, came across to where Emma was sitting and put one hand caringly on Emma's shoulder. 'It's because I know that you both care so much that I don't want to see you hurt,' he said softly.

Emma turned to look at her husband who was leaning against the doorpost, his brawny arms crossed over his wide chest. 'Do we really have to stand by an' see Tom an' John carted off again?' she half-whispered to him.

Sam shook his head wearily. 'I dunno, Emma, I really don't. All this bunkum about rules and regulations is way beyond me.' Then having thought for a moment he said, 'We could apply to look after them, don't know if we can but it's worth a try.'

'That might be an avenue for you to explore sometime in the future, Mr Pearson,' Inspector Clarke said, getting to his feet to signify that he wanted to be on his way. 'We have the matron from the Kentish home coming here with a member of the board and two people from the welfare department will be accompanying them. They won't be arriving until late this afternoon or possibly tomorrow morning. By that time we should have established whether or not Thomas Yates is to be admitted to the nearest hospital or if he is fit enough to travel. John Kirby will definitely be going to Pinewood Children's home.'

'You can't separate them just like that,' Emma said forcefully. 'Not after all they have been through together.'

'Mrs Pearson, will you please try to understand? Every stone has been overturned. Both these lads were abandoned at birth. There are not any relatives to be found in either case. Therefore the law states quite clearly that the courts have a responsibility to care for these children until they reach the age of fifteen.'

'All right all right, you've made your point,' Emma said irritably, thinking he didn't have to speak to her as if she were totally stupid.

Then a thought struck her and she blurted it out without thinking. 'It's more than likely that Tom will be going to hospital this afternoon, at least that's what Dr Hamilton said he was hoping to arrange, so please, will you allow John Kirby to stay the night with us?'

The inspector arched his eyebrows again. He wasn't about to show too much sympathy, not in front of his sergeant, instead he covered his mouth with his hand and cleared his throat.

'I think that is very kind of you to make such an offer, Mrs Pearson. Yes, I'm sure everyone concerned would be more than grateful to accept your offer for tonight. It would save a lot of unnecessary rearranging. Thank you.'

Emma, who had been holding her breath, hearing that at least they were going to be able to keep John for the rest of the day and night, puffed out her cheeks and let her breath out in one long gasp.

'No need for thanks,' Sam answered quickly, 'you've just made my wife a very happy woman.'

The next day Emma was standing at the sink, washing up the breakfast things just before ten, when she heard a car come to a halt at the corner of the road. Horse-dawn carts and carriages could come further down but car drivers never wanted to manoeuvre their vehicles over the cobbled stones.

By the time she'd dried her hands, there was a knock on the door. She opened it to find there were four adults standing on her doorstep.

'Do you . . . want to come in?' she stammered.

'Not if the young boy is ready,' a stylishly dressed young woman answered her.

Emma was all at sixes and sevens because she had never set eyes on any of this group before in her life, yet neither one of them had offered to introduce themselves. It was as if they had just called to pick up a parcel and were querying whether or not it was ready. She took a nervous glance up the road, Sam had taken John to buy some sweets for the journey and Emily and Bella had insisted they walked to Mr Cadman's shop with them.

'My husband is out with the children, he shouldn't be long. Would you all like to come in?' Emma asked again, nervously plucking at her apron strings, wishing she had taken it off before opening the front door. 'I could make you some tea or coffee if you would like,' she said, unable to control her embarrassment.

'Thank you, Mrs Pearson, but we'll wait here, as soon as we collect John Kirby we'll be on our way.'

Emma felt her temper begin to rise. The woman who had

so sharply replied to her offer was middle-aged, one could say she looked a motherly type and Emma assumed that she was the matron from the children's home. This business was all so cut and dried. It was, as she had previously thought, as if they were here to pick up a parcel in stead of an abandoned young lad that was badly in need of some love and care.

No one living nearby needed an explanation as to why four strangers were standing on the Pearsons's doorstep. Neighbours were standing in every doorway. Yesterday's news had travelled fast. No one liked what was about to happen, no one agreed with it, but there seemed little that anyone could do. The wait seemed endless and Emma had a great urge to close the door hurriedly, take herself out the back way, find Sam and warn him. What good would that do? she asked herself, feeling very aggressive.

'Can you tell me how Tom is? Is he going to remain in hospital?' Emma ventured to ask.

'I'm afraid I don't have the answers but I am sure your local doctor will be along shortly to bring you up to date about Tom Yates.' This time the words came with a kindly smile and Emma thought maybe she is good at her job and that thought gave her courage. 'Will you give me the address of the children's home if nothing else?' she pleaded.

Emma didn't get her answer. The sound of Sam whistling and children laughing could be heard and minutes later they came into view.

Nothing in Emma's life had prepared her for the pain that this parting was going to bring. She had worried for months over these two boys and the joy at them coming back to her had been so short-lived. She reached behind and picked up a small attaché case in which she had packed a few clothes for John. She had also put in a pack of sandwiches and a box of her home-made cakes. The three children had not uttered one word, their faces were chalk white but they watched as Sam withdrew a coloured tin from his pocket and passed it to Emma, saying, 'Joe and Lucy Cadman had that ready when we got to the shop, it's full of boiled sweets.'

Emma undid the clasps of the case and slid the tin inside then placed the case down on the ground near to John's feet.

He still had not spoken. Emma caught hold of his two arms and pulled him close to her, she kissed him two or three times and the mere touch of her lips on his cold cheek sent her reeling. 'Promise me you will let us have your address this time, you will, won't you?' Her emotions were choking her and she had a job to get the words out.

It was no better for John. If he had ranted or raved it would have been easier to bear. His silence and the tight grip he had on her arm only emphasized his sorrow which made her own ten times worse. What had he said when he and Tom had turned up the other night? 'We've nowhere else to go, Aunt Em!' Now she was turning him away and it felt like a knife had been stuck into her own heart.

She released her hold on him and stepped back but the two of them had their eyes locked and in that look there was nothing but heartbreak on the part of the young boy and the middle-aged woman.

'Bye, John,' both Emily and Bella said, but their voices were little more than a whisper.

Sam hugged him tight, then patted his shoulder. The last words he said were, 'No matter what anybody tells you, we will always be here for you an' Tom. You move heaven an' earth if you have to but you stay in touch with us from now on. Understood?'

John's big blue eyes were sad, brimming with tears as he nodded his head. Words were beyond him.

It was a sad and sorry family that Doctor Hamilton walked in on later, and the news he brought didn't do much to help. 'It is as I feared, young Tom has pleurisy. He will be staying at the cottage hospital until a bed can be found for him at a Chelsea hospital, south of London.'

'Why would they be sending Tom to that hospital?' Sam asked warily.

Dr Hamilton sighed, he had hoped no one would pick up on that but Sam Pearson was a good intelligent man and he deserved a straight answer. 'The hospital is known as the Brompton Hospital, it comes under the district of Chelsea and deals mainly with chest complaints.'

Now Sam was worried. He looked gravely at Dr Hamilton and took a deep breath. 'I understand that where Tom is concerned my wife an' I have no legal rights. But we care. I don't suppose we shall be allowed to visit him even while he's still at the hospital, will we?'

Dr Hamilton shook his head, he could barely bring himself to answer. 'I'm afraid not,' was all he managed.

It wasn't enough for Sam. 'I appreciate that you are in a difficult position, doctor, but I can tell that you are worried more over Tom than you are letting on. Surely it won't hurt for us to know how the lad is doing?'

'All right, Mr Pearson, I have just come from Basingstoke and I was allowed to see Tom's X-rays. I'm so sorry but young Tom has pleurisy, and a chance it could be tuberculosis.'

'So that's why Tom is being sent to this special hospital,' Sam murmured thoughtfully. 'Thank you for telling us, doctor.'

'Believe me, Mr and Mrs Pearson, Tom couldn't be going to a better place and if in the future I am able to hear of his progress I will certainly come and tell you.'

Sam went to the front door with the doctor. Their handshake was firm as they said goodbye and Sam felt that Doctor Hamilton really did care about young Tom.

Back in the living room Sam told the girls to get themselves ready because after they had all had lunch he was taking them into Basingstoke to the cinema.

'Must do something to cheer them up,' he said, turning to Emma and touching her cheek. 'I am so proud of you, the way you showed John and Tom how much you loved them. I promise you we will keep track of them from here on, no matter what it takes.'

She looked up at him and smiled. 'You'd better keep that promise because I am more determined than ever that some day our family will consist of two girls an' two boys.'

The next few days seemed endless. People came and went, they talked a lot but in actual fact said nothing. Nothing that is about what really was happening to Tom or John. It was a week later before they were finally told that Tom had tuberculosis. He would receive all the appropriate treatment but unfortunately it meant that he was set for a lengthy stay in hospital.

One small grain of comfort. They had received a short

note from John telling them that the new home was much nicer in many ways than the one in London had been. He had ending by saying, 'I will always love all of you,' followed by a row of kisses. Needless to say two adults and two young girls had had to wipe their eyes after reading that message.

Knowing it was absurd to feel shut out by men in authority, Emma and Sam still resented all the red tape that banned them from looking after the boys. The powers that be deemed that until the boys reached the age when they could face the outside world and earn their own living they must remain in the care of the Kentish Care Home.

In desperation Sam had contacted the City of London branch of the Toc H. With the backing of this mighty organization he and his wife had been granted limited privileges. Letters to and fro would be allowed and visits could be arranged. It was good to receive this much authorization but it didn't cover nearly as much ground as they would have liked; still it was a step in the right direction and John would be allowed to leave the home when he reached the age of fifteen and Tom just one year later. Meanwhile Emma and Sam were determined that both Tom Yates and John Kirby would henceforth be regarded as members of their family. Nothing or no one would be allowed to interfere with their special relationship.

Emily and Bella were delighted. No persuasion would be needed to ensure that each girl wrote a weekly letter to the lads.

Today had been one long round of talking. Each one had wished for more concessions but as a family they were at least grateful they had been recognized as the nearest thing to next of kin.

It was eleven thirty before Emma went to bed and she was having a hard job to get comfortable. Her mind was still in a complete whirl although all annoyance and bad feeling had finally left her. 'Oh dear God, bless us an' keep us,' she prayed.

All she wanted from now on was to be able to say that she and Sam not only had two daughters but they also had acquired two sons. Maybe they were not legally their sons but whatever happened in the future they would never again lose touch with either one of them. Having made this vow she plumped her pillows up and settled down.

Still she found herself repeating, 'Oh, Tom! Oh, John!' until at last she fell asleep.

Part Two

Eighteen

Emma Pearson gnawed her bottom lip anxiously, unable to control her thoughts. In two months' time her two daughters would celebrate their birthdays. Emily would be eighteen on the 20th of March and Bella seventeen on the 10th April. She and Sam had had such big ideas for their girls' futures but lately with the news as bleak as it was she dreaded the probability that they might choose to leave the sleepy village of North Waltham and seek bigger prospects in a large city.

Every day her fears become greater. Everyone seemed to be talking of a second world war. It wasn't possible surely? According to Sam it was very much on the cards and it was all down to a fellow called Adolf Hitler. You couldn't pick up a newspaper without being bombarded with news of his Nazi regime. If such a catastrophe were to come about the young boys and girls even, according to the Government, would be called up to serve their Country.

The past two years had seen England torn apart. King Edward the Eighth had abdicated. Giving up his Crown to marry an American divorcée, Mrs Simpson. His brother, the Duke of York, had become King George the Sixth and while all this drama was taking place the depression worsened. Untold numbers of men were finding it impossible to find employment and they and their families were facing starvation.

In May 1937 the new King and his wife Queen Elizabeth were crowned in a colourful traditional ceremony at Westminster Abbey in London.

To Emma, still well satisfied to be living in the village in which she had been born, but some would say was the back of beyond, it was a case of haves and have-nots.

Against all the pomp in London the commentators on the wireless would explicitly tell of the horrors that the Jarrow

Marchers and thousands more from all over England were suffering. Hungry desperate men who were asking not for charity but for the right to be employed. Since the shipbuilding yards and the iron and steel works had all closed down, these men had walked from the North East of England into the City of London without even a decent pair of boots on their feet or a good meal inside their bellies. And yet, on their arrival to London Stanley Baldwin had refused to receive them at Number Ten.

With all these thoughts whirling around in her head Emma found herself trembling. Stop it, for God's sake, she chided herself. As Sam was so often telling her she was too fond of meeting trouble halfway. The rattling of the letter box caught her attention. She got up from her armchair and went through to the front of the house to pick up the midday mail that was lying on the mat.

There were two letters and a postcard. Emma smiled broadly as she looked at the picture card showing the Tower of London on the north bank of the river Thames. Many years ago it had been a prison and had held many notable prisoners, nowadays it only held the Crown Jewels! She needed no telling who the card was from, bless his heart, her Tom never failed, every fortnight she received some form of communication from him unless he had earned a bit of overtime in which case he would be coming home for the weekend.

The message was short and sweet, 'Hope all is well at home. See you in ten days' time. Love to everyone, Tom xxxx'.

There wasn't a day that she wasn't thankful that all those years ago she and Sam had taken the boys into their home for a fortnight's holiday. Tom had contracted tuberculosis but a lengthy stay in Brompton Hospital had put him back on his feet.

There had been at times when both she and Sam had felt they were drowning in despair and anxiety. Would the boys never know a normal life? For months on end it had seemed like that. In an institution for children who have no parents there is no remittance for good behaviour.

John had been the first to be turned out to fend for himself at the tender age of fifteen and one year later Tom had been given the same treatment. Naturally each boy in turn had come directly to North Waltham.

Emma paused in her reminiscence. God, what a day that

had been when John arrived! Royalty had never received a better welcome! Flags, balloons, whistles for him to march with through the lanes. The villagers had turned out to let the lad know that they cared and that North Waltham was his home.

And they did it all over again, one year later when Tom had come home.

All's well that ends well, so the saying goes. It had been a hard struggle but by Jove it had all been worth it. Today she was able to say that both boys were part and parcel of her family. Brothers to Emily and Bella and sons to her and Sam. Maybe not legally but a strong bond held them all together. They all loved the boys so dearly.

Emma stood the postcard up on the mantelshelf and left the rest of the post unopened, Sam would see to it later. She went through to the scullery to start preparing the vegetables for dinner. The day hadn't brightened at all, if anything it was getting colder and she knew quite early in the afternoon it would be dark. She had finished scraping a pile of carrots and had opened the back door to put the bowl of peelings on top of the shed ready to go into the swill bin when the sheets she had pegged out earlier this morning were caught by the wind and flung forward over the top of the shed.

I'd better shift myself, go down the garden and fetch all the washing in, she told herself. When she tried to pull the sheets down and take out the clothes pegs, it was all she could do to hold them, the wind was so strong. 'Talk about battling against all the odds, I'm not going outside this house again today,' she said aloud as she came back indoors, dropped the pile of washing on to the kitchen table and went to warm herself by the stove. 'I must be getting old,' she said to herself. 'I never used to feel the cold so much as I do now.'

'Well, would you believe it?' exclaimed Sam, as he came down the stairs. 'My wife is not only talking to herself, she is admitting that she is getting old.'

'I didn't hear you come in. How long have you been home?' Emma asked.

'Of course you didn't hear me, you were down the garden having a battle with my long johns and wrapping sheets round your shoulders.'

'Oh, so you think I was playing silly-beggars down there, do you? Been a lot more useful if you'd come down an' given me a hand.'

'Now why would I do that? You were managing quite well.' He grinned. 'You look great, never better with your rosy cheeks an' that soppy woolly hat.'

Emma didn't like to be teased. 'You're rubbing me up the wrong way, Sam. If you want any dinner tonight you better put the kettle on an' make me a cup of tea.'

'And meanwhile what are you going to be doing?'

'Folding all the washing and getting it ready for ironing. For us women work doesn't stop like it does for you men. You come home, sit in the chair, read the paper an' wait to be fed.'

Sam's grin spread even wider now. 'You look gorgeous when yer rattled,' he said, staring at her intently until she dropped her eyes from his. 'God above, Emma, I didn't think it was possible to love you more than I already do, but as the years have gone by my love gets stronger. I just wouldn't know how to live without you.'

Emma had loved every word he had said, but wondered if he was just mucking about. Yet as she lifted her eyes again he did appear to be serious.

He took a step forward and suddenly his arms were around her, the look on his face was soft and tender.

'Is it allowed for a man to make love to his wife in the afternoon?' he asked, but not giving her time to form an answer he kissed her. Her cold lips turned warm as he covered them with his own and the tighter he held her the more she loved it.

She forgot that it was the afternoon, that she had all that washing dumped on the kitchen table, that she had only just started to do the vegetables for tonight's dinner and that it wouldn't be too long before the girls would be coming home. Nothing mattered but the fact that her Sam still loved her, still wanted to make love to her even in the middle of the day.

'Sam,' she whispered, 'Are you sure you're not having a funny turn?'

He didn't loosen his grip but he did laugh loudly. 'I know our lovemaking hasn't been so frequent of late, we both seem to take each other for granted but the old flame is still alight, at least it is with me, but if you rather we didn't, you only have to say so, my love.'

Emma was so full with love for this brawny great husband of hers that she was choked up, unable to utter a sound. She looked about her, feeling a surge of affection for this lovely old cottage. They had been married just seven days when he had brought her here to live and he had carried her over the doorstep. Both their daughters had been born in the front bedroom upstairs. Suddenly she felt herself blushing, remembering those first seven days of married life they had had to spend with her mum and dad because this cottage wasn't ready for them to occupy. The blessed Jesus himself was the only one who could have known of her feelings each night when they had got into that single bed in the box room which was right next door to her parents bedroom. The walls had been paper thin. Embarrassment, shame, dirty, painful and horrid. That would have been her true description of her first week of married life.

How things had changed once she'd been carried over the doorstep of their own home. She could still recall exactly how she had felt that first night alone with Sam. Trusting him. Liking him as well as loving him, finding out just how gentle he could be yet terribly afraid that it wouldn't last.

It had though! Oh yes it had!

Sam kissing her again brought her back to the present.

'Well?' he asked pointedly, not waiting for an answer but taking her hand and leading her to the foot of the stairs.

Once upstairs and inside their bedroom he laid her down on the bed and kissed her so gently that she forgot all her anxieties and found that the years had rolled back.

For the next hour it was as it had been in the year 1919. She was just twenty years old and Sam was twenty-three.

Much later Sam took his wife's face between his two hands and asked, 'Mrs Pearson, would you like that cup of tea now?'

'That would be much appreciated,' she told him, continuing to lie back with her head resting on the pillows.

Emily and Bella arrived home together and almost immediately they wanted to know why the table wasn't set for dinner and come to that why was it that they couldn't smell anything cooking.

Emma didn't dare to look at Sam as he said, 'Because I

am taking my three lovely girls out for fish and chips.' He saw the look that passed between Emily and Bella and he quickly added, 'It will give your mother a rest from cooking.'

The events of the afternoon and Sam's decision to take them all out had driven the arrival of Tom's postcard clean out of Emma's head. It wasn't until they were back home that Bella saw it propped up on the mantelpiece, took it down and read it out loud.

'Great!' Emily declared. 'He'll be able to help us organize our birthday party. By the way, Mum, have you heard from John?'

Emma looked at her and smiled happily. However much she tried to cover it up it was common knowledge that Emily was known to thirst for at least ninety per cent of John's attention whenever possible. The light shone in Emily's eyes at the very mention of his name, the sun rose and set on his head, at least for her it did. 'No, not recently, pet,' Emma said tenderly, 'but we are about due for a letter. Don't forget he hasn't quite finished taking his exams.'

The girls went up to bed first and while Emma was setting out the breakfast things and putting the porridge in the saucepan to soak in milk so that it wouldn't take so long to cook in the morning she fell to thinking once again about 'their two boys'.

There was Tom. 'Bless his heart,' Emma said out loud as she continued to stir the oats into the milk. He had been working at Woolwich Arsenal since he was fifteen years old. He was lucky to have found a caring family to board with even if they were a bit loud-mouthed and brash. She shouldn't be thinking thoughts like that, she chided herself. She and Sam had met Daisy and Donald Gaskin just the once over the August bank holiday weekend last year. They seemed to think the world of Tom, which in her book made up for a lot of their shortcomings.

The Gaskins lived in London close to the Royal Arsenal which made it handy for Tom. No travelling expenses to and from his work. Their house hadn't been very tidy and it was in a very run-down neighbourhood but she and Sam had been made very welcome and Tom always said that Daisy had a heart of gold.

Then there was John. If those two boys had been born brothers they couldn't have been closer. Emma was in no doubt that each would lay down his life for the other, yet they were also as different as chalk and cheese.

Tom was still cocky, knew what he wanted out of life and was prepared to go after it. He even walked with a bit of a swagger and that always brought a smile to Sam's face.

When John had been taken back to Pinewood without Tom it had almost been the finish of him. The family had tried to explain in their letters that if Tom did not stay in Brompton Hospital and receive specialist treatment that only they could give, he would most certainly die. Shock treatment had its effect on John. He had worked and studied hard. Long before the time came for him to be out in the outside world, he had made known his preference to join the army. With help and a push from the Toc H he had been allowed to sit a number of examinations. Having passed each and every one he sat and had volunteered to be in the Army Cadet Corps.

At a prize-giving event a military spokesman had announced that John Kirby had beaten off formidable competition to win his scholarship on his own merit.

There were no two people sitting in the hall that day that were more proud than Mr and Mrs Pearson.

Both their girls were doing well, though it was their mother's belief that neither of them had yet settled. Emily had travelled to find a job and because she had done well in chemistry at school which was remarkable for a girl, she had been offered a job in the only chemist shop in Basingstoke.

Last week Emma had raged at Sam. She had mentioned that Bella was thinking of joining the forces and asked him to have a word with their youngest daughter because she felt it was a ridiculous idea. Sam had only laughed and gently questioned his daughter the next morning at breakfast. 'Now, Bella, what's all this I hear about you intending to join up? Chosen your uniform already, have you?' he'd joked brightly as Emma placed a breakfast in front of each of them.

Bella, being the baby of the family, knew she could get away with murder where her dad was concerned. Her eyes were dancing as she looked him in the eye.

'Well, what do you expect me to do around here?' she cheekily asked.

'I thought you were happy working in the dairy up at Corner Farm,' he said astonished.

'Well, you thought wrong, Dad. I only took the job cos Mum kept on to take it until something better came along. If I wait for that something to happen I'll be old an' grey an' fit for nothing. At least in the forces I might get to see something of the great big world instead of only ever knowing the limitations of living in this village.'

Emma was appalled. She'd had no idea that her youngest daughter felt that way. With great difficulty she kept her mouth closed. Events would unfold soon enough.

She had silently prayed. *Please God, let the powers to be think hard, before taking our country into another war. We have already had to live through the war that was supposed to have been the war to end all wars. So many young lives had been sacrificed then. Please don't let it all have been in vain.*

Nineteen

'So, what do you want to talk about?' Emily asked, turning over from lying on her back on to her stomach and staring up at John. 'Oh, I know, let me guess, about how lucky you are to have scraped through another exam an' that now you aren't going to have any trouble getting into the Royal Military Academy.'

John sighed. 'No, I don't think that at all. It would probably be easier to rob the Bank of England than it will be for me to be granted a place at the Academy.'

Emily could only stare at him in disbelief. 'But John I thought it was all cut and dried,' she finally managed to say. 'Mum and Dad think the same.'

'So did I,' he said sadly. 'I slogged a good many hours away to get through those exams, but it seems that the powers that be who are responsible for allocating places are taking their time in deciding whether I am in or not.'

'Oh, John, I am so sorry,' Emily sympathized with him, 'but you don't really know one way or the other, not for sure, do you?'

'No, but the three years I was granted a scholarship to stay in the military college for further education are up an' I have been given two months' notice.' He saw her downcast look and added, 'I suppose I could always join the regular army. I can't believe they never gave a thought to all the planning and preparation I put in before I was allowed to sit the exams.'

'What on earth will you do?'

John didn't answer. He rolled away from her and got to his feet.

Emily sat up, never taking her eyes away from him. *Was he upset? Of course he is you daft thing*, she rebuked herself. He had worked towards this goal for years and if what he was saying turned out to be true it would break his heart. Life could be so unfair!

Just staring at him made her heart yearn for him to take her in his arms. Why oh why did he always have to treat her as if she really was his sister? She had always imagined that one day he might look upon her with a different kind of love. He looks gorgeous now he has filled out, she thought. Tall, well built and fair-haired with those brilliant blue eyes that always set her heart pumping nineteen to the dozen.

'Strange how things have turned out, there's Tom whom Dad said would never settle down to a humdrum life, and he's kept that job at Woolwich ever since he got turfed out of the home.'

'Yeah.' John's whole attitude changed, his face was wreathed in smiles and his eyes were twinkling. 'Our Tom will never starve, he'll always have more than one string to his bow an' come hell or high water he'll make his way through life an' leave his mark to say he's been here.'

It was now the first week in March, the end of the month couldn't come quickly enough because then the girls were going to have their joint birthday party. John had arrived yesterday and was staying for the best part of four weeks. Tom would be coming home in two weeks' time. They had been lucky with the weather, so far it had been unusually warm and sunny for March and they'd been making the most of this spring-like spell. Having laid out a blanket on the grass in the back garden they'd been content to be idle as long as they had each other for company.

The uncertainty of John's future had cast a cloud over both of them but John's remarks concerning Tom had them both chuckling as they walked arm in arm back towards the house.

From the moment Emma had opened her eyes this morning she had felt guilty. Last night's BBC news report had been frightening to listen to. Every single day there were more reports of men being thrown out of work, men who had wives and children to care for but were having to stand by and see them go hungry.

Good God, I just can't begin to imagine it, she thought as she put her dusters and the tin of mansion polish away in the cupboard. She'd done enough dusting and polishing for today. To have your children sit up at the table and not have any food to put in front of them just did not bear thinking about. They had a chicken house and a closed-in-run out in the back garden and two dozen chickens. They were able to go to the bottom of their own garden each day and collect newly laid eggs.

She couldn't rid herself of this feeling of guilt, her family had so much. Indeed all the inhabitants of North Waltham were counting their blessings. More so as each day the news from all over the country seemed to be grimmer. It served to remind everybody that all this suffering was bypassing North Waltham. Most of the villagers agreed that while they were not rich, and didn't have posh houses filled with beautiful furniture and valuable possessions, they did have wide open spaces for their children to play in and a source of good food on their doorsteps. Moreover if anyone was feeling the pinch folk were kind, always willing to share.

There were collection boxes at many bus stops, railway stations and hospitals. Most folk spared a few coppers, some a sixpence or even a shilling. Soup kitchens had been set up all over London, manned by women volunteers, to feed the hungry marchers.

Emma shook her head, angry with herself; at times it seem as if all these disastrous happenings were taking place else-where, certainly not on her doorstep and she felt the village was not offering to help enough.

'Not completely true.' Sam had been quick to set her to rights when she had voiced some of her concerns. 'Our local farmers have made several trips to Hyde Park in London deliv-ering, free of charge, churns of fresh milk to be given to the unemployed.'

It was then that she had had a brainwave. Not totally convinced she asked herself a question.

My girls' birthday party! Could I turn the event into some-thing that a lot of people might benefit from but at the same take away nothing from the enjoyment of the day from Emily and Bella?

Of course she could! And she was in no doubt that she would receive help from every corner of the village.

Once the idea was set firmly in her mind she knew she had to act quickly. She had left it rather late and time was short.

Who did she know who was a great fête organizer? Kate Simmons would take a lot of beating and so she decided there and then Kate was going to be her first port of call.

Once inside Kate's comfortable living room, with a steaming cup of coffee in her hand, Emma took a deep breath and began.

'Kate, we were wishing to hold a birthday party for our two girls in our back garden. Now with little more than three weeks I would like to change the plan.'

Emma paused to give Kate a chance to consider what she had said.

Kate, as always, was quick on the uptake.

'Oh, where exactly do I fit in with your change of plans?' Kate asked smiling.

'You're more used to dealing with the parish council than I am. I wondered if you could persuade them to let us use the market field and instead of the family party I had planned we could invite everyone and turn the event into a traditional village fête. I haven't even discussed this with my Sam yet, I know he will insist on it not being forgotten that it is for the birthdays of both Emily and Bella. Could we manage that and still make money which we could give to the unemployed?'

'At last!' Kate exclaimed loudly, allowing her frustration to show. 'We've finally got to the purpose of all this.'

'And you don't approve?'

'I never said that. I do approve, wholeheartedly, as I'm sure most of the villagers will. So what part in this scheme do you want me to play, apart from persuading the councillors to grant you the use of the market field for one day even though you haven't put in an application?'

'Not one day, two at least, three if possible,' Emma shot back cheekily. 'If we do things properly, beg help from anyone who is willing to lend a hand, we may be able to have lots of bunting put up, loads of games and rides for the children. Definitely an ice-cream stall and Joe and Lucy Cadman and their ever-popular home-made sweets. They might even consider making toffee apples for us.'

By now Emma was flushed with the prospect of success, she leaned forward and picked up her cup again, the coffee was still warm and as she sipped it she enjoyed the taste of the local cream Kate had poured on the top.

Kate smiled as she watched Emma lick her lips and replace the cup back on to its saucer. 'I'm sure members of our Women's Guild will be only too willing to man a stall with home-baked tarts and pies not to mention cakes and scones. We have a meeting the day after tomorrow, would you like me to get members of our committee to help with the organizing?'

'Oh, Kate, would you? I hesitated before asking you for help but I am so glad that I did.'

'Well – ' Kate smiled broadly – 'we shall have to make good use of what time we have. I'm sure folk will come up with lots of good ideas. Anyway I shall pay a visit to Councillor Maurice Johnson, and if he is not in I shall try Robert Chapman, let them know of your plan, ask if they will put forward a proposal that you be given the go-ahead to use market field.'

'You think it likely they will skirt round the normal rules and regulations?'

'I shall point out that in the main it will be a private birthday party, we'll get John Brown to make a couple of huge banners, one saying 'Happy birthday, Emily' and another one for Arabella, they can be stretched right across the entrance. But – ' Kate paused and looked slyly at Emma – 'I'll dangle the local press under their noses and emphasize that all profit is going to be used for the good of the unemployed. Councillors are full of their own importance and they are never loath to feature prominently in the newspapers. By the time I have used my powers of persuasion they'll welcome the chance to be part of your fête, you'll see.'

Emma chuckled to herself all the way home. She had heard Sam often say that there was more than one way to skin a rabbit. Up until now she had never known the reasoning in that saying.

It would be some time before she'd be able to look into Kate Simmons's eyes without remembering their conversation and laughing to herself.

Twenty

E mma looked round her kitchen. A feeling of satisfaction swept over her as she took a deep breath and sighed with contentment. The smell was gorgeous.

This party-cum-fête was going to be such a success. So many folk had come forward, saying they were only too pleased that Emma had thought of a way that would enable the whole village to contribute to the many charities set up to benefit the unemployed.

It seemed that everyone had chipped in one way or another. Men had rushed to do the heavy lifting, carpenters had stalls erected in no time at all. The women had worked hard to ensure the event ran smoothly.

With all this goodwill surely nothing could go wrong.

All members of the local council had been in total agreement that permission to use market field for the fête should be granted.

The real fairground people also appeared. The travellers had heard of the event on the grapevine and had turned their caravans about and travelled in this direction only too willing to lend a hand. Lionel Trenfield had been standing at the entrance to his property on the look out for their convoy of wagons and caravans. Several colourful characters jumped down from the first wagons to greet Lionel as an old friend.

Handshaking and hearty back-slapping finished, Lionel told them to park up and settle in to the adjoining field that they regularly had use of when they were in this neck of the woods, which was normally the week that the annual fair was held.

Marion Trenfield had come out from the Big-House to join in the welcome greetings. A few councillors looked as though their feathers had been ruffled by the arrival of such a large assortment of vehicles. But, with each and every one of their vehicles, their entire families, plus numerous dogs and horses parked up on land that was owned by Lionel Trenfield they were powerless to object.

On being informed of the full circumstances for this fête, two young ladies' birthdays to celebrate combined with a need to raise money for the needy unemployed, the Romany folk had readily agreed to erect all rides, swing boats, the ever-popular ghost train and several side shows and were willing to give thirty per cent of their gross takings to the overall fund.

Councillor Maurice Johnson had suggested that they should at least deduct their running costs before the thirty per cent was calculated.

This offer had been met with a cheerful but flat refusal.

By noon of the next day the market field was well under way to being given a complete transformation. Men were swarming everywhere and volunteers queued up to offer help. A St John's Ambulance team set up a medical tent. A beer tent had been one of the first to be erected and a sign writer had been generous with his talents. The board, on which he had drawn and painted a background of the buildings of a farm surrounded by cultivated land, was huge. To the forefront of the picture two typical weather-beaten farmers were shown raising a foaming tankard and beneath them a notice which read: CIDER A SHILLING A FLAGON. OLD ALE 4d A PINT.

Farmers themselves were not to be outdone. A huge bonfire was erected, children of all ages had gleefully collected rubbish and wood to add to the pile. It would simply need a match put to it on the day that the fête would be declared open. To the side of the fire a spit had been set up using several long thin metal rods on which a whole pig would be skewered for roasting.

It was now nine o'clock the night before the big event, just thirteen hours before the fête would be declared open. Emma wondered where Sam had got to. Last minute jobs up at the field, she supposed. Emily, Bella, John, Tom and herself had all eaten earlier though it had only been a scratch meal because she'd still a lot of baking and clearing up to do. However she decided that she would take five minutes and make herself a cup of tea.

Her moment of peace was shattered by a series of loud thumps from above. Her mouth was set in a grim line as she went to the kitchen door. Opening it wider, she shouted loudly, 'What are you lot up to? You do know you almost came through this ceiling.'

She stood listening for a few minutes, giggles and laughter as if they were four or five years old, then Emily's head appeared around the top of the stairs.

'Sorry, Mum, Tom fell off the bed,' she said, trying not to smile.

'Oh, I might have known it was him playing about,' she said, raising her voice. 'You listen to me, Tom, you're not too big to feel the weight of my hand. I don't know why you're not still up the field helping out with the finishing touches.'

John stepped gingerly past Emily and came down the stairs. By the look of his hair you'd think he had been pulled through a blackberry bush backwards. 'Sorry, Aunt Em, Bella was trying to make Tom tell her what he had got her for her birthday, she got a bit overexcited.'

Emma had a job to conceal her own smiles. They were still her kids, all four of them, not really grown up at all.

'Ever the peacekeeper, aren't you, John?' She grinned ruffling his unruly mop of hair. 'Tell me, why did you come home at six, was there nothing more to do?'

'Not a lot anyway, an' so many wanting to put in the finishing touches. We thought we'd be best out of the way. Though Uncle Sam has said he has a load of jobs lined up for me an' Tom tomorrow, once the day gets underway.'

'John, tell me, do you think Emily and Bella mind that their birthday party has been practically taken away from them?'

'No, I don't, Aunt Em, honestly I don't. To be truthful we, me and Tom, think they're over the moon about it. As Emily has so rightly said, it isn't every day that the whole village turns out to help to prepare a party for a girl's birthday.'

'Ah, thanks, John. I did at one time think we could have kept it secret like, but it got out of hand, kind of snowballed, they could tell for themselves it wasn't just for them. I do hope they won't feel cheated.'

'Aunt Em, will you please stop worrying. There are still quite a few surprises in store for both Emily an' Bella. For one thing Sam wouldn't let the banners be put up until after we'd left, they don't know about them but they'll be the first thing they set eyes on tomorrow. And the banners are going to be surrounded by dozens of coloured balloons.'

'And?' Emma raised her eyebrows and stared at John.

'And what?' he asked, feigning innocence.

'Now, son, don't you come the old malarkey with me, I'm too old in the tooth to be taken in. You said there are a quite a few surprises for the girls an' so far you've only told me one.'

'Oh, you poor old soul, been left in the dark, have you?'

John just managed to duck as the teacloth that Emma had been holding whipped past his ear. 'I was going to tell you, but now I won't,' he said as he ran round her and flew back up the stairs.

It would have been hard to tell who was laughing the most, Emma or John.

Before I do another stroke I will have that cup of tea, she thought. Going to the sink she half-filled the kettle with cold water and placed it on the gas. As the kettle came to boil she heard the back door open and popped her head round the scullery door to see Sam kicking off his muddy boots.

'You timed that well, Sam, the kettle's just boiling.'

'Thank God for that, I couldn't spit a sixpence,' he said, coming into the kitchen and sitting down in his armchair.

Emma poured the steaming water over the tea leaves she'd already spooned into the pot. Having poured some milk into a cup and a lot more into a large brown mug she filled them both with the scalding tea. Placing the mug beside Sam she sat herself down and picking up the cup she gratefully sipped her tea.

Ten minutes later, with her cup well drained, she wrapped a thick kitchen towel around her hands and opened up the oven. 'Lovely,' she said beaming as she took out trays of sausage rolls and meat pasties which were all cooked to a lovely golden colour. Reaching down to the lowest shelf in the oven she prodded the joint with a carving fork and said, 'That needs another quarter of an hour.'

'Smells gorgeous,' Sam said, his mouth watering. 'What is it?'

'Your favourite,' Emma said laughing. 'Boiled ham.'

Sam shook his head. 'If it's boiled what's it doing in the oven?'

'Special occasion, isn't it? It was partly boiled, then I coated it with melted butter an' topped it all over with brown sugar. It will give it a nice glaze being in the oven for a little while.'

'I'm impressed,' Sam said as his wife handed him a plate with two sausage rolls and two pasties on it.

'Why are you suddenly impressed? Don't I always bake savouries for you?'

'Course you do, luv, but while yer back was turned I had a peep beneath all those white tablecloths. From what I hear by the time you an' all the other women in this village are finished there should be enough food laid out tomorrow to stretch from here to Basingstoke an' back.' He quickly added, 'You haven't roasted any pork, have you?'

Emma gave a hearty laugh. 'No, none of us are that daft. We heard days ago there was to be a whole pig roasted on the spit.'

'Well, what exactly have you chosen to do?'

'Three chickens, two veal, ham and egg pies, a sirloin of beef and an ox-tongue,' she told him, sounding weary for the first time. She had been on the go since five o'clock that morning after all.

Sam immediately noted how tired she looked. He drained the remains of his mug of tea and stood up. 'Come on, my lovely,' he said, placing his arm across her shoulders and guiding her out of the kitchen towards the stairs.

'Let's get you up to bed. I won't be far behind you. Stop worrying, tomorrow is going to be a great day.'

He wasn't exaggerating.

It was barely daylight and the whole house seemed to be in uproar. 'Even Christmas Day hadn't ever been as bad as this,' Emma mumbled to herself as she placed two plates on to the table, each piled high with buttered toast.

'Hurry up an' finish your porridge before the toast goes cold,' she ordered.

Sam looked at the boys and winked. 'What, yer sending us out without a cooked breakfast inside?'

The girls giggled. 'Terrible, isn't it, Dad? And it's supposed to be our special day an' all,' Emily said, moving aside her porridge bowl and reaching for a slice of toast.

'None of you will starve, I'll lay odds you'll be eating all day long, there's me home-made plum jam or marmalade, take your pick an' then we'd all better start to make a move.'

'Hey, wait a minute, Mum.' Bella's voice had risen to being almost a shriek.

'In case all of you have forgotten, today is actually my birthday. What about all my cards? I've seen you, Mum, hiding them after the postman's been these last couple of days.'

None of them could contain their laughter as Sam reached beneath the table and produced a cardboard box that he'd had tucked between his knees.

Bella's face was covered in smiles as she read the labels on five packages. Mum and Dad, Emily, Tom, John and Auntie Agnes. The next fifteen minutes of sheer childish madness had Emma turning away to wipe her eyes on the corner of her apron. Sam wasn't much better, he'd sniffed a few times. The look that passed between them needed no words. They felt they were truly privileged. Their two girls were growing up fast and their family had increased by two. Two wonderful lads. There wasn't a day that passed that they didn't feel thankful to be able to look upon these boys as if they were their own sons.

Bella's voice broke into their private thoughts and snapped them back to the present.

'Thanks, Mum an' Dad,' she said, throwing her arms around her father's neck because he was the nearest to her. 'I was envious when I saw the handbag you brought for Emily and I'm so pleased you got me the same.'

'Different colour,' her mother hastily butted in. 'We don't want any arguments.'

'As if,' Bella said grinning. Would I fight with my dear sister?'

'No, you wouldn't, but only because you know that I always win,' Emily said, shoving Bella so hard that if Tom hadn't grabbed her she would have fallen to the floor.

'Heavens above, what has got into you lot today? Bella, will you please stop acting the fool an' open your other presents or the day will be half over before we even get to the fête.'

'Mum, you weren't watching, you were miles away, yours wasn't the only present I opened. John has given me this beautiful silver locket an' chain, an' look at this, it's from Tom. It's a watch but not a wrist watch, it's one you pin to your dress or jacket. Emily's present is this pretty basket, it's filled with lovely smellies and perfume.'

Emma had to stop herself from saying, I hope it's not make-up. I don't want either of you using a load of muck to paint your faces.

'Last one,' Bella cried, tearing the brown paper off of the biggest of the parcels. 'Oh, isn't that beautiful,' she murmured as she held up a bolero. It had obviously been hand-knitted, the wool was soft to the touch, the colour of the very palest baby blue and around the edges, including the cuffs, the most intricate, decorative crocheting had been worked.

'Mum, did Aunt Agnes make this herself?' Bella asked, sounding almost as if she couldn't believe it.

'Yes, she did love,' Emma answered before turning to her eldest daughter.

'I know Aggie gave you lovely slippers for your birthday but she asked me to tell you that if you would like a cardigan or a jumper you only have to choose the pattern an' she will make it for you. She just didn't have time to knit two before your birthdays.'

'Mum, it's all right. I'll talk to Auntie, let her know that I really like my slippers but I will take up her offer if she will let me pay for the wool.'

'Well, as long as you're both all right about it. Now, are we going to clear this table, get ourselves ready and go to this fête or not?'

'Try stopping us,' a chorus of voices answered as chairs were pushed out of the way and a scramble to see who could be the first to make it up the stairs began.

When the kitchen was finally empty, Sam and Emma took a moment to stand still with their arms around each other.

Each knew that they were both counting their blessings.

Twenty-One

They were still ten minutes walk away from market field when the sound of the music could be heard, loud and clear. Their arrival was something that neither of them would ever forget.

'Happy Birthday, Emily. Happy Birthday, Arabella.'

The two-foot high banners were stretched side by side across the entrance and there were bunches of balloons flying high attached from one end to the other of both signs. Jesters dressed in colourful outfits, wearing three corner hats that had bells jangling from the brim, were walking on stilts to greet folk. Clowns, some with chalk white faces, other with faces painted red and black noses were handing Union Jack flags to children as they passed. Gypsy Rose Lee, wearing more gold than you would see in a pawn shop, was begging folk to come into her tent and cross her hand with silver.

Friends were gathering round to greet the birthday girls, all offering a card, some had presents. Sam looked over their heads and grinned wickedly at his wife. 'Looks like all we're lacking here today is the flipping Pearly King and Queen.'

Jack and Joyce Briggs from Corner Farm were just passing, each loaded down with trays of food, and Jack, having heard Sam's remark paused.

'Hang about, Sam, today nothing is going to be impossible, who's to say the Pearlys won't turn up in time for a royal lunch?'

'That would make the day,' Sam remarked, to a chorus of laughter.

'I'd better take myself off to the food tent,' Emma said reluctantly. 'I know the reverend picked up all our contributions early this morning but they'll need many pairs of hands to sort everything out.'

'Mum, you don't sound too enthusiastic,' Emily said. 'Do you want me to come with you?'

'Certainly not. This is your and Bella's day, so, off you go an' enjoy yourselves. I'll catch up with you later on.'

'We'll come an' find you if you don't,' John softly said.

'As soon as we're hungry, Aunt Em. Remember you denied us any breakfast.'

'Tom, you're a cheeky whelp. Trust you to come out with something like that,' Emma said, taking a swipe at him. However, Tom was too nimble on his feet to fall for that one.

'Morning, Emma,' a number of voices hailed her, before she had even set a foot inside the huge marquee.

'Looks like we're preparing to feed the five thousand by the look of this lot,' Kate said, pointing towards several trestle tables that were already heavily loaded with every kind of food one could imagine.

'Well – ' Emma laughed – 'perhaps we should thank the good Lord that we haven't got to do it with five little fishes an' five small loaves.'

'Stop yer laughing an' get yer sleeves rolled up,' Dorothy James called out in a voice that was uncharacteristically jovial.

Seems like a bank holiday atmosphere is going to rule here today, Emma thought as she tied her white apron around her ample body.

'There's a plan laid out on this small table,' Aggie called. 'Come an' give it the once-over an' you'll get some idea of what we're tackling.'

Emma joined her friend, taking a couple of minutes to say how pleased Bella had been with her bolero. 'I'd seen you knitting it but I hadn't seen it stitched up an' pressed, it is beautiful.'

'I'm pleased Bella liked it,' Aggie answered, blushing a little but nevertheless showing how much Emma's praise meant to her. 'Come on then, cast your eyes over this lot an' then we can decide where we'd like to work.'

'Work? Good God! I thought we'd done our bit all day yesterday.'

'Well yer thought wrong, me old mate. Look – ' she ran a finger over the typed page – 'it says cold meats, poultry an' pies for table one; sandwiches, sausage rolls an' pasties for table two; jellies, trifles, gateaux and pastries, for table three.'

'And what about all the roasted meats? Where are they going to be put?'

'Don't be silly, Em, that's where the glory boys step in. Didn't your Sam tell you? A lot of the men have begged borrowed or stolen chef's outfits. They'll be outside doing the carving an' helping the farmers out with that ruddy great pig which they started turning on the spit before five o'clock this morning,'

'Do you know if my Sam has a chef's uniform?' Emma asked.

'According to Janet Swimford, he has. Janet borrowed two outfits, wanted her husband to wear one but he's more the skinny type an' the whites as they call them were far too big. Apparently one set fitted your Sam a treat, wait till you see him in his tall white hat!'

'Wait till I do,' Emma mumbled, sounding slightly aggrieved. 'But how come you know all about it?'

'It was last night, I came down with several tins of cakes that I had made, there was all sorts of costumes on offer an' the men were having a good old laugh trying on various outfits to see which suited them the best.'

'No wonder he was so late home last night, playing silly buggers with chef outfits while I was slaving over a hot stove. And as for that John! The sly monkey knew full well what was going on but didn't see fit to let me in on it. Right, John Kirby, that's one I owe you.'

She followed Aggie down to where Kate said they were needed the most. She couldn't wait to do her stint here and get outside to mingle with the crowds. She had a feeling that her Sam acting as a chef was not the only surprise she'd let herself in for, before this day was over there would probably be plenty more.

It was ten thirty before news started spreading about the biggest surprise of all. It wasn't a Pearly King and Queen that were coming to the fête but it might as well have been, the pleasure the news had given everyone.

The whole marquee was agog with the news and it was growing with the telling!

'Do you want to make the announcement?' Kate kindly asked Emma. 'After all you set the ball rolling, it was your idea.'

'In the first place it might have been, but who in their wildest dreams would have imagined it would turn out to be an affair as large as this. No, please, Kate, you try calling for folk to listen an' you tell them what is happening.' Then shaking her head in disbelief, Emma added, 'It's all got way beyond me.'

Kate Simmons smiled. She had never baulked at a challenge before and she wasn't about to start now. Outside, she walked tall, determination showing all over her face. She climbed the few wooden steps that had been erected to enable one to get up on to the platform. To the front of the stage three large cardboard boxes were set in line. One box was filled with every kind of fruit available, the second one contained a bottle of Scotch whisky, a bottle of brandy and a bottle of ruby port wine. The third was a food hamper containing enough goodies to feed a family of four for a good many days. All three boxes were to be raffle prizes. John Brown was making himself hoarse trying to sell tickets for the raffle.

'Five tickets for a tanner,' he bellowed, as two lady volunteers, who were seated one each side of him, were being kept busy collecting money for the tickets.

Kate had a quick conversation with John.

Smiling broadly he stepped back. 'And the best of luck to all of us.'

Kate spoke in a voice that commanded the crowd's attention. 'Ladies, gentlemen and children, each and everyone of us here today is playing a part; we hope as the day progresses we shall continue to enjoy ourselves. However, to begin with this event was to be on a much smaller scale, to celebrate the birthday of two young ladies whom all of you know have graciously agreed it could be turned into something larger in order that we might make some money. All of which will be donated to the needy unemployed.

'It is absolutely amazing, that with only very short notice and due only to the generosity and hard work of the residents of this village, this tremendous fête is up and running. You don't need me to tell you that for the past three years unemployment has worsened. In other parts of the country folk are so desperate. Faced with scenes of human misery such as out-of-work miners scrabbling through slag heaps in the hope of finding scraps of coal to heat their homes with. We find it hard to imagine, don't we?

'And the thought of not having any food with which to feed our children is beyond most of us. Always, the residents of North Waltham have felt privileged to live in Hampshire. At times it is almost seems as if the outside world passes us by. Today we are sharing our good fortune with those who are suffering so badly and as it has turned out we have friends in high places.

'Just listen to this, Mr Lionel Trenfield has used his influence with some of the union bosses and they in turn have notified the press and all of us had better be ready to greet two coachloads of unemployed men. Men who are at their wits' end, their whole families affected by the never-ending unemployment. Men who are not seeking charity but the right to earn a living. When they arrive let's show them we care.'

The silence had ended. Questions were being shouted. Cheers were ringing out loudly. Everyone was clapping. Kate waited a couple of minutes before she spoke.

'I know I don't have to ask you to make these men feel that they are indeed most welcome. Talk to them, make sure they have a good meal.'

Again the response from the crowd was overwhelming!

'Both coaches will be arriving somewhere around midday,' Kate stated, looking round at the sea of smiling faces below and she couldn't resist adding, 'I don't suppose the reporters that turn up here will be from the intellectual newspapers, so be warned, be on your best behaviour. Now, get yourselves a good feed, spend what you can afford and most of all make sure that when our guests go back to London late tonight they will take with them the knowledge that there are people in this country who *do* care about their plight.'

At twelve fifteen two red busses came to a halt on the grass verge opposite the market field. For a few minutes it was as if time stood still, the band ceased to play, people stopped talking and cast their eyes downward as the men slowly began to file out of the busses.

My God, what a sorry sight! The words on everyone lips as they watched. Not one soul would have dared to speak then.

It was as if these painfully thin, shabbily dressed men were wearing a uniform. Each man wore a flat cap. A collarless shirt, the top which should have been fastened with a collar stud, flapped open showing raw, scrawny collar bones. Their dark jackets and trousers were threadbare and the boots they wore had seen better days. The overall picture was of a line of gaunt, skinny, undernourished men.

The older women of the village turned away, their eyes brimming with silent tears.

It took a while, but after numerous mugs of hot tea and the overwhelming offer for them to help themselves to food, the ice did get broken.

It was a strange day. How those men's hearts must have ached to see all that food, more so when the chefs began to carve roasted joints of meat. The greatest roar rose up when Marion Trenfield handed her husband a carving knife that had an extra long blade and Lionel, very dramatically, carved the first slice from the roasted pig.

For the latter part of the afternoon help from all the women folk of the village was enlisted to help make up boxes of food.

By seven o'clock, when the men boarded the buses for their journey back to London, they were certainly looking a much happier bunch. As each man received a box containing all sorts of wholesome food they in turn shook hands with those who had adopted them for the day. Most were unable to verbally express their thanks. Their throats were clogged up.

Later Sam said to Emma, 'How sad it was to see grown men reduced to such a state.'

Emma answered wisely. 'Because of today a lot of people now had a better understanding of what poverty actually means.'

A week later Kate Simmons read out a copy of a letter sent to the Women's Guild and to every organization in the village that had participated in the running of the fête.

The gross profit from the fête had been more than they could have ever dreamed.

That same evening, Emma reported the good news, word for word, to Sam.

'The council might have thanked the newspapers for all the good coverage they gave,' Sam said, sounding very cynical.

'The headline on the front page of the *Herald* was great,'

Emma said, picking up the local paper and starting to read aloud.

UNBELIEVABLE!
THE LARGEST DEMONSTRATION OF SOLIDARITY THIS AREA HAS EVER SEEN.

When Sam didn't bother to give an opinion Emma couldn't resist a sly smile.

'I know what's eating you, Sam Pearson.'

'Oh, you do, do you, Mrs Clever Clogs. Well, let's hear it.'

'Come off it, Sam, you're niggled because a photograph of you in your beautiful chef's uniform has not appeared in our local paper.'

Emma didn't wait to see her husband's reaction to that. She thought she'd be much safer if she left him alone and went to put the kettle on.

Twenty-Two

E mma was thoughtful as she stood tackling a pile of ironing. For a brief moment she smiled, her girls might have grown into young ladies but their mum was still expected to do their washing and ironing. Nice to be thought of as useful though and she knew she wouldn't want it to be any other way.

She shook the creases out of Sam's best white shirt and laid it flat out on top of her ironing blanket. Now *he* was giving her cause to worry. From the start of this year he'd been different. Not nastily different, at least not to her and the girls, more like quietly different. Serious. He never missed listening to the six o'clock news on the wireless and he scanned from the front page to the back page of the newspaper. Always summarizing the most important news for her.

'Emma, you're not paying attention,' he would often shout.

She could hardly reply that she didn't want to know, that would get his back up. Too often he accused her of burying her head in the sand. Maybe she did but she didn't feel the need to meet trouble halfway.

Even John never came to visit without having a deep conversations with Sam, especially about the way the Jewish people in Germany were being treated, especially since Hitler's troops had invaded Austria. All Jewish judges and state attorneys had been forced out of their jobs and Jews were forbidden to leave the country. The part of the news that had affected Emma most was being told that the elderly Jewish folk were being forced to leave old people's homes and were left wandering the streets. Frightened, bewildered, no food, no money and no one to turn to. How could these invaders sleep at night? Had they no notion of what they were doing?

This was certainly turning out to be a terribly uncertain year except for the weather. The summer had been glorious and as a family they had had many picnics, trips to the seaside and had even been to London twice. Both girls had stuck with their jobs yet neither would give the assurance that they were truly settled.

With September almost ended, the news was that the Prime Minister, Neville Chamberlain, together with the leaders of France, Italy and Germany had met in Munich at a conference designed to solve the problem of Hitler's claim to territories in Czechoslovakia. According to the BBC the meeting had lasted from lunchtime into the early hours of the morning, when they had emerged with a settlement.

The prime minister was met at Heston Aerodrome by the Lord Mayor of London, the entire Cabinet and thousands of cheering people. Neville Chamberlain waved in the air a piece of paper, which he said would guarantee peace in our time.

Five days later Hitler sent his troops into territory that he had long coveted. Sam had almost blown his top as he'd listened, believing they were all being lulled into a false sense of security.

Emma tried to look at it from another point of view. At least to her way of thinking Chamberlain had bought the country some time. Not that she would dare to express that view to Sam. With the run up to Christmas about to start all she wanted was to have her entire family under her roof and spend what most would probably describe as an old-fashioned Christmas.

Hitler or no Hitler she was going to aim for just that, she decided as she folded the last shirt and rolled the ironing blanket up ready to be put away in the linen cupboard.

It was Guy Fawkes Night on Saturday. Both boys were home for the weekend, much to the delight of Emily and Bella. The four of them had just gone out, up to the hills where a pile of wood and rubbish had been steadily growing for days in readiness for the evening's bonfire and firework display.

'As it is Saturday, how about you coming with me for a drink?' Sam suddenly suggested.

He had just had a look around the kitchen. Emma never ceased to amaze him. Everything was prepared for tomorrow's roast dinner, and he could see the results of the start of long-term preparations for the Christmas celebrations. Soon Emma would be asking him to fetch home a heap of holly with lots of red berries. He would also go up the top of the yard behind his smithy and tear away from the wall long strands of dark green ivy. Emma did love to see the whole house decorated, and as usual he would see Jack Briggs about delivering a tree in good time.

'What's got into you, Sam? You don't usually ask me to go to the pub with you.'

'Well, I am asking you now. Come on, take that ruddy overall off an' go upstairs to put yer best coat on.'

'Why my best coat? Are we meeting someone special.'

'No, my love, we are not, but that coat that you insisted that I buy you has hung in your wardrobe for donkey's years. Only ever sees the light of day if we're going to a wedding, a christening or a funeral. Now will you stop asking questions and get yerself ready.'

Emma didn't bother to form an answer, she was bubbling inside. For Sam to ask her to go to the pub with him on a Saturday night he had to have something up his sleeve.

The lounge bar of the Fox was a great deal more cheerful than sitting at home by the fire. There was a jolly atmosphere and there were a few unknown faces at the bar.

'Hello, Emma, dear. Great to see you out, I'll let Alice know you're here at soon as she got a free moment.' Ted Andrews sounded really pleased to see her.

In the small bar, always referred to as the snug, a noisy party was already well under way. Young men in smart jackets, leather patches at the elbow, shirts worn with a tie, and well pressed trousers were gathered round the bar. Their fashionable girlfriends with posh accents had probably driven over from Basingstoke to see the fireworks. Emma overheard one of them mentioning the drive and it got her thinking.

Sam came back from the bar saying, 'Aggie served me, said if she gets a break later on she'll come over and join us.' He set a pint of old ale down for himself and a port and lemonade for Emma. 'We were lucky to find this unoccupied table, probably because it's small and in a dark corner,' he moaned.

Emma didn't mind. The whole place was lively and an open fire burned at the far end of the room.

Sam said, 'Cheers,' as he took a mouthful of his foaming pint. 'Are you glad you came?'

'Yes, yes I am, and, Sam, there is something that I wanted to ask you about.'

'You didn't have to come to the pub to ask me, did you?'

'No, of course not, but I've just overheard something one of the young ladies said and it just reminded me. How old does a girl have to be before she is allowed to drive a car?'

'Same age as a lad, I suppose. I don't really know. Why?' Sam's forehead was wrinkled as he tried to work out why Emma had asked such a question. Then it came to him!

'You're on about our Emily, aren't you?'

'Well, yes I am. She said she had spoken to you about it but you didn't like the idea. Have you a reason for that?' Emma waited, but when she got no reply, she gently said, 'Sam you do realize that in five months' time our Emily will be nineteen years old.'

Poor Sam. Emma took note of the look on his face and she felt so sorry for him. Daughters were always the apple of their father's eye, and fathers never wanted their little girls to grow up. Sam Pearson was no exception.

'Yes, luv, I do know an' yes, Emily has already asked me if she may have driving lessons.'

'And your answer was?'

'I told her to leave it for a while, but she's not going to be fobbed off for too long. How do you feel about it?'

'Well, suppose you did pay for driving lessons, where will that get her? Next thing she'll be wanting a car, where's the money going to come from for that?'

'Emma, both our girls have their heads screwed on the right way. They are fully aware that when each of them was born your mother took out an insurance policy for each of them. It was an endowment policy which matures with profits when the girls reach the age of eighteen.'

'You've been paying them both for the last eleven years since my parents died, haven't you?'

'Well, yes, it wouldn't have been good practice to allow the policies to die out. The payments are only a shilling each per week.'

Emma thought hard for a good few minutes. Just think, soon her girls might have a car, be driving about on their own. She deplored the fact that there were never any of these privileges around when she was a young girl.

'So, how much would Emily's policy pay out if you did agree?' Emma finally asked. 'Would it be enough for her to buy a car?'

'I haven't the slightest idea, I don't think I've ever bothered to look at the policies. We would have to ask Mr Finch, he's the collector for the Prudential but he only calls round once a month now.'

Their conversation was interrupted by the arrival of Aggie.

Sam leapt to his feet straight away, insisting that she took his chair. 'I'll get you a drink an' then I'll go round to the public bar for a while, see who's there, might even get a game of darts. What would you like to drink, Aggie?'

'I'll have an orange juice please, Sam.'

'Are you sure? Yer more than welcome to have something stronger.'

'No, really, Sam, I try not to drink when I'm working, but thanks all the same.'

'How about you, Emma, top your glass up or do you fancy something different?'

'Same again will be fine, thanks, Sam, but you can spoil both of us if you feel like it and treat us to a packet of Smiths crisps.'

'Oh, I think I can just about manage that,' he said, laughing as he elbowed his way to the bar.

'Christmas must have come early,' Aggie said smiling, 'otherwise how come yer here tonight?'

'To tell you the truth I haven't worked it out myself yet. I was flabbergasted when Sam suggested it.'

'Well, it's great, you don't get out often enough. I've been meaning to ask you if you'll come into Basingstoke with me, help me choose what to get the kids for Christmas.'

'Course I will, shopping on my own is not one of my favourite occupations but together we'll have a laugh.'

'Good, set a date then an' I'll ask Elsa next door to give my three their tea if we're not back in time. Be a bit of a job knowing what to get for the boys, an' with Mary coming up to being ten years old she's getting a bit choosy.'

They both went quiet as Sam set their drinks and two packets of crisps down on the table and told them he'd see them later. Emma had to stop herself from saying to Aggie to wait until they got even older and start thinking about buying a motor car!

They each took a sip from their drink, tore off the top of the crisp packet and delved about inside looking for the twist of blue paper that held the salt. Having found it the salt was sprinkled over the crisps and the bag given a hearty shake.

After they had each munched a few Emma said quietly, 'You did my Sam a favour coming over in your break to sit with me.'

'How d'you work that one out?'

'He couldn't get away quick enough, he'll have far more to say to his friends than he ever takes time to say to me.' Emma's voice was sharper than she had intended and Aggie looked slightly shocked.

'Something wrong between you two? It's not like you to have a go at Sam.'

'Oh, I'm sorry love, no, there's nothing wrong.' Seeing the look on her friend's face she quickly added, 'Honestly, it's not Sam, it's me. I can't be bothered with keeping up with the news all the time but Sam reads every word in the papers and always has his ear glued to the wireless; in fact he's convinced that before very long this country will be at war again.'

Aggie sat up straight and pulled her shoulders back. Emma wondered if she had offended her, she was such a long time answering.

'You know, Emma, your Sam might well be right,' she eventually said. 'But I'm a bit like you, never worry trouble till trouble worries me. Yet working behind the bar you meet up with folk from all walks of life, some talk a lot of sense, others I wouldn't give the time of day. All I will tell you, Emma, your Sam is not the only one that is thinking along those lines an' I'm talking about men in high places. Nothing will happen this side of Christmas but come the New Year we might have to start thinking about being prepared. Anyway, sufficient unto the day is the evil thereof, that's what the Bible tells us, so let's drink up an' cheer up.'

Emma tried her best to smile as she picked up her glass but for a few minutes silence hung heavy between them.

Loud singing could be heard coming from the snug. They both smiled then as they listened to the words.

Bless 'em all, bless 'em all, the long and the short and the
     tall. You'll get no promotion this side of the ocean.
          So cheer up, my lads, bless 'em all.

Aggie stood up, 'I'd better get back to work. Ted said I can
have a couple of days off for shopping so I'll let you know
which days, see if they suit you.'

'All right, I'll look forward to it.'

Emma was happy enough sitting there with her drink; there
was plenty going on around her to keep her curiosity satisfied, but she couldn't help wondering what the reason was
that had moved Sam to bring her out tonight. She didn't set
eyes on him again until after Ted had called time.

It was one o'clock in the morning before Emma heard her
brood come home. She buried her head in the pillow smiling
as she listened to the clowning and horseplay going on downstairs as they ate the supper she had set out for them. Thank
God they were all safe and sound, Sam was dead to the world
and now she could close her eyes and go to sleep.

It was the first week in December before Emma and Agnes
set out for their shopping expedition to Basingstoke. Emma
was so grateful that Sam hadn't wanted to go hunting for presents with her. After about an hour he'd get short-tempered.
Moan about how long it was taking for her to make up her
mind about which colour suited Emily the best and what
present she was going to buy for Bella. He'd complain about
the crowds and demand that they get the next bus back home.

But shopping with Aggie wasn't like that. It was a happy
day. In and out of shops they went, like a dose of salts, making
snap decisions one minute but then spending half an hour
making up their mind whether it should be a blouse or a
jumper for the girls.

The presents piled up, bundled into brown paper bags. An
Aran cardigan for Sam, a jersey for Tom and the same for
John. A warm hat, scarf and fur-lined gloves for Mary.

Agnes couldn't think what to get for her boys and neither
could Emma come up with a suggestion, but they still had a
while to think. They had each brought loads of little presents,
some useful, some funny and some downright daft. They had
each brought a couple of boxes of chocolates to give to friends

and they had shared the cost of a bottle of Elizabeth Arden Blue Grass perfume which came in a box that was padded and lined with blue satin. That was to be a gift from the ladies in the village to Kate Simmons to show how much they appreciated all the work she put into running the Woman's Guild.

When Aggie said she needed to go to the toilet, Emma saw her chance. There was a very good craft shop just across the road from where she was standing and she made a bee-line for it. Weeks ago Aggie had expressed delight at a pattern for a twin-set in *Woman's Weekly*. Emma had cut the pattern from the book and hid it away but she had made a note that it would need fourteen one-ounce balls of wool and eight buttons to make the set. She came out of the shop absolutely delighted by her purchases. The shop assistant had been so helpful, even down to finding buttons for the cardigan that exactly matched the wool.

Agnes wasn't there, so Emma was able to take her time pushing her purchase to the bottom of one of her bags.

'Look, I remembered wrapping paper,' Agnes called as she hurried towards Emma, waving brightly coloured rolls. 'The shop is only two doors down if you want to get some an' we could both of us probably do with getting some ribbon an' gift tags.'

'All right, let's go an' have a look, but then I think we had better find somewhere to have a hot drink before we get on the bus. My feet are beginning to ache.'

'That, my friend, is a very good idea, we've both got an awful lot to carry. Let's hope the bus is not too crowded.'

Much later when they finally arrived back in North Waltham, the bus conductor helped them off with all their bags and parcels and wished them both a happy Christmas.

'That,' Agnes said, as they parted, 'was what I call a jolly good day's shopping.'

'I heartily agree,' Emma answered, giving Aggie a big hug.

Walking the few yards to home Emma was longing to kick her shoes off, and put her feet up. She hoped that Sam might make her a nice cup of tea.

Twenty-Three

S am had got up very early on Christmas morning to put the turkey in the oven. That's all he had to do, just slide the big roasting tin on to the middle shelf of the oven and close the door.

Emma had prepared everything last night, made stuffing with sage from the garden, onions and chestnuts bound together with two of their own fresh eggs. The breast of the bird was coated in butter and she had used strips of streaky bacon to cover the whole of the bird.

Sam hadn't lingered, he'd gone straight back to bed. It had just turned seven o'clock and Emma decided she couldn't lie in bed any longer. Actually she had been reminiscing about past Christmases. At this hour in the morning the house would not have been so quiet, by now the girls would have been in their mum and dad's bed shouting and screaming with delight at the presents they had found in their stockings.

It was one o'clock this morning before Emily, Bella, John and Tom had arrived home. It was no more than she and Sam had expected because Ted Andrews had applied for an extension and being Christmas Eve it had been granted, allowing him to keep the Fox open until midnight. Let them be, she thought to herself, they'll get up when they're ready.

All those years when the boys were so young, and not a soul wanted to lay claim to them, what had their Christmases been like? Perhaps as they had never known family life they didn't miss it. She shook her head hard. They must at times have felt robbed, really hard done by and very lonely.

At least this Christmas is going to be really great! she thought positively. *Well, it might be if you shift yourself, get washed and dressed and get down those stairs*, she laughingly reprimanded herself.

Their living-room had never looked so cosy or so wonderful.

The fire was well banked up, logs on top of the coal flamed and crackled, red candles in white candle-holders were dotted around the room, sprigs of holly and green ivy adorned the walls and the masterpiece was the tree. Set in the corner of the room its branches glimmered with silver baubles and strings of tinsel, a tiny fairy doll crowned the top branch, her wand promising the world to those who wanted to believe it was a magic wand.

They all attended church and Emma's heart almost reached breaking point as she listened to Tom sing the Christmas carols. The clock for a few moments was turned back as she recalled a scruffy lad singing in this very same church almost nine years ago.

Ten people sat around the dinner table for Sam had insisted that Agnes and her three children should join them. Aggie was thrilled. Her brother John and his wife Mary had invited her and the children to their cottage for Boxing Day but Christmas Day they were spending with Mary's aged parents, which was only fair.

Afterwards, in the sad years to come, whenever Emma looked back over that Christmas she felt she should have been aware that it was all too good to last.

Red crackers set the white tablecloth off to a treat, paper serviettes and place mats were the same red colour, to be special for Christmas. As for the folk who sat around the table, Emma thought they had all made a great effort.

Sam sat at the head of the table, in his big old Carver chair, with his daughters seated one each side of him. It was only today that Emma noticed that over the years Bella had slimmed down, lost her puppy fat. She and Emily were as alike as two peas in a pod, both slim, with thick long glossy chestnut hair, beautiful healthy skin yet showing a different taste in dress. Emily looked sophisticated in a long-sleeved beige dress, wide brown belt which emphasized her small waist and three rows of amber beads around her neck.

Bella looked younger, though there was less than a year's difference in age between the two girls. She wore a sleeveless white chiffon dress with the pale blue bolero that Agnes had made for her around her shoulders.

Tom and John each looked every bit like successful well-dressed adults. They had grown up pretty fast. They had not been given much choice, had they? Though Tom was the youngest by nine months he was taller at six foot one to John's five foot eleven. Nothing much had changed, no two lads could be closer, yet still, no matter what the situation, it always appeared that Tom was in charge.

Agnes had made a supreme effort. Although she wore no make-up or jewellery, her thick dark hair had been washed and set at the hairdressers and waves framed her face while the hair at the back was turned underneath to lie neatly on her shoulders. Her green eyes were her finest point and the navy-blue dress she wore with an emerald green scarf wound around her neck complimented them to the full.

Emma smiled as she glanced at Lenny and Sidney. Nobody knew the contrary ways of these two boys better than she did. She guessed they would not have got dressed up without some words of complaint. They were wearing long trousers, white shirts and a jersey, Lenny's jersey was a bright blue and Sidney's was grey.

Mary had them all smiling. Pretty as a picture, but then she had been from the day she had been born. Agnes had certainly gone to town on her. Bright as a parrot in a red dress, her dark curls were as lovely as ever. To set off the dress Agnes had knitted her a sweet cardigan, using white angora wool. Its softness and fluffiness had her looking like a small princess.

Emma herself had made a special effort and had made a black velvet skirt; the length was longer than she usually wore, it almost reached to her ankles, with a white blouse which she had smartened up by replacing the collar with a new lace one. She felt her outfit was very festive.

She, too, had splashed out and had had her hair done at the shop in the village. She had been persuaded by Margaret, the owner of the salon, to have her long hair put up in a French pleat; the finished look had almost frightened her. Used as she was to winding her hair into a bun, this new look made her look kind of sophisticated. Because she had wanted it to look nice for today she'd tried to sit up in bed last night but of course she had finally fallen asleep and this morning she had thought her hair looked a mess with so many long strands having escaped from the pins.

'Don't you dare take all the pins out an' let it down!' Emily had screamed at her. Yet it was Emily, bless her heart, that had stood over her while she had got dressed and then using a tail comb, the likes of which Emma had never before set eyes on, she had set it back to perfection.

At least that was what Sam had told her, as they'd walked arm-in-arm to church that morning.

At the other end of the table Sam was really spruced up. Everything he was wearing, with the exception of his check trousers, had been a Christmas present. A fawn shirt from the girls, a brown striped tie from Aggie, the Aran cardigan she had bought for him, socks from John and slippers from Tom.

Everyone sitting around the dinner table had given and received gifts. Tom and John had repeatedly had a chuckle during the morning because when they had finally woken up they had found that Father Christmas had left each of them a well-filled stocking!

There was no shortage of conversation or laughter as the delicious feast was eaten and Emma felt that all the weeks of preparation had been well worthwhile. By the time the dinner plates were cleared from the table she was fully convinced that Emily and John only had eyes for each other. From time to time Emily would look up and catch John's eye, and he would smile as though they shared some splendid secret, and raise his glass to her, and sip Sam's home-made elderberry wine.

Of course there was more to follow. Emma's Christmas pudding that had taken weeks of preparation, her brandy butter, mince pies and dishes of thick cream which had come straight from Corner Farm that morning. This was followed by dishes of nuts and fruit along with chocolates and marshmallows. Of course Sam had to ask, 'Where is my Turkish delight?' and he had been taken aback as Bella got up and produced the largest box of his favourite sweet it was possible to buy. They had purposely hidden the box behind a family photograph on the dresser.

It was time for nuts to be cracked, dates and figs to be eaten, tangerines and Cox apples to be peeled and crackers to be pulled.

Emma, Sam and Agnes exchanged glances, as they watched Agnes's three children and their four, who liked to think they were grown ups, roll about the floor playing the fool.

With silly paper hats worn lopsidedly and soppy jokes and

daft riddles being read aloud the room was in uproar. Then came the games. The arguments over whether the dice thrown really was a six or if somebody was cheating.

Out of the blue, John announced that overall Mary had won the most games. Sam was delegated to do the honours and present her with a prize. He did as he was bid, and bending low to kiss her cheek he said, 'You are the prettiest girl I know and it has been lovely to have you with us for Christmas.'

Mary said, 'Thank you, Uncle Sam.'

He handed her the present, and the eyes of everyone in the room were on her as she tore the wrapping paper from a cardboard box. She lifted the lid, removed some sheets of tissue paper and finally discovered a pair of red shoes.

Emma knew that for weeks Aggie had considered buying these shoes for Mary, they went so well with her pretty dress but they were also sturdy and she would be able to get a lot of wear out of them. However the cost has been more than Aggie was able to afford. Emma had mentioned the fact one evening and it had been John and Tom's idea to go half each and buy them for Mary as a Christmas present.

To see the look on Mary's face and her mother's eyes almost brimming with unshed tears as she thanked the lads "was money well spent" according to Tom.

Christmas Day was drawing to an end and it was time for the Brownlow family to leave. Lenny and Sidney scrambled amongst the torn paper, sweet wrappings, broken nutshells and cardboard boxes that littered the floor. They were making quite sure that none of their presents were left behind. Their aunt Emma had found them a large bag in which they could put all the presents they had been given.

From the Christmas tree Emily cut down three chocolate Father-Christmas figures and three silver-wrapped Snowmen and passed them to Lenny. 'Put these in with your presents, it's two each for you to eat tomorrow.'

Lenny's face beamed.

Sam was standing by the front door, his overcoat on, a big scarf wrapped round his neck and holding his corduroy cap in his hands.

'Oh, Sam, you don't need to turn out this time of night,' Aggie protested. 'I've got the boys, we'll be fine, really we will.'

Sam swept Mary up into his arms. 'Come on, as if I'd let you walk on your own even if it is only a short walk.'

'Well, thank you, Sam. Thanks also for a wonderful day.'

Nobody needed telling that Aggie wasn't far from tears as she moved around the room, kissing everyone, saying thank you and calling out good night. At the door, she turned.

'What can I say, Emma? Nobody ever has had a better friend than you. You an' Sam have given us a wonderful day.'

'Aggie, you know how much we enjoy your company. I was a bit worried as to whether Lenny an' Sid might have been bored but as it turned out John and Tom kept them amused and I think they've enjoyed the day.'

'Oh, I know they have. I can't thank all of you enough.'

'Then stop trying an' get going or else my poor Sam will freeze to death standing out there in the cold waiting for you.'

'All right. Good night. God bless.'

'Good night, Aggie, have a good day with your brother tomorrow.'

Emma stood at the doorway, watching the little family go off with Sam, and she felt so sad that Aggie had had her husband taken away from her when they were both so young and the boys had lost their father. Poor little Mary had not even known him.

It was almost as if Tom caught on to the fact that she was having a sad moment. He came up beside her and put an arm around her waist. They stood staring out into the dark night for a while before he said, 'Smashing Christmas, isn't it?'

'Yes,' Emma agreed, snuggling him up closer in her arms. 'But, Tom, you said that as if it weren't all over yet.'

'Well, it's not, is it? It's Boxing Day tomorrow an' we're all going t'make the most of every day of this Christmas.'

Hardly had he got the words out of his mouth before he broke free from her grasp, ran outside down to the cobbled roadway, with his head flung back and his arms stretched out wide.

'Emily, Bella, John, get yerselves out here. It's snowing!' he yelled.

What a perfect way to end a perfect day.

Twenty-Four

The coming of the New Year had never meant much in the way of celebrations to Emma and Sam. Years ago when they were much younger they used to go to the pub and stay until after midnight but not these days. Proper old pair of stick-in-the-muds they had become.

This year Emily and Bella had gone to a dance up at the village hall and Sam and her had had a quiet night. It might have been different if the boys had been able to stay on but Tom had to be back in Woolwich and John still had two more exams to pass before his future could be decided.

The weeks were flying by. Just two weeks to go and Emily would be nineteen years old.

'All right, all right,' Sam said irritably, staring hard at his eldest daughter, 'I've already told you Emily, that I have written to Hampshire County Council asking for them to send the necessary forms you need to apply for a driving licence.'

Sam had every right to sound disgruntled, Emma was pressing him so hard over this.

'Thanks, Dad,' Emily said, her father's words had gone a long way toward pacifying her. 'Did you ask Mr Kershaw if he'd be willing to give me driving lessons?'

'Not yet I haven't, why are you in such a mad rush? Freddie is pretty busy at the moment, he told me more an' more vehicles are being brought into his garage for a check up. He also said that if this country does go to war the first thing that will be rationed is petrol. Won't be much good you owning a car if you can't get any petrol to run it on.'

'Oh, Dad, why do you always have to be such a rotten pessimist. Mr Kershaw is already giving driving lessons to my friend, Nancy Ingram, an' she said he is ever so good, has loads of patience.'

He'll need every ounce he can rustle up if he takes you on!

Sam thought. What he said aloud was, 'Could you please drop the matter now until the forms arrive.'

'Just one more thing, please, Dad,' Emily said as she crossed the room to stand behind her father who was sitting at the table, his newspaper spread out in front of him. She wrapped her arms around his shoulders, leaning forward across one shoulder.

'When Mr Finch comes for the Prudential money will you ask him how long I will have to wait for the pay out of the policy that Grandma left me?'

Emily was well aware that normally she was able to twist her father around her little finger, but today, somehow her charm wasn't working.

'You listen to me, young lady,' her father said, freeing himself from her arms. 'A big company like the Prudential runs its business like clockwork, when your policy becomes due they will write to you stating how much the policy was taken out for an' how much interest it has incurred. Until then I would be grateful if you would, just for once, keep your pretty mouth shut. At least about *your* money, *your* driving lessons and *your* bloody car, cos I've just about had enough.'

Emma knew that Emily was looking at her but for the life of her she wasn't able to meet her daughter's gaze. Instead she took herself off into the scullery to start the washing up. It was all she could do to stop herself laughing outright.

It wasn't often that Sam let it be known that when it suited him he was the master of this household!

Everything seemed to bear the hint of uncertainty. Even in this quiet village there were signs that Sam wasn't the only one that thought another war was inevitable. A trip into Basingstoke had both Emma and Agnes thinking along the same lines. There were notices on display everywhere.

NATIONAL SERVICE. WE'VE GOT TO BE PREPARED.

Prepared for what? Not one person in authority would stand up and say that we are approaching a second world war. Nevertheless, leaflets were being thrust through letter boxes suggesting that older men should become Air-Raid Wardens. They would be trained to know what to do should England ever get bombed. Local councils were making an offer to households to accept an Anderson shelter, sheets of corrugated iron that families were being told to erect in their gardens or backyards to shelter in if or when Germany should decide to send bombers over England.

'If we didn't laugh we'd all end up crying,' Aggie remarked to Emma as they stood staring at a picture of an Anderson Shelter that was pinned up outside the town hall in Basingstoke.

'Leave the safety of our homes to all be huggled up in that tiny space. I don't think so.' Aggie sounded defiant, which was all very well, but it might be a different story if German planes were flying overhead and dropping bombs.

The increasing threat of war was gaining recruits, particularly young men who wanted to be sure of serving in the regiment or corps of their choice. The Military Training Act was passed which started a conscription process requiring all men between 20 and 21 to register for service in the militia. This was not for the army alone, it included the navy and the air force too.

Emma didn't know whether to feel thankful or not when Tom told them that he would not be called up as he had been granted exemption, his employment being classed as a reserved occupation. You didn't have to think very hard now to know what work the Royal Arsenal would be engaged in.

Tom was put out. He had fancied himself flying a plane and if he had been able to volunteer for His Majesty's Royal Air Force he might have been successful with the training and might have ended up being an officer.

Sam had been of two minds when Tom had related these thoughts to him. He was in no doubt that Tom was a good worker but only if he were interested in what he was doing. But Tom as an officer with men under his command, somehow he just couldn't picture that.

Then again if a second world war was on the cards, and with every passing day it seemed more of a certainty, then events would move swiftly and the men would quickly get sorted from the boys.

The months dragged by and Emma never wanted to listen to the news. The first week of July brought some of the best weather that England had ever had. The Women's Guild held their meetings out in the open air because it was so hot and stuffy inside the village hall. Every person you met looked really healthy, the local women still loved to meet up and have a good old gossip but the news was a subject on which they all preferred to stay silent.

Emily's head was in the clouds!

Within two weeks of Emily's birthday, Mr Finch had brought her a cheque for a little over two hundred pounds. She had already worked it out that over the eighteen years the total amount paid to the Prudential Assurance Company by her grandma and then her father was forty-six pounds and sixteen shillings!

Mr Finch had gone to great pains to explain that the policy her grandma had chosen was 'with bonus profits'.

Emily didn't care two hoots what the policy was called, the pay out was beyond belief.

For three months she had been taking driving lessons with Mr Kershaw. The ninth of July had been scheduled for her driving test and today was the day. Her father was going with her.

This morning while the two of them were eating their breakfast, Emma had wisely decided to keep well out of the way. Emily was like a cat on hot bricks and all Emma kept thinking was if she's like this now what the hell will she be like if she fails this flipping test?

Emma watched them drive away in the car, an Austin Seven that belonged to Freddie Kershaw, the car that Emily had been using twice a week during her driving lessons. She hoped to God that Emily would pass because there would be no living with her if she didn't!

Ten fifteen was the time set for Emily's test. Emma was concerned about the result.

I'll go stark staring mad if the hands of that ruddy clock don't move a bit faster, she thought. *And if our girl comes back and starts playing up cos she hasn't passed I'll murder her, I will. If it's the last thing I do. Because she's had all of us walking on eggshells for three months ever since she started learning to drive. Even Bella, bless her, has had enough of hearing about nothing else than her sister and that ruddy car.*

Aggie stepped through the open back door, calling, 'It's me, Em.'

'Oh, come in, Aggie, I've just made myself a coffee. Do you want one?'

'Yes, please, but I'll make it. Suppose it's too early for Sam and Emily to be back yet, isn't it?'

'Much too early, they haven't been gone long an' there's me tearing me hair out. Honestly, Aggie, our Emily has changed since she started learning to drive a car, she's almost driven Sam mad. Bella walks out of the room when Emily starts and I've done me best to ignore the whole business, but today, well . . .'

'Dear God, Emma. What on earth's the matter with you? It's not like you to let things get on top of you. I'll tell you what we'll do. First you can roll your sleeves down an' take that pinafore off, change those slippers for a decent pair of shoes, wash your face an' comb your hair. Then when you've calmed down we'll go down the village an' treat ourselves to a coffee an' a doughnut.'

By the time Emma came down the stairs she had brightened up and Aggie smiled, but even she silently prayed that Emily would pass her test.

An hour and a half later they had walked the length of the village high street, had done some shopping and had now ended up in Holloway's, the baker's shop, where they had gone through to the back room. Coffee made with fresh milk and an apple doughnut had made them both feeling a lot better.

As Aggie was at the counter paying their bill, Emma was standing at the open doorway when the Austin came down the road. Sam must have spotted his wife because he was leaning out of the car window on the passenger side and as the car drew level he grinned and gave the thumbs up sign.

Emily puffed up with success took her cue from her dad and hooted the horn twice.

'Thank God for that.' Emily's words were said from the heart and she wasn't the only one that was giving heartfelt thanks.

Aggie was relieved, mostly for the sake of Sam and Emily, though to be truthful she couldn't see why there had been so much fuss made over a young girl wanting to learn to drive a car.

But then Agnes Brownlow had no way of knowing that before the year was out young women as well as young men would be called upon to serve their country and it would not be unusual for either sex to be called upon to drive military vehicles and military personnel.

Twenty-Five

The opening shots of the Second World War were fired on the Friday morning of the first of September when German troops crossed the Polish frontier.

What a weekend that was! Rumours were flying everywhere, newspaper editors rushed a midday edition on to the streets, the headlines all being similar:

WAR IS INEVITABLE

Most folk, at regular intervals, had their ears glued to their wireless sets and those who could not afford such a luxury crowded into their neighbours' houses.

Yet no official announcement came over the air until the following Sunday. Prime Minister Neville Chamberlain, who just a year ago had promised the nation 'Peace In Our Time', had announced a state of war now existed between Great Britain and Germany.

Within hours of this declaration air raid sirens sounded in many parts of Britain. It was a false alarm but a grim reminder that civilians should be prepared for the ordeals which lay ahead.

No such sound was heard in North Waltham because the village had never been equipped with an air raid siren. On Monday evening an emergency meeting of the local council was called, prompting a motion to be carried that whenever an emergency occurred the bells of St Michael's Church would be rung by Reverend Coyle.

Once again the folk who lived in this Hampshire village had good cause to believe that the outside world would pass them by, but from the moment war was declared, Sam's predictions became reality. Petrol became a defensive and offensive weapon. Without petrol tanks, aeroplanes and staff cars would not be of the slightest practical use. From day one, only motorists with a special permit were able to buy petrol and the price shot right up to one shilling and sixpence per gallon.

Working horses, that many had forecast would have no part to play in the modern world of the motor car, were suddenly back in favour. This could only be good news for Sam Pearson who was the only farrier within miles. Now forty-two years old, Sam wasn't sure if he would be called to serve or whether he would be regarded as being too old. He would have to wait and see.

Air Raid Precaution posts, soon to be casually referred to ARP posts, were set up in all parts of Britain including North Waltham and the older men were ordered to attend in order to learn about incendiary bombs and how to use a stirrup pump.

Each man was issued with a tin helmet which had a W painted on the front.

Kate Simmons soon had the women of the village well-organized. They met in the village hall where sewing machines had been set up ready on sturdy tables. They were working hard making not only their own blackout curtains but also the same for the church, the doctor's surgery, the village hall. Each and every window had to be blacked out, not the tiniest hint of light from the edge of a window could be allowed to show. It might be seen by German planes and so guide them as to where their bombs might do the most damage.

One other big difference in the village was the local policeman's familiar helmet had been replaced by a tin hat!

The press reported that all the major cities were evacuating their children, though so far none had been brought to North Waltham. It was Emma that wisely said, 'Not all mothers would want to part with their young kiddies.'

As the young men left their jobs for military service, rather than wait to be conscripted, so women were called upon to take over. Working in munitions factories, as bus conductors, even in the shipyards and railway sheds. The post deliverer soon became a girl, as did the milkman. Many young women were volunteering to join the forces and the medical profession was crying out for nurses and aid workers, they were going to need all the help they could get.

Almost immediately the Food Ministry was set up. There was talk of rationing. Folk would be able to take their ration books to any butcher and grocer of their choice and register with those shops for the duration of the war. Food was already in short supply and if the word spread that such and such a shop had any off-ration items in minutes a long queue would form.

North Waltham residents had always thought of themselves as almost self sufficient. As regards farm produce they were. Yet as time went on they were to find out that having farms locally, gardens and allotments did not provide everything that a family needed in order to survive.

Nearing the end of the year folk were not very enthusiastic about Christmas. As Emma remarked to Aggie, 'It won't be so festive this year, will it?'

'How could it be, Emma? A great many able-bodied young men aged from twenty onwards have already joined up.' Aggie got to her feet, stretched her arms above her head yawned and went into the scullery. 'What do you fancy to drink? I've got a bottle of Camp coffee but I haven't got much tea,' she called out loudly.

Emma rose and went to join her, 'Joe Cadman said we'll be better off when we have to start using our ration books, he'll get a regular supply of tea according to the number of people that register with him.'

Aggie laughed as she spooned the black liquid from the bottle of coffee into two cups. 'I don't know about you, Em, but I think it's strange. No sooner did Chamberlain declare that we were at war with Germany than everything disappeared from the shops, and I mean *everything* and yet it doesn't seem as if we are at war. No bombs, no sign of us being invaded, makes yer wonder, don't it?'

'Well, don't forget money talks all languages, I bet the big wigs aren't going short, but I tell you what Aggie, if you don't take that kettle off the range the flipping thing will boil dry.'

Aggie turned round quickly, grabbed a padded iron-holder and lifted the hot kettle, and half-filled each cup. Pouring a large amount of milk into a saucepan she then lit the gas beneath the pan.

'It will boil quicker on the gas,' she said, 'that's one thing we have to be grateful for, we're always going to have plenty of milk. I hate bottled coffee but at least it's drinkable as long as we make it with half milk.'

They sat now with a half-decent cup of coffee and suddenly the prospect of a day spent on their own was not unattractive. 'I need to get some more wool if we're going to continue kitting socks for the forces. What about you, Aggie, have you got enough wool?'

'So far, but I don't feel knitting is much of a war effort. If we lived in a town I would volunteer for proper war work.'

'Oh yeah, an' what exactly is your idea of proper war work?'

'No idea really. What I would really like is to have the same chance as your Emily. During this war it's going to be different, women are going to play a big part.'

The room had gone dark, Aggie got up, struck a match and held it to the gas mantle. It was then they heard the rain bucketing down, beating loudly on the corrugated iron sheeting that formed a roof on an old shed, which was just outside of Aggie's back door.

'That's put paid to us going too far afield, better wait a bit an' see if it's only going to be a shower or if it's set in for the day.'

'I've got something to tell you,' Emma said cautiously, as if she had been pondering whether or not to tell Aggie her news.

Aggie raised her eyebrows, but made no comment. She sensed that it was going to be something delicate.

'John has joined the army.' Emma's face, as she said these five words, showed the depth of the heartache she was feeling. After a lengthy pause she carried on. 'When the boys were down last year John told me he might not finish his exams. I told him not to be so silly, not to do anything rash. He said there would be time enough for him to sort his future out when we had settled this war with Germany.'

'So way back John has kind of known that war was coming,' Aggie remarked sadly.

'I think he has always been influenced by Sam.'

'Who can blame him? Sam was and *is* the only father figure those two boys have ever known.'

'Since we got the letter from John, Sam and I have talked a lot. You wouldn't believe what that young man has told Sam. Really opened up his heart he did but I've only just got to hear about it. Seems every interview that he went to he was made to feel inferior. With no known family background and an institution upbringing Sandhurst would be out of the question he was informed. After all the effort he put into his studies, worked his damn socks off and why, because he was encouraged to do so and come the final, well . . . I don't know, I really don't.'

Aggie could tell that Emma was on the verge of tears. What could she say to her? Life can be so unfair at times and she knew that better than most. Poor John, a nicer lad you'd be hard to find. To be told, even if not in so many words, that you were of inferior stock and not fit to be officer material would have been like throwing a bucket of dirty water over him!

'Do you know when he volunteered? And what regiment he has gone into?' Aggie finally managed to ask.

'He enlisted almost as soon as he got back to London after having spent those four days with us. He was sent to Aldershot for training. As for a regiment, Sam read it out to me but I can't remember, I think he said it was the First East Surreys, but maybe he was only joining them for his training period. Sam did say he will get some leave before he is finally posted.'

Aggie really was at a loss for words. She loved that boy almost as much as Emma and Sam did. Tommy too, come to that, though he was a different kettle of fish entirely. He wouldn't have been hurt if someone had suggested that he wasn't good enough for a specialist job. If he were hurt he wouldn't have shown it. He'd still have swaggered as he went on his way. Most people loved Tom for what he was, happy-go-lucky, he could take care of himself as he'd learned the hard way.

One thing Aggie would state her life on, both John and Tom regarded the Pearsons as their true family. Their blood might not run through their veins but they were kith and kin every inch of the way and God help anybody that tried to tell either one of them any different.

The rain had stopped and Emma was just about to suggest that they did brave the elements and go for a walk when there was a knock on the door. Aggie was so startled that she almost dropped the dirty coffee cups that she was taking to the scullery to wash. She put the cups back down on the table, saying to Emma, 'Like you, nobody hardly ever uses my front door. Who can it be?'

'Only one way to find out,' she said grinning.

Emma was already halfway down the hallway. She undid the top bolt and opened the door, noticing how bitterly cold it was. Standing on her doorstep was a young woman, maybe in her early twenties, slim and of medium height. Her appearance was so unusual that for a moment Aggie was taken back. She had very dark hair, cut in a fringe which peeped out of a bright red woolly hat. She wore a military-style mackintosh and muddy black Wellington boots. A tartan scarf was wound round her neck, framing a face that was beautiful and entirely without make-up. Her cheeks were rosy, probably even more so because of the cold, and her eyes were deep set and a very dark brown.

She smiled. 'Hello. I'm Hazel Osborne. I hope I'm not disturbing you, but I've been given two addresses by Bella Pearson, one was her mother's but she isn't in, the other one was this address. She told me her aunt lives here.'

Aggie hadn't idea who she was or what she wanted and her confusion must have showed clearly on her face. 'How can I help?' she asked shivering and wishing she could close the door.

'I am going to be a Land Army Girl and until billets are ready we have been advised to seek shelter with folk in the village. Bella Pearson and I met three days ago, we've become friends already and she suggested I came to see you.'

'Oh.' Aggie made a great effort not to appear too astonished. She stepped back, holding open the door. 'Do come in out of the cold. Bella's mother is here with me.'

Hazel Osborne hesitated. 'If you've got a visitor . . .'

'It's all right, Mrs Pearson is a great friend. Come on in and get warm.'

Hazel stepped through the door, and Aggie quickly closed it behind her. 'Do you mind coming into the kitchen, there's a nice fire going in there?' She led the way. 'I can offer you a cup of coffee but it will only be from a bottle of Camp.'

'That would be great if it's not too much trouble. I'm frozen, I didn't realize it was so far to walk from the farm. At one point I thought I was going to fall flat on my back, it's so icy.' She followed Aggie into the kitchen, bent over and started to remove her dirty boots.

Emma had been in the scullery washing their coffee cups, she came forward and Aggie quickly said, 'This is Hazel

Osborne, she is going to be working locally on the farms. She has already met your Bella.' Then turning her head she said, 'Hazel, this is Mrs Pearson, Bella's mother.'

Hazel removed her bright red woolly gloves and they shook hands. 'So, are you going to be a Land Army young lady?' Emma asked smiling.

'Yes, I went to a recruitment office in London and they gave me a choice of Wales or Hampshire, so here I am, but no billets have been sorted out yet. That is where your daughter came in. She suggested that one of you might take me in until some sort of quarters have been built.'

'Oh, my dear girl!' Aggie's hand flew to cover her mouth and she stood there staring at Hazel's feet.

Having removed her boots a pair of thick dark socks were on show and so was one big toe that was sticking out through a rather large hole.

Hazel wasn't the least bit embarrassed. 'Must get round to doing some darning,' she said laughing, then added, 'missing Mother already.'

'Take your mac off an' sit by the fire. I'll get you that coffee I promised you,' Aggie said, feeling glad to have something to do. She left Emma to do the talking as to whether or not one of them could offer the young lady a spare bed.

A very pleasant hour flew by. Between them they had worked out that Aggie hadn't really got any space to spare, her three children were not old enough yet to have to leave home and fight for their country. Although Aggie was afraid, having done her calculations she reasoned that with Sidney coming up to being seventeen and Len fifteen she prayed to God that the war would be over and done with long before they could be recruited.

Meanwhile Emma was fully aware that Emily hadn't gone to work today but had taken herself off to London for the third time. There would be no stopping that girl! Even Sam agreed with her on that point. So if Emily was going to be a Wren or anything else in His Majesty's forces then her bedroom might as well be made use of.

Lifting her head and looking straight at Hazel Osborne, Emma asked, 'When did you arrive in the village?'

'Three days ago, it was arranged in advance for me to stay temporarily at the pub, the Fox.'

Aggie looked surprised at this piece of information. Nobody had said anything to her but then as she worked behind the bar it didn't really affect her.

'So there is, at the moment, just you an' my Bella as female workers up at Corner Farm, is that right?' Emma was making sure she had all the facts straight before she committed herself.

'Yes, Mrs Pearson, but from what I have heard there will be at least two more Land Army girls arriving soon and probably more going to other farms in the area.'

Emma turned swiftly to Aggie. 'Has your brother got his call up papers?' Then without waiting for an answer she went on. 'I thought your John would have been safe an' sound where he is. An experienced farm worker must surely be graded as exempt from being called up, there's enough posters urging us to dig for victory.'

'John thought so too,' Aggie said sadly, 'but when he went before the board he was told that women were able to do what he does an' therefore he is eligible for conscription.'

'Going to take a while to erect enough buildings to house all of you,' Emma sounded as if she were talking to herself. 'Meanwhile I can't offer you a room in my house until I know what our eldest daughter is doing. I am sorry, Hazel, but if you ever have any free time an' our Bella is coming home do come with her. You would be most welcome.'

'Thank you, Mrs Pearson, and thank you Mrs Brownlow for the coffee,' Hazel said, as she struggled to put her wellies back on.

Aggie went to the door to see her off and as she came back into the kitchen she smiled. 'Who was it said the war was not going to affect our village way of life in any way? I took one look at that young lady standing on my doorstep an' I knew straight off the things were about to change.'

The two friends couldn't have known how right Aggie was, if they had they might not have laughed so loudly.

'Nearly lunch time,' Emma said, pulling herself together. 'Shall we go out and treat ourselves?'

'Why not? We could go to the pub for a change, have a sandwich or Alice makes a jolly good steak an' kidney pie. We'll also have a real drink before they ration that.'

'Lunch in the pub?'

'Do you mean that?'

'Course I do.'

'Oh, Aggie.' For a ridiculous moment, Emma felt a bit weepy, but she brushed her fingers over her eyes and came round the table, put her arms around her friend and hugged her tight.

As they broke away Emma thoughtfully said, 'Don't know why I'm getting so upset, surely this war can't last for long.'

Twenty-Six

Christmas and the New Year came and went and still it didn't seem as if the Germans were going to strike against England. A saying sprang up, mostly because of the shortages of everything in the shops. If a customer were to ask a shopkeeper or even a barrow boy, why no eating apples, or even a bar of soap was not available the answer was always the same.

'Don't forget there's a war on, missus.'

When goods were purchased there was never any wrapping paper or bags available. Emma and Aggie took to carrying a pie-dish or even a smaller bowl, there was always the odd chance that their farm shop might have some liver or even a couple of kidneys and there was nothing worse than slippery offal sluicing around in the bottom of their shopping bags.

Things still couldn't be worked out to either Emma's or Agnes's satisfaction. There was no battle going on. Not a single soldier from another country had set foot on British soil. No German planes had had been spotted or heard from the village. And yet every British citizen had been issued with a ration book and a gas mask.

What a sorry sight it was for Aggie to watch each morning as her daughter, Mary, now eleven years old, set off for school, surrounded by six or seven of her friends and each child had to have a square cardboard box slung over their shoulders which held a gas mask.

And what did the future offer her two boys? It was a question that she often asked herself. Too old to be children now, yet too young to be men. Sid was working as a telegram boy at the post office and Len had got a job with the Ministry for Agriculture and Fisheries in Basingstoke. Their uncle John had managed to buy each of them a bicycle, both second hand but in very good working order. Of course, both bikes being of the same colour the pair of them had had to bicker about which one was theirs. Aggie's brother John had soon solved that problem he painted each one a different colour. Sid had insisted that his bike was to be painted red, the same colour as the bikes supplied by the post office. It wasn't until weeks later that Aggie found out that Sid was using his own red bike to deliver telegrams and for that he was paid an extra shilling a week!

Old men and men that were employed in a reserved occupation were anxious to be seen to be doing their bit for their country and they readily joined the Home Guard. Sad to say no provision was made to arm this band of loyal men but they soldiered on stepping in to help with all sorts of problems.

The villagers of North Waltham still counted themselves extremely fortunate when it came to natural foods. However, Joe and Lucy Cadman saw the shelves in their shop grow emptier by the day.

Sugar had become a heartache. Home-made jam an impossibility.

Dinner was over, Emily had gone out with her friends and Bella hadn't come home from work yet. Emma and Sam were seated on each side of the fireplace. Sam had the evening paper and Emma was sorting out her needlework basket.

Emma looked up at the clock, the hands showed five minutes to seven. 'Our Bella is late tonight, I don't know whether to put her dinner in the oven or not,' she said suddenly.

Sam laid his paper down. 'I met Jack yesterday and he told me that our Bella has been a godsend since the lambing season has started. I wouldn't worry about her being late, Joyce Briggs will see that she gets some dinner. Bella won't starve,' Sam said grinning.

'Did he say anything about him being allocated women to work on his farm?' Emma asked, shaking her head slowly.

'Well, not exactly, sounded a bit worried though. Aggie's brother John, has been before a selection committee and they listed him as expendable which means he can jump the gun and volunteer now or wait until his call-up papers arrive and then he'll have no choice but to go to whichever regiment they send him to. Whichever way you look at it, Jack is going to miss John, there isn't a job that he can't tackle, makes yer wonder how girls that are being drafted to work on the land will cope. Anyway, what made you ask?'

'I was in Aggie's house today when she had a visitor. It was a young lady, named Hazel Osborne. Apparently she arrived in the village three days ago, she's needing a room until billet arrangements are sorted out.'

'Emma,' Sam loudly interrupted, 'will you please put that sewing down. If yer going to tell me something please talk to me properly.'

'I thought I was till you butted in.'

'No, you were rambling an' I couldn't make head or tail of what you were saying except that a female named Hazel Osborne is looking for accommodation.'

'Oh, I'm sorry, I'll start again. This Hazel has been sent to Corner Farm, she's become a Land Army girl. It's like the forces, known as the Woman's Land Army an' according to this young lady more females are to follow. I think I've got it right. They won't only be working at Corner Farm but at all farms in the district when an' wherever they are needed. And I want you to do something for me.'

Now Emma had got her husband worried because he had caught the hint of fear in her voice. He gave her his full attention. 'Fire away, love, I'll do my best.'

'What I want you to do, Sam, is go up to Corner Farm an' have a few words with Jack. Ask him if he *is* having recruits from this WLA and if he is whether he would consider making our Bella one of them.'

Sam gave a sigh of heartfelt thanks. He knew now what was running through Emma's mind and he thought all the more of her. She was like a mother hen when it came to her children.

'We both know that our Emily won't be here much longer. John is already in the forces, God alone knows when we'll get to see him. Tom's work in London is as dangerous as it can be an' I thought if Bella could be put into real war work, proper like, as a member of this WLA but at the same time stay working locally at least you an' me will have one of our brood still with us.'

Sam wanted to laugh. Poor Emma, if she hadn't got something to fret about she'd invent something. He didn't laugh though. He had too much admiration for his Emma to do that.

'That is a brilliant idea, Em. Our Bella could be billeted, as they call it, right here under our own roof. I'll tell you what, I fancy a pint so I'll walk along to the Fox, it's quite likely Jack might be in there. If not I'll ask Ted if I may use his telephone and I'll give Jack a ring, see what he has to say, that way you'll be able to go to sleep a darn sight easier tonight, won't you?'

'Thank you, Sam, I've been wanting to ask you ever since that Hazel turned up on Aggie's doorstep.'

Sam was already up on his feet walking through to the scullery where his outdoor jacket hung behind the back door. He stopped and turned to face Emma. 'Well, you've asked me now an' I will see to it. By the way, what was this Helen Osborne like?' Jack was now shrugging his arms into his jacket. Emma didn't reply to his question but he heard her laugh so he came back into the living room.

'What's so funny?' he asked, watching Emma trying to smother her laughter by covering her mouth with her hands.

Emma took a real deep breath but finally managed to answer. 'Just let's say that young lady is different to any of the girls in our village.'

'And what is that supposed to mean?'

'Sam, take yourself off if you're going, you'll be able to judge for yourself when you meet her.'

Sam knew that he wasn't going to get any more information so there was no point in arguing,

Emma had changed into her nightdress and dressing gown and had made herself a cup of cocoa. As soon as she had finished drinking it she planned to go to bed. She heard the click of the back door and voices, glancing up at the clock she saw it was only ten minutes past ten. For a silly moment she thought the pub must have run out of beer, Sam rarely came home as early as this. He was with Bella.

'Hi, Mum, you look cosy,' Bella said, as she unwound her scarf from around her neck. 'It's still pretty cold out there tonight.'

'You all right, luv. Have you had any thing to eat cos if not it won't take me long to heat up the dinner I put aside for you?'

'Yes, Mum, I'm fine an' yes I have had my dinner with Joyce.

I'm sorry I couldn't get word to you that I was going to be late but we've had seven lambs born today and every one of them is really bonny. Give it about a week an' you should come up to the farm, those born at the beginning of the week will be well away by then an' they will be a grand sight to see.'

Bella was kneeling down on the hearthrug, warming her hands in front of the fire. Emma looked over her head and saw that Sam was smiling and holding two thumbs up to her.

Emma's excitement boiled over. 'Really, Sam, do you mean what I think you're telling me?'

'Ask Bella.' It was Sam's turn to grin.

'Well, Bella – ' Her mother took hold of her shoulder and gave her a little shake – 'will one of you please tell me. Was Jack Briggs in the pub?'

'No, Mum, he wasn't but I was. I was having a celebratory drink with Hazel Osborne.'

'Oh, for the love of the Almighty, will one of you get to the point and tell me what's going on?'

Bella smiled sympathetically at her harassed mother. She realized that it hadn't been easy for her, John joining the army, Emily doing her best to do the same and Tom forbidden to leave his employment because it was regarded as vital war work. That leaves only me, the baby of the family and if Mum couldn't have the other three around her at least she was doing her best to keep me at home where she can keep an eye on me.

'Mum, calm down an' I will tell you what has happened. As soon as I got to work this morning Jack broached the subject. We had a bit of a chat. He told me that he wanted to keep me on but it would mean he would probably have to share me with Farley's Farm because they are one hundred per cent a dairy farm. He asked me how I felt about that an' also asked if I had any yearning to go into the forces.'

Emma almost jumped up out of her chair, she couldn't resist butting in. 'I hope you told him you were better off at home here with me an' your father.'

'Mum, will you sit yerself down again an' let me finish.' Bella waited a minute for her mother to settle.

'That is exactly what I told him an' also that I realized I would have to go wherever the work was according to the seasons.'

'Good girl, I knew eventually we'd find out that one of our children has a sensible head set on her shoulders.'

Bella looked at her father, he sat back in his armchair looking as pleased as punch and they both raised their eyebrows.

'Jack had got the forms, he has already filled them in an' all that remained was for me to sign them. I am now all set to be enlisted to work on the land for the duration of the war. In other words I'm going to dig for victory. Oh, by the way, there is what you, Mother, might regard as a downside to all of this.'

'What's that?' Emma asked quickly, fearing the worst.

'You might have to put up with me still living at home.'

Emma gave her daughter a real hard look. 'I haven't said I would agree to that,' she said sharply, but not meaning it at all.

'Oh, going to play hard to get, are we, Mum?' Bella asked, giving her mum a cheeky grin. 'Anyway, I'll tell you what has happened, see if you're happy with the arrangements or not. There's a huge place a few miles from the village, some sort of warehouse I think. Jack said the powers that be heard about it, sent their scouts out to vet the building and decided it could be changed into living quarters for war workers more quickly than temporary buildings could be erected. The outcome? Well, Jack's been told the whole place has been requisitioned.

Jack also said he and several other farmers have written on their application forms stating their preference for local girls who were already in their employment. In my case he has added two more good reasons. One that I was working for him even before I left school and two that the address at which I lived with my parents was very much nearer to Corner Farm and he requested that I be allowed to continue to live there. The requisition building allocated as being a suitable billet for Land Army women being some distance outside of the village.'

Emma didn't know whether to laugh or to cry.

Sam muttered, 'Women,' as he stood watching his wife and daughter hug each other and saw a tear run down Emma's cheek. At least this wretched war wasn't taking all four of their children. Emma would still have one at home to love and fuss over.

A fact that he was more than grateful for.

* * *

Just fourteen days later, half past nine in the morning and
Emma was out the front polishing her brass door knocker and
letter box when a man in a fawn coat overall climbed out of
a big green van which he had parked at the corner of the road
and started to walk towards her. He had a clipboard in his
hand and seemed to be checking off the house numbers against
the form that he was holding.

He drew abreast with Emma and said, 'Miss Arabella
Pearson live here, does she, missus?'

'Yes, yes she does,' Emma answered, straightening herself
up.

'I got a large box and a bicycle to deliver for her,' he
muttered. 'Have to get me trolley out, can't carry that lot down
over all these cobbles.'

Won't be an easy job pushing a trolley, Emma thought to
herself but he was the delivery man and he should know his
own business best. As to why Bella should be on the receiving
end of a bike and a big box she couldn't wait to find out.

It was so annoying, her Bella had only been gone a half
an hour or she could have opened the box. She'd have to wait
all day wondering what was in the box and who in God's
name would be sending Bella a bike.

Emma couldn't contain her curiosity. She decided to walk
down to Sam's forge, it was quite a while since she'd paid
him a visit and she did like to stand and watch him heat up
iron in his furnace. Besides she was dying to tell him about
the delivery that had come for Bella. Once the decision was
made she moved quickly, taking off her apron and tossing it
over the back of a chair. She was wearing a decent brown
tweed skirt and a fawn twin set that Aggie had kitted for her,
all she needed from upstairs was her coat and a stout pair of
shoes. Almost ready she glanced in the mirror and decided
she needed a hat to finish the outfit off. At the back of the
wardrobe she found a fawn hat with a wide brim that was
trimmed with a band of brown velvet. She put it on her head,
pulling it down over her ears.

Emma took another look at her reflection and smiled. For
a middle-aged old biddy you don't look too bad, she decided.
As long as Sam thought she was feminine and attractive then
everyone else could keep their opinions to themselves.

The long walk did her good, it was still bitterly cold but

there was some weak sunshine and it was dry which was the main thing. The minute she set eyes on Sam she thought there couldn't have been a better way to spend the day. Sam looked great. He was wearing a leather apron over his shirt and trousers, the top three buttons of the shirt were undone, his sleeves rolled up as far as they would go. His skin glistened with sweat and this big man, who she was so proud of, looked the picture of good health.

'Why are you sweating?' was her first question.

'Trust you, my luv, just cos you can't see me doing anything, does it look as if I've been lazing about?'

'No, I'll give you that. You look like you've walked through that furnace an' come out the other side.'

Sam let out a hearty laugh. 'Actually that is not a bad description, I have shod three shire horses an' three from Mr Trenfield's stable, the last one has just been collected.'

'Well, then you deserve a drink an' I will make us both one. While you're taking a breather you can listen to my news.'

Emma boiled the kettle on a gas ring that Sam kept in the little room at the back of his forge. She poured a generous amount of blackcurrant cordial into two glasses and topped them up with the boiling water. When they were both seated on two upturned crates with their drinks in their hands, Emma relayed the news that a large box and a bicycle had been delivered that morning addressed to Miss Arabella Pearson.

'And you can't work out what they are?' Sam asked. 'Not much of a detective, are you?'

'Well, if you're so clever you try telling me,' Emma said sharply.

'All right, don't get out of yer pram, my luv, it's easy when you think about it. The bicycle is provided by the organizers of the Women Land Army. Bella has already been told that she will have to work on other outlying farms. The bike is the only means of transport that they are going to provide for these lasses. No staff cars for our country girls.'

'And what's in the box, I suppose you're going to tell me that it is a uniform for our Bella to wear?'

'Got it in one, I'd say, although I might be wrong.'

'Oh, no, Sam Pearson, that's not possible. You may not always be right but you are never wrong,' Emma said airily.

They both laughed.

Sam moved his crate so that he was able to sit closer to Emma's side and when he was settled his hand went out to close over hers. 'You worry yerself sick over the kids an' you'll end up making yerself ill,' he said quietly, gazing closely at her.

Emma forced a brief smile, aware of the heat of his hand.

'I just wish that they didn't have to be split up,' Sam continued. 'It doesn't seem that long ago that we were fighting the authorities to let us visit the boys.'

'We were not allowed to adopt them, were we?' Emma quietly stated.

'Emma, look at me,' he almost growled, 'has it made any difference to how they feel about us?' Emma made no answer and Sam carried on. 'John told you that he had put us down as his next of kin in his military papers an' when it comes to Tom I defy anyone to argue with Tom that he hasn't got a family or any real parents. You an' I both know who would come off the worst.'

Still Emma couldn't bring herself to answer.

'My love, all four of our children, and I mean *four*, are now adults. They've had to accept that fact quicker than they, or us, would have liked, but it has been the same for families the length and breadth of this country. None of us wanted this war but all we can do is pray that it will be over in a very short time.'

Emma sat there, shoulders drooped, knowing that every word Sam had said was the truth and she had to accept that or she would go under.

'Come on, my old love, you wash these glasses an' I'll see to the furnace an' lock up. I've done enough work for today. I shall take my lovely wife home but we shall stroll through all the lonely country lanes where there is no one to see us.'

And where it's far to cold to dawdle, she almost said, but second thoughts told her it would best, if for once she kept quiet.

Even before Bella came through the back door she was complaining.

'All the other girls were moaning that they had been sent a man's bike an' I was hoping I might be the exception. That bike propped up outside the back door has got a saddle bar.'

'Have you given a thought to the fact that it will be men's work that you will be doing half the time,' her father told her, thinking it was better to indulge her rather than start an argument.

'Come on, Bella, dinner won't be ready for another half an hour, you've got plenty of time to open your box,' her mother urged her.

So thick was the packing material that it took Sam several minutes before Bella was able to delve into the contents. The top layer of clothing consisted of smaller items, three pairs of thick knee-length socks, one green shirt-like blouse, one green cardigan and a very smart fitted brown jacket. The next article Bella held up brought different reactions from her parents.

Her mother said, 'Oh my God!'

Her father remarked, 'Perhaps your duties will include being a jockey. I don't think even a war will stop our royal family from attending horse race meetings.'

Bella's remarks were at first unprintable but she smiled as she held the riding breeches up against herself. She knew there was a special name for these trousers but she couldn't think of it.

As if reading her thoughts her father said, 'They're called jodhpurs.'

'Thanks, Dad, any more useful information will be gratefully received,' Bella said sarcastically.

'Is the box empty now?' her mother called from the scullery.

'Not quite,' Bella answered her, 'there's a pair of very heavy shoes, a pair of Wellington boots and there's a hat. It's not too bad, brown, seems to be the only colour the War Office knows. It has a very wide brim and a badge on the front.'

I've not heard any mention of underwear. Isn't there any?' Emma as always was being practical.

'Doesn't seem to be, Mum. Perhaps I should be grateful for that. I don't want a commanding officer telling me to lift my skirt up so that he can see if I'm wearing regulation fleecy-lined passion-killing knickers.'

'Bella!' her mother shrieked. 'We'll have less of that talk. Now clear all that mess up, but mind you save the brown paper, then you can lay the table. I'm almost ready to dish up the dinner.'

'Yes, Mum,' Bella answered politely, wondering what her mother would have to say when she heard the rumours that troops might be billeted in the woods outside of North Waltham. *She'll have my father coming to the farm to walk me home every night just to make sure that I am safe!*

She had a huge grin on her face as she set the knives and forks out on the table.

Twenty-Seven

O n Sunday morning Tom whistled happily as he pumped up the tyres of Bella's bicycle. It had turned out to be a very pleasant Saturday evening, and he smiled to himself as he remembered how John and Emily had slipped away from the dance during the interval.

Aunt Emma had been emotional when he and John had arrived at midday yesterday but as it was the first time that the family had seen John in uniform it was only to be expected. As Sam had said, it is all right talking about joining the forces or even reading about it in a letter but seeing John all geared up brought the war right home to their doorstep. John had got seven days leave and was going to stay at home in North Waltham until next Friday whereas he needed to be back for a night shift tomorrow and would have to catch a train early this afternoon.

Aunt Emma had cheered up, seemed quite happy with the fact that she would have John for seven whole days. Sam's thoughts ran deeper, like his own, Tom admitted to himself. Was this seven days his embarkation leave? If it was John wasn't saying. Like a good many more young folk he seems to have adopted an attitude of live for the day.

The wind was blowing pretty fiercely. It is still only March, Tom reminded himself as he tightened the screw beneath the saddle of this sturdy bike. He gave the bell a bit of a polish, wiped the dust off the saddle and decided the bike was in good working order. He gathered up his tools but at the same time he was doing some mental arithmetic. John had volunteered before war was declared, about the first week in August of last year, that made it eight months he had been in the army. He knew quite a bit of that time John had spent at Catterick Military Camp in Yorkshire but surely that didn't qualify him to be sent abroad already!

I'd better keep my thoughts to myself, he decided. What I need now is a damn good breakfast. He smiled as he pushed open the back door and stepped into the scullery. As he stood rolling his sleeves even further up his arms Emma followed him in. She picked up the simmering kettle and poured the hot water into the tin bowl that was lying in the large stone sink.

'Tom, what kind of work is it that you do?' she asked with a hint of fear in her voice.

'Now, aunt, you really don't need to know and I'm not about to tell you,' he said jokingly before adding, 'it's obvious you don't live in London. You can't turn around without seeing a poster that warns, "CARELESS TALK COSTS LIVES". He grabbed the bar of Lifebuoy soap and dipped it into the water.

Emma stood behind him as he scrubbed his hands and fore-arms. He still wasn't much more than a lad, she thought sadly. It was the same with John. All that learning and exams and now what? Learning to kill? It seemed as though the whole world had gone mad.

'Shall I set the table, Aunt Em?' he asked as he reached for a towel to dry himself with.

'How many do you think will be eating breakfast with you at this time in the morning?' Emma queried, smiling broadly.

Tom was at a loss to know what she was talking about and his confusion showed clearly on his face.

'Tommy, lad, when you live in the country you learn to make the most of the daylight hours. Five of us had our break-fast at eight o'clock, it is now twenty minutes to eleven.'

Tom poked his head round the door to enable him to check the time by the clock which stood on the mantleshelf. 'God, I didn't realize it was that late, it's this rotten shift work that upsets my routine. I came off a night shift at eight o'clock yesterday morning, had a bath, changed me clothes, met John at twelve, had a bite to eat and a pint, then we travelled down here and last night we all went dancing.'

'Stop it, Tom, for goodness sake, you rattle on without ever stopping to take a breath. We all knew you were whacked out an' that is why we let you sleep in this morning. Anyway, my darling boy – ' she paused, came to stand in front of him, stood up on her toes and taking his face between her hands she kissed first one cheek and then the other, then stood for

a moment hugging him, her face resting against his broad
chest – 'I am going to cook you the biggest breakfast you
have ever seen, because we aren't having dinner until this
evening an' only a scratch meal at lunchtime.'

'Oh, aunt, you don't have to go to all that trouble for me,
a couple of slices of toast will do me fine.'

'What after that wonderful box of goodies that you brought
down for us. I wonder that the smell of real coffee didn't
wake you up this morning. I was making the beds when I
heard you come down. Now, what will it be, tea or coffee?'

'I'll make a pot of tea for us both while you cook my breakfast,' he said smiling, before going to the sink to fill the kettle.

'Oi you, watch it my lad!' Emma couldn't say any more,
her emotions were getting the better of her. She loved this
boy so much, the feeling went beyond words, it was the same
for John but somehow that was a safer love. Tom had a frightening effect on her, she was always afraid that she might lose
him. He was always loveable but a bit of a rogue. A lovable
rogue though! These days he never seemed short of money
and you only had to mention that you were feeling the shortage
of something and a parcel would be delivered containing whatever it was you were missing. How had he come by all that
food? His parcel had contained tea, marmalade, jam, two tins
of corned beef and gorgeous freshly ground coffee.

She knew better than to ask!

It *was* a big breakfast. Emma sat at the far end of the long
kitchen table sipping the cup of tea that Tom had made for
her and told herself to make the most of having all the children home at the same time.

'I could make a fortune if we could get the eggs from your
hens an' some of yer neighbours back up to the smoke. There's
nothing like a real fresh egg. These are smashing!' Tom said,
smacking his lips.

'Tom, don't talk with your mouth full. Just get on an' clear
your plate. As to you selling our, or anyone else's, eggs, you
do realize that those of us that keep chickens have to have
families registered with us. We have Agnes an' her three children an' Dorothy James an' her husband.'

'Sounds double Dutch t'me. What do you mean by regis-
tering?'

'We take the coupons out of their ration card so they can't

get any eggs from the shops an' we have to give all the coupons up, including our own, when we need to buy chicken feed and corn. In return we are able to supply them with eggs which is much better for them than relying on the shops. Mostly the shopkeeper can only allocate one egg per ration book per week, and there are times when retailers don't receive a delivery of eggs.'

'Complicated life, ain't it? I thought it was only in the big towns that we had to beg off Peter to pay back Paul. Cor that was a smashing breakfast,' Tom added, getting to his feet and taking the teapot with him. 'D'yer want another cuppa, aunt?' he called from the scullery.

'No thanks, Tom.'

'Is it all right if I do, what I mean is 'ow are you off for milk?'

Emma chuckled. 'That's one thing we don't have to bother about, every other day Bella is up at Farley's Farm. Some of the old farmhands have been recalled back to work an' one old boy is teaching Bella to drive a tractor an' an old lorry they had lying about up there. But for the moment she an' another girl are driving a horse an' cart. They leave the farm loaded with four churns of milk. Two they leave at the top of our lane for collection by the Milk Marketing Board an' the other two they drop off at the local dairy shop where folk can buy their ration. We always know the night before if Bella is going to be on that milk run an' if she is either me or Aggie wait up at the corner. Bella hands us down a strong bag with two pints of milk wrapped up inside.' Emma chuckled again, more heartedly this time.

'Now, what's tickling you?' Tom impatiently asked.

'Our Bella skims the milk she is bringing for us straight of the top of a still churn.'

Seeing the bewildered look on Tom's face Emma explained. 'A still churn is one standing in the dairy. Fresh milk straight from the herd of cows. By skimming the top Bella makes sure we get a good amount of the cream.'

'I don't know.' Tom was shaking with laughter. 'I thought all the ducking an' diving only went on up in the smoke. This war has 'ardly got off the ground yet an' already there's young girls an' old women fiddling the books.'

'I won't warn you again, our Tom, watch what your saying.

I might be doing a bit of harmless fiddling but an old women I am not.'

Tom was on his feet in an instance. Bending low from the waist he bowed and mockingly said, 'I wasn't referring to you, o gracious lady.'

For an answer Emma lightly boxed his ears.

It was at that moment that Bella and her father came in through the back door.

'What the hell's going on here?' Sam couldn't believe what he was seeing. Tom had Emma in an arm lock and they were both laughing fit to bust.

Emma broke free, straightened her dress and did her best to tidy her hair by patting it. Eventually she asked, 'Good service, was it? Were there many people in church? By the way, where are Emily and John?'

Sam gave her a funny look. 'You been drinking?' he asked sternly.

'No, I have not. I'll have you know I've had a cup of tea an' nothing more.'

'So why fire three questions at me and not wait for one answer? However in the order that you asked, yes, Michael gave us a very good service, yes, the church was almost full, and as to where Emily an' John are, yer guess is as good as mine. John did say that they wouldn't be coming back for lunch but they would be home in time for dinner this evening. And here is a bit extra for you. Michael asked about Tom, we explained that you were too tired, that you have to go back to London tomorrow. He sent you his best wishes, Tom. Said he looks forward to seeing you next time you manage to get down.'

Bella quickly cut in. 'Loads of people asked me about you, Tom, all the old dears said they would be praying for you.'

'God help us!' Emily muttered. 'What is it with all you youngsters that you suddenly refer to nice middle-aged ladies as old dears?'

Suddenly everyone was laughing. Bella turned to her father and said, 'Shall we get the sherry bottle out or shall we all go up to the Fox? If those two – ' she pointed to her mum and to Tom – 'haven't been drinking then it must be that they are badly in need of a drink! So what's it to be?'

'Well, I'll tell you one thing my girl!' Sam bellowed. 'It

isn't going to be the blasted sherry bottle. Ted Andrews might
be short on the spirits in his pub but I know he had a delivery
of beer yesterday. Come on, Tom, let's get going, we might
even get a crafty one in before the womenfolk turn up.'

John squeezed Emily's hand as they walk away from the
village. He had been really touched by the number of people
who had approached him and wished him well. He shouldn't
be surprised though, he had been coming here for some years
now, ever since that first holiday fund had sent him and Tom.
*God, what a blessing that had turned out to be. We both gained
relatives, a whole loving family, all the money in the world
couldn't buy what he and Tom had found here.*

'Which way shall we walk?' John asked, when Emily hesitated at the top of one lane.

'I thought you an' Tom had sorted out your favourite haunts
years ago.'

'We had, but to be honest they mainly consisted of fields
an' orchards where things grew that we could eat.'

'John Kirby, are you telling me that our mother kept you
two short of food when you stayed with us?' Emily had done
a good job of sounding horrified.

'Oh, Emily, of course not!' Then he saw that she was
giggling. 'You rotten tease,' he muttered, giving her a playful
slap.

Emily broke away and ran ahead. 'Come on slow-coach,
this way leads to the lovely village of Steventon. As we go I
shall give you a history lesson.'

'Oh, wonderful,' he mocked but within the hour he was
ready to change his tune. Steventon was indeed a most
delightful village.

Emily led him down lanes boxed in each side with high
hedges, where they finally came to the remains of a forsaken
derelict house. What seemed really strange was the fact that
what must have once been the garden attached to this property was still lovely. A bit wild and overgrown in places but
still an old-fashioned English garden. In a secluded corner
there stood a tree, its branches not bare but not yet leafy.
Around the trunk of the tree was an old oak seat. They made
for this seat and the first thing Emily did was kick off her
shoes, lift up her legs and stretch them out across John's lap.

'Years ago this must have been a beautiful house,' Emily remarked thoughtfully. 'It was a vicarage an' the vicar was the father of Jane Austen.'

'What, Jane Austen the author,' John said delighted.

'Yes, and in the springtime this small garden is always ablaze with flowers, mostly daffodils. It is as if someone tends the garden still.'

'Wonder why the old house has never been rebuilt?'

'Bella and I used to wonder that. Such a shame, isn't it? To see the remains so dilapidated and discarded.' Emily turned her attention to the small holdall she had brought with her. 'I brought two of Mum's pasties with me . . . I thought one each would be enough seeing as we're going to have dinner tonight. I also boiled some milk an' made up this small flask – ' she paused and gave John a wicked grin – 'using some of the coffee that Tom brought down with him.'

'He probably nicked it,' John said smiling.

'John, that's not nice,' Emily said, sounding cross.

'Maybe not, but it's a dead cert he never bought it.'

'Probably not, but he may have had something that the person who had the coffee wanted an' they did a swap.'

'Pigs might fly. Take it from me, Emily, our Tom is going to have a lovely war. One thing I am pleased about is that he won't ever see you an' the family in need. Remember when Tom an' I ran away from the institution? Well, I would have starved many a time if it weren't for Tom, he's a real good friend to have when you are in need.'

'I think he's a good friend to have at anytime,' Emily said quite huffily. 'You would never involve yourself in the kind of tricks that Tom pulls, is that what you're saying?' she asked mischievously.

'No, that is not what I am saying an' if you would please pass me that flask I will pour us both out some coffee, compliments of Tom.' The last three words sounded cynical.

Emily fished a small beaker out from her coat pocket. 'Here, I remembered that flask only has one cup to it.'

While they were sipping their coffee and munching on a pastie silence reigned for quite a while until Emily spoke.

'I loved dancing with Tom last night. He's a great mover an' I wasn't the only lass at the dance that thought so.' She was deliberately teasing John.

'Yes, you have to give our Tom the credit, he knows how to play the field.'

'What about you, John, when it comes to *classical* ball-room dancing you are far better than Tom. Do you like to play the field?'

'I thought you knew me better than that,' he said sounding peeved.

'I was only joking, John.'

'That's my trouble,' he replied with feeling. 'No one ever takes me seriously.'

'I do, John.'

'You can't do or else you'd know how I really do feel about you.'

'Why didn't you ever tell me?'

'Because I was sure you knew full well. I wish you would realize just how much I care about you. Don't for a moment think it is brotherly love. The way I feel about you goes much deeper than that.'

'Why then have you never showed how you felt?'

'I like to think that I have shown you how much I care but that I would never take you for granted.'

'So the only reason that you have never told me outright that you love me was in case I rejected you?'

'Now you're being silly. The way I have always felt for you has always been special, but I've always felt afraid to overstep the mark. Your mum and dad regard me and Tom as family and for that I . . . well I can't put it into words, it is unbelievable. The day that Tom and I arrived in North Waltham honestly changed our lives. No great change happened straight away but your parents never gave up on us.'

'So you never let me know in case you got hurt in the process?'

'Yes, that's partly it, but now there are other things to be taken into consideration.'

'Such as?'

'Well, I'm in the Army now.'

'What's that got to do with it?'

'Supposing I get crippled or that I don't come back home at all? Where would that leave you?'

'Listen to me, John, we are told this war is going to be as bad for civilians as it is for servicemen. In any case I hope to get my own papers soon. None of us know if we'll be around tomorrow or the next day. All any of can do is get on with our lives an' hope this war doesn't last long. Just pray we will come through. Wouldn't you like to know that I will be here waiting for you? Won't you be thrilled to get my letters, show my photograph around to your mates, let them see how lucky you are?'

John's mouth fell open. 'Why you sounded almost as big-headed then as our Tom does.'

'Who knows, perhaps it is catching,' Emily answered confidently.

'Emily, will you really write to me regularly?'

'On my honour, at least once a year!' She still persisted in teasing him.

For his answer he took her into his arms and a kiss that began as a soft gentle kiss suddenly changed and they both knew that their feelings for each other were strong and would hopefully stand the test of time.

Twenty-Eight

Life seemed to go on normally. But what was normal these days? To Emma it was like living on a knife's edge. It was now just over two months since they had seen John, three weeks since they had seen Tom and a fortnight since Emily had been home.

Thank God for Bella!

One postcard had arrived from John, bearing a postmark which said 'Military Post Office'. There was very little space for the sender to write and John's message had been short.

> Hope all is well at home. I am fit and well. Always with my love, John

'Does that postmark mean that John is not in this country?' Emma asked cautiously.

Sam didn't answer for a moment and when he did there was a break in his voice. 'Probably, but, Emma, it would be best if you didn't ask that question an' certainly don't talk about it outside of the house. Of course you can always talk to me.'

'Oh, Sam, things get worse by the day don't they?'

Sam's immediate thought was that they'd get a damn sight worse before they started to get better, but thoughts such as that were best kept to himself. Instead he changed the subject. 'We've had a great piece of news this week, haven't we? At least Emily seems to have fallen on her feet.'

'Yeah, pity that you weren't in the Fox when she telephoned. It was nice that she got through an' left a message for us but if you'd been able to talk to her she might have told you a whole lot more as to what was going on. Now I suppose we'll have to wait until she comes home to get all the details.'

She stopped. Sam waited.

'This war, it seems everybody's going to be in the thick of it except us.' Emily sighed. My conscience has been pricking me every day since we said goodbye to John. I can't get the picture out of my mind of him and Tom saying goodbye to each other. Those two lads were hugging, slapping each other on the back. Heartbreaking to watch it was.'

'Oh, come on, Emma, it wasn't all doom an' gloom, remember what the boys said?'

'I know they told each other to take care but then everyone is saying that.'

Sam forced a laugh. 'Tom came out with the saying that they'd both be fine because the devil looks after his own. John was just as quick off the mark too, his reply was "In that case, my old mate, you will live forever."'

That did bring a smile to Emma's face.

Sam thought that was good. 'I've suddenly hit on what is your problem,' he told his wife. 'You haven't got enough to do. No children around the house, only you an' me an' Bella coming home to sleep. I think a little of what our Bella is doing wouldn't do you any harm.' He paused to see what effect his shock tactics had had. He wasn't disappointed.

'What! You want *me* to volunteer to join the Land Army?'

'On a much smaller scale,' he finally managed to say. 'This afternoon why don't you and I take the time off an' go into Basingstoke. I will buy you a pair of rubber boots an' all the equipment you will need to dig for victory. No, No . . .' He held his hands up to stop her from butting in. 'Hear me out, please. Behind the chicken run I can dig you a trench for runner beans, too late to sow them from seed but I'm sure I can beg quite a few plants and they'll soon be climbing up the back fence. I'll have a word with Clifford. I reckon he'll let you have some tomato plants as well. Too late for new potatoes but you could certainly set some down now, ready for the winter and maybe a few cabbages. What d'you think?'

Emma was amused. The more she thought about it the more she liked the idea. It might be rather fun to take her home-grown vegetables to the Women's Guild. She felt grateful towards Sam for having suggested it and she felt relieved to finally have found something worthwhile to do.

She had been going to do Bella's washing this afternoon

and she did have a pile of Sam's shirts waiting to be ironed, but she realized all that could wait until later. It wasn't every day that Sam offered to take her out, and she wasn't going to miss this offer. Who knows what he might end up buying her when they got to the shops in Basingstoke.

Emma walked the length of her garden, looking up at the sky. It was a clear beautiful blue colour, not a cloud to be seen and the sunshine was quite warm. 'What a really lovely day,' she said out loud. Going behind the chicken's run she reminded herself to look in the hen boxes and pick up the eggs on her way back. Give yourself a pat on the back, she thought with pride as she gazed at the neat rows of runner beans and peas even though they were only inches tall. Thanks had to go to Sam, he had done all the heavy digging and sieving of the earth. Old Clifford and John Brown had been a great help. Both men were known as the village odd-job men and with all the young men called to serve their country there were numerous jobs that folk were grateful to have their help with. Only this morning John had dropped some roots of beet outside her back door and this afternoon she was going to get them into the ground. We all love beetroot in salads she thought. Sam loved it boiled and pickled with slices of raw onion in the same jar, with a good bit of strong cheese and a hunk of fresh bread it made a darn good supper.

Suddenly she snapped her head round and stared up towards the house. Their wireless had come on, she could hear it, yet there was no one in the house. She had been on her own all morning.

'Emma, are you upstairs?' She heard Sam calling her.

Of course he couldn't see her, tucked away behind the old shed and the chicken house she was hidden from view. But what was Sam doing home in the middle of the morning? she asked herself as she hastened to scramble back to the house.

For the past weeks all had been quiet. No air raids. No invasion.

'Come and listen to this, Emma,' Sam said breathlessly as he turned up the volume of the wireless.

They listened together in silence. It was unbelievable!

Emma hadn't caught all of what the newscaster was saying but as he went on she got the gist of it all.

Our British Expeditionary Force is stranded in France.

Thousands of our troops are pinned down in outlying towns and villages of France. It was the 20th of May 1940. Hardly a shot had been fired and the war that hadn't started was over.

The Germans had defeated us! Had they?

There were some that thought so, including many high ranking army officials. There were however a great number of English people who declared, 'Never.'

There wasn't much work done that day. In shops, offices, factories, town halls and ordinary houses the news was repeated at regular intervals. Every bulletin was listened to.

Our troops were in trouble across the channel. Dover was only twenty miles from the French coast, practically the front line.

By the 24th of May the order had gone out that all our troops, using what ever means possible, should make their way to the beaches. A great evacuation was to be got underway.

Boats were needed. Pleasure steamers, fishing boats, lifeboats, motorboats, yachts, everything that could make it across the channel, the broadcasting announcer pleaded, even rowing boats! Men were also needed to man the ships and the boats and to aid the wounded. Who would volunteer to go? Nobody knew what to expect, but men from all walks of life volunteered.

By six o'clock that evening an assorted line of vehicles left North Waltham all filled with volunteers from the village. Even Len and Sid Brownlow were on board one of the open-backed lorries. They were told that they would not be allowed to put to sea but that their help with the wounded on shore would be greatly appreciated.

Bella Pearson was driving Jack Briggs's old lorry with five older men sitting on the floor. Leading the line of vehicles was Reverend Coyle. John Brown, Joe Cadman and Sam Pearson were his passengers.

Portsmouth harbour was bustling with activity. Even the Hayling Island ferries, navy patrol boats and old battleships which were in dock had all been pressed into service. As the first stream of boats returned, the men in charge were able to offer valuable information. Thousands of men were stranded on the beaches of Dunkirk.

Dunkirk Harbour could not be used to evacuate our men because the Germans air attacks at that spot were heavy and continuous. Larger vessels would not be able to get close enough to the beaches to lift off our wounded men. Therefore it was especially important that little ships should go over. Craft small enough to get close to the beaches to lift off the wounded men. Dunkirk was easy to find, the volunteers were told. A huge pall of smoke from burning oil tanks hung over the shattered port.

For days, boats and ships made return journeys. All over Southern England men who had no knowledge of the sea left their desks, their garages and their shops. An unbroken line of vessels could be seen carrying the men back home across the channel.

The Luftwaffe gave them no leeway. Raining bombs down on them as craft after craft disappeared. So near and yet so far from home.

In nine days almost 350,000 allied troops were brought back to England.

It was to be almost a month before Mr and Mrs Pearson was notified that sadly John was not one of them.

Twenty-Nine

After the death of John time seemed to go slowly. Such a long time, Emma thought as she stared down the lane. She couldn't bring herself to act bright and cheerful, it was as if her hopes were as dead as John was. It hurt most that there had been no body brought home. No funeral, no church service. There would be no party for his twenty-first birthday. No future for John.

Sam kept saying they would be notified where he is buried when the war ends. Suppose he had died at sea, she reflected. His body might never be found. It was the not knowing that was the hardest to bear.

Then one morning Emma woke to a brighter day. She put on her dressing-gown and padded down the stairs, through the kitchen and into the scullery to fill the kettle. While she waited for it to boil she let her thoughts wander.

About the same time as the evacuation of our troops from Dunkirk, Neville Chamberlain had resigned in Britain and was replaced by Winston Churchill. That very fact had given folk renewed hope. The threat of invasion seemed to have passed away and for the first time in weeks Emma felt she had something to look forward to.

Emily had been given a weekend pass and Tom was travelling down with her. How she longed to hold them both. It would also be good for Bella to see her sister and Tom. John's death had hit her hard. She had talked to her father, but parents aren't always on the same wavelength as the youngsters and Emma hoped it would help Bella a lot to be able to draw some comfort from her sister and for her to give comfort to Emily in return. God knows Emily is the one who needs it most.

Tom being here for the weekend would be an added bonus. He probably won't let his real feelings show. More than likely he'd still play Jack-the-lad. The news that John had been killed must have hit him hard though.

They were two brothers in so many ways. From birth they had been cast aside, not one living relative had laid claim to either of them. They had found each other and stuck to each other through thick and thin. Two lads, in many ways as different as chalk and cheese, and yet there had been such a powerful bond between them. Nobody could work it out. You just accepted it, that binding cord was there for everyone to see.

Tom must have felt that his right arm had been cut off when he received the letter from Sam. They hadn't seen him since. It was nearly seven weeks and in a way both she and Sam were relieved he hadn't come before. What if he had come home? How can you console a person when your own heart is breaking?

Knowing that Tom and Emily had been able to meet was something to be grateful for. Also the fact that they would be travelling down by train together was good news. *I know I go on about them all as if they were still small children, but what mother doesn't?* Emma asked herself.

Once the hugs, the tears and the emotions had settled down it was three grown-up children who were waiting for their mother to dish up the dinner and their father to open a bottle of his home-made brew.

Emily wrapped her arms across her chest. 'What a delight it is to get out of uniform an' into civvies,' she said, smiling down at the floral skirt and a pale pink short sleeved blouse she had dug out of the chest of drawers in her bedroom. 'But this is best of all,' she said, leaning back in her dad's old armchair she raised her leg and twiddled her foot. 'A pair of soft leather shoes. My feet feel they have died an' gone to heaven.'

'I know the feeling,' Bella told her, 'my feet spend hours tucked into Wellington boots, but you're lucky you get a change of uniform.'

'No we don't,' Emily quickly retorted. 'What made you think that?'

'You wrote in one of your letters that you get a "parade" uniform and a working set of clothes.'

'Bella, love, that was when I first went into the Auxiliary Territorial Service but as soon as my training period was over I got sent on a Motor Transport Course. The second set of clothes we were given was overalls and dungarees.'

'Well, that's a lot better than we get.'

Tom was listening to all of this and made a mental note to talk to the girls when their parents weren't around.

'Sit up to the table,' Emma called as she carried in dishes of vegetables and Sam carried the big meat dish.

Emily stretched her neck forward as her father set the dish at one end of the long kitchen table, she closed her eyes and took a hefty sniff. 'Mmm, that smell takes me back,' she murmured. 'Roast rabbit and it's stuffed with sage and onions, isn't it, Mum?'

'Yes, it is. I'll tell you something you might find hard to believe. Emily, do you remember old Clifford Watson?'

'Of course I do, Mum, always coming to the back door with fresh vegetables that he had just dug up an' wanted you to buy them from him.'

'That's right, luv, different story today though. Can't get hold of onions for love nor money, leeks are all right done in a cheese sauce but they're a poor substitute when you're making stuffing. Cliff had three rows of onions, almost ready for digging up but one morning last week when he went to his allotment the whole three rows had gone, leaving just shallow trenches of earth.'

'What, somebody had dug them all up and nicked the lot!' Emily was appalled.

Tom could hardly believe it. 'Disgusting,' he snapped. 'Who'd stoop so low as to pinch a few onions?' he asked, mistrusting what Emma had just said. 'What hell this war has caused when even in a lovely place like this yer can't trust anybody.'

'You've got all the weekend to tell the kids about the spicy life we live in this village. I've cut the rabbit into portions so will you please pass your plates and let's get on with the business of eating, shall we?' Sam said. Without waiting for any reply, Sam added, 'Tom, you take that big spoon an' start doling out the vegetables before yer mother takes to telling you in detail how she grew each an' every one of them all by herself.'

Smothered giggles could be heard but no one dared to disobey their father, not when his tone of voice told them he was losing his patience.

Emma lowered her voice to a whisper as she bent near to Bella. 'Sorry, love, but you're nearest, I've forgotten the jug of gravy. Go and fetch it, will you, please?'

By the time every single morsel of the first course had been eaten and the dirty dishes stacked away in the scullery everybody had calmed down.

That was true until Emma had squeezed past Bella and returned carrying a huge enamel pie dish in which she had baked a bread and butter pudding. The top was golden brown and smothered with fat juicy sultanas. Everyone moved to one side so that Emma could lean over and place the dish in the centre of the table.

Turning her head in Bella's direction and without thinking, she loudly said, 'Where did you hide that big jug of cream you brought home?'

Emily, Tom and Bella looked at each other trying so hard to keep a straight face but it was impossible.

The pudding went down a treat, covered in thick cream and Tom even got to scrape the pie dish!

When all the washing up was done, the table cleared, Sam made the coffee and when Bella told Tom how great she thought his fresh coffee was and she passed him the jug of cream that was still half full they again fell about laughing.

Bella had certainly grown up since she had been in this Land Army. 'I've found out that God helps those that help themselves.'

Tom gave her a smug look. 'Too true, Bella, my darling, but always remember one thing, sometimes it's a question of Christ 'elp those that get caught 'elping themselves.'

Bella threw herself at him, playfully punching him. He grabbed her arms and held her tightly against his broad chest, rocking her back and forth as if she were a baby.

Emma had been standing in the door way and just watching them had brought the tears to her eyes.

After they had been notified that John would not be coming home she had cried so many tears that she hadn't thought she had any left to shed. These were different tears, hopeful happy tears and once again she prayed that this awful war would soon be over.

'Right, who's going to let me buy them a drink?' Sam's voice was hearty as he stood at the bottom of the stairs and four pair of eyes turned to look at him.

'What came over you, Dad? You've got yourself all spruced up,' Emily said with a winning smile.

Sam's answer was to say to his wife, 'Come on, love, no saying yer too tired, you are coming to the pub. We're all going, as a family.'

'Thanks, Sam,' she whispered as she squeezed passed him to go upstairs and get herself changed.

The saloon bar was pretty full. They found seats for Emily and the two girls but Sam and Tom stood at the bar waiting not only to be served but for Alice or Ted to recognize that Emily and Tom were home.

What a wonderful welcome. Aggie came through from the snug, the locals slapped Tom on the back and kissed Emily, Ted and Alice insisted that the first round of drinks were on the house. After the first ten minutes it was as though neither Emily nor Tom had ever been away.

Much later that night, as Emily lay in her bed in the same room as Bella, they turned the gas mantle right out and in the black darkness they started to talk.

'Bella, do you like being in the Land Army?' Emily began.

'Well, I think I made a wise choice. At least one of us is able to be home with Mum and Dad, at least most nights so far,' Bella said, sounding a little apprehensive. 'Though if the Germans do send their planes over then it might be another thing altogether.'

'Have you been asked to do the night watch?' Emily asked quickly.

'No, not yet, we have all been trained to use a stirrup pump which apparently is the only thing to use if incendiary bombs are dropped.'

'How about you, Emily? Does army life suit you?'

Emily gave a small laugh. 'Different times of the day, different feelings.'

'What's that suppose to mean?'

'Well, let's start at the beginning of the day. Early parade in the half dark. Back to one's hut to polish shoes an' boots, strip our bed an' lay blanket and sheets in a nest pile. God help the recruit who hasn't learnt how to fold bed linen. I do a lot of driving which is no hardship to me. I really like driving an' it does get me out of a lot of other tedious jobs.'

'I think it's funny. Sweated blood while you waited for your driving test result, didn't you, Emily? While me, I've never had a lesson from a professional an' I always thought that I would only ever drive a horse and cart. Just goes to show, doesn't it? When I drove to Portsmouth an' back at least seven or eight times in one week during the time that we were doing out best to evacuate our boys from the beaches of Dunkirk, nobody bothered to ask whether I had ever passed a driving test.'

'You're doing great Bella, I really admire you.'

There followed an uncomfortable silence until Emily whispered, 'I get homesick, Bella. More so since I know that John is not going to come home.'

Emily's voice was so full of sadness that Bella felt her own eyes fill up.

She threw the bedcovers off, swung her legs round until her feet touched the floor and in two strides she was standing beside her sister's bed.

'Move over, pet, I know it will be a bit of a squeeze but both of us need a cuddle.' Emily did as she was asked and within minutes the two sisters had their arms around each other and both were sobbing their hearts out.

Bella was grieving for a small boy who had come to them from nowhere and over the years his love had bonded until he had become her beloved brother.

Emily was still bewildered and heartbroken although she had done her best to put on a brave face when her mum and dad were about. She was lost. She had *lost* a future that had promised so much. A husband who would have loved her until the end of his days. The chance to have their own brood of children, their very own family. Something that John might never have known if he hadn't stayed with her family.

She had lost the chance of all of that. 'I'll never love anyone as much as I loved John,' she whispered.

'Oh, Emily don't say that, never is a long time.' Bella's voice held a note of pleading.

'John had such plans for both of us. He was too young to die! I've asked myself a hundred times, what did he die for?'

At that moment neither of the sisters was capable of answering that question.

'Night-time is the worst of all,' Emily suddenly said, as she wiped her wet cheeks with the sleeve of her nightdress.

'Why, luv? Because you can't sleep?' Bella sympathized.

'No Bella, it's not that. It's just a daily routine that I can't get used to. Every night in the camp they play 'The Last Post'. Sounding out across a quiet base where only the sentries are on duty, it never fails to make me feel homesick an' now, since John, well it is as if they are sounding it just for him.'

'Oh, Emily, my love, come here.' As they clung to each other Bella said, 'Damn this bloody war.'

It was a sentiment with which her sister wholeheartedly agreed.

Breakfast the following day might have been a very more sombre affair if it had not been for Tom. He was already tucking in to his fry-up when Emily and Bella finally put in an appearance. They took their dirty tea cups out into the scullery and then took their place at the table.

'Look – ' Tom used the edge of his knife to point to what he was eating – 'real eggs, these are, really really real. Laid in clean straw in boxes which are housed at the bottom of this very garden. Did you know that?'

'Of course we did, you daft fool,' Bella told him bluntly.

'I wasn't exactly talking to you, Miss Bella, you work on the land an' you live off the land. You come home at night so that Mummy and Daddy can spoil you rotten. Where as your poor sister spends her days driving bigwigs around Whitehall, which, if you don't know, is in the centre of London an' when, and if, it becomes possible for her, or me come to that, to sit down an' have a good old English break-fast, do we get real eggs from home-bred English fowls? Do we heck! We get eggs from a packet! Dried egg. With compli-ments from the Americans and no one can say that we are not truly grateful to the good old US of A. Whether you prefer scrambled egg, poached egg or fried egg it is one an' the same. But having a boiled egg an' soldiers is not possible.'

Emma looked at Sam. They were both having trouble stifling

their laughter. Emily and Bella were ignoring Tom, at least they were trying to as they tucked in to their breakfast.

Emma had the last laugh. 'You finished, Tom?' she asked.

'Couldn't eat another morsel,' he said, patting his flat stomach. 'It was smashing.'

'Well, stand up. I want to have a look at you before we set off for church.'

Tom did as he was bid, as he pulled himself up to his full height he gave Emma a mock salute. 'Do I pass muster?' he asked grinning.

'You most certainly do, my lad. 'I can see there's no shortage of clothing coupons where you come from. That's an entirely different outfit to the one you wore yesterday, isn't it?'

All eyes were on him now and he played the part of a dandy to a tee. He looked down at his fawn trousers, the crease so fine you could almost cut your fingers on it. The shirt might not have been hand-made but it was a certainty it had not come from a market stall. His brown jacket was well tailored, from material the likes of which Emma had never come across before. The seams were hand-finished, each sleeve had four buttons running upwards from the cuff and the brown and fawn striped silk tie set the whole outfit off perfectly.

Emma cast her eyes down. 'Why, you've nothing on your feet,' she cried.

Tom lifted one foot up. 'Yes I have, a pair of Wosley fine wool socks,' he said with pride.

'Where are your shoes?'

'Upstairs, still in the box, don't worry they are quite fine to wear to church. They're not red, pink or blue, just ordinary brown leather brogues.'

'God give me strength,' Emma muttered.

To the amusement of the girls he planted a kiss on the top of Emma's head as he dodged past her.

In church that morning Emma looked at her daughters, both wearing their uniforms and she prayed as she had never prayed before. She wasn't on her own, everyone was beginning to feel apprehensive about where this war was leading.

The weekend was over far too quickly. It had been arranged in the pub on Saturday night that John Brown would drive Tom and Emily to the railway station.

Bella was going to the station to see them off. There was no room in the car for anyone else to go. Sam kissed and hugged Emily. He shook hands with Tom, then changed his mind and dragged him close, holding him in a great bear hug.

Now it was only left to Emma to say her goodbyes. She stood in front of the pair of them and gazed up into their faces. 'I love you both, we all do. I want you to remember that. God bless you.' She kissed each in turn and after that there was neither the time nor the opportunity to say anything else.

Sam had his arm around Emma's shoulders as they stood and watched the car disappear out of sight.

'Wonder how long it will be before we see them again,' Emma said sadly.

Probably best that we don't know the answer, was Sam's immediate thought. Also best that he didn't voice his thoughts aloud. He'd keep those thoughts and opinions to himself. He'd had to do a lot of that lately!

Once the car was out of sight Emma sighed heavily. 'I think I shall go upstairs an' have a lie down,' she said softly.

Sam knew that when Emma admitted to being tired something was worrying her and while her mood seemed so strange there would be no point in questioning her. Instead he kissed her, calmly and gently. 'Good idea, my love, you have a good rest.' His thoughts were sad as he watched her climb the stairs.

As soon as Emma was alone in their bedroom she opened the bottom drawer of the chest of drawers and took out a small collection of photographs. Settling down on the bed she drew the eiderdown across her legs and rested her shoulders back against the pillows. She spread the photographs out in front of her. They were pictures of the family when there had been two girls and two boys, taken on the day they had all gone to Southsea. Emily and Bella, both as pretty as a picture, Tom playing Jack-the-lad and John looked so well and handsome.

Dear God, why was life so unfair? It had taken years, heartbreaking years before she and Sam had finally been able to claim John and Tom as their own sons. It had never been a legal agreement. Even so, wasn't it a much stronger bond because it had come about from choice on all sides? Lifting one of the photographs up into her hands she let herself remember every detail of that day. Hot sunshine, a picnic, hands covered in sand, splashing in the sea, so much laughter.

From the time that each lad had left the institution they had been a complete family. The boys tormenting the girls yet caring for them in every way possible. It had been a gloriously happy time when they were able to get together, not a cloud in their sky, they'd had everything they needed. Happy, happy days, she thought. Why had the country had to go to war? If every member of this family lives to be a hundred years old, not one of them would ever forget John. He had had such a rough life to begin with and then when he had gained a family who loved him so dearly he had been taken, dying like so many other young men in this cruel war. Both she and Sam had known that Emily and John had fallen in love and who knows what might have happened? All just wishful thinking now, yet there would never be a day when she would have regrets about taking those two lads into her home. She knew Sam felt the same way so she must be thankful for small mercies and look back with happiness.

In spite of the struggle they'd had to prove they were worthy to add two lads to their existing family neither she nor Sam had any regrets.

No, definitely no regrets.

Thirty

Tom was worried about Emily. For the first month after John had died she had grieved and it had been terrible to watch her. He didn't get to see her as often as he would have liked but when he did he thought she was acting as if she were a zombie. Going through the motions of living, obeying orders but when he looked straight into her eyes he knew her feelings were dead.

He'd had a word with Daisy and she had good-heartedly suggested that he bring Emily home to their place when she had some off-duty time.

He thanked the Lord for the day that he had met Daisy and Donald Gaskin. He had answered an advertisement in the local paper offering a room and full board. At first he had thought that it was a stopgap. He'd had no intentions of stopping there for long. He had soon changed his mind.

Living with Daisy and Donald, within walking distance of the Arsenal, made it easy for him to get to work. Never in his wildest dreams had he thought that when war had been declared he would not be allowed to join the forces.

When it came to 'Reserved Occupation' and 'Exemption' top of the list had been Woolwich Arsenal and there was nothing that he and all the other men and women who were working there could do about it. Object and the powers that be would more than likely have you shot!

Daisy and Donald had five children. Three had married but were still living in the same street as their parents, the other two had moved away to live and work on the other side of the Thames. There had to be a good reason if any of them failed to turn up at their parents' home for Sunday tea with their offspring. The Gaskins had taken Tommy to their hearts and he had become number six when they were counting their children.

One thing that had pleased him a lot was the fact that Aunt Emma and Uncle Sam had got on so well with the Gaskins. It was a wonder they had! Two very different backgrounds. North Waltham was worlds apart from Woolwich! The Pearsons had only visited the Gaskins twice and then only for the day, but both families had kept in touch and Daisy and Donald, who had always told John that their street door was always open to him, had been really broken up when they learnt that John had been lost at Dunkirk.

Tom was on nights this week, he'd come off a shift at eight o'clock in the morning, was in bed by nine but found he was unable to sleep. Deciding it was useless to lie there tossing and turning, he went downstairs to find the house empty.

After he had washed, shaved and dressed he had gone to Covent Garden Market, to the only café for miles around where anyone could still get a half-decent breakfast.

Before pushing open the door, he paused to throw his half-smoked cigarette into the gutter. When at home in North Waltham he never smoked, never even gave it a thought. Most likely because nobody in the family smoked. He doubted that Aunt Em even possessed an ashtray.

Bit different in London though. Donald rolled his own and Daisy was hardly ever seen without a cigarette in her hand. That reminded him, Donald had said he was low on baccy, while he was in this part of the world he would pick up some tins of Old Holborn and a few hundred cigs. He'd plenty of cash on him but he wouldn't be too choosy when it came to which brand of cigs he was able to lay his hands on. Daisy wouldn't be fussy, she'd said only last night that the way this war was going with all its shortages, she'd likely end up smoking old rope before it finished.

Emily had seen Tom before he'd seen her and she lowered her head staring into her cup of coffee. It made no difference. Emily Pearson stood out in a crowd, she always had. Tom stood stock still, it was the first time that he had seen Emily in officer's uniform. It made a world of difference!

Her new cap lay on the table allowing her shiny auburn hair to show. Tom sighed, Emily had had such lovely thick long hair which John had always admired.

Army regulations had insisted that it be cut, the length now barely reached to the lobes of her ears. Her face was lightly made up and she was wearing lipstick. She looked so much older.

Tom walked quickly to her side, bent and kissed her cheek.

'Emily, what a lovely surprise. How come you're here by yerself?'

She grabbed hold of Tom's hand and squeezed hard, not letting go until he had slid in and was sitting down facing her.

'I've had a couple of hours to kill. Am waiting for a high-ranking official, have to stay in the vicinity. It gets a bit boring.'

'How will you know when he's ready to leave?'

'A runner will be sent, he knows where I'm waiting.'

'So, in the meantime you can sit and watch me eat my breakfast. I'll just go up to the counter an' give my order, no waitresses these days.'

'No,' Emily said laughing. 'There's a war on.'

'Really? I'd never have guessed. Want a coffee refill? Come to that have you had anything to eat?'

'Yes, I have eaten but another coffee would be nice.'

Tom stood up. 'All right, I won't be a minute.'

When they were both settled again Tom brought up the subject that Daisy had invited her to join the family for tea, if not on a Sunday on any day that she was free.

'You'll like Daisy and Donald,' Tom assured her. 'Very different to our mum and dad but still nice good people.'

'I think I have met them,' Emily said thoughtfully. 'It was when you first left the institution. Mum and Dad brought Bella and me up to London for the day. It was a long time ago but I'm sure we all got on well.'

'Mum and Dad have met them a few times over the years, they always keep in touch.' Tom stopped eating his breakfast and gleefully said, 'See what I meant when we were last home. *No eggs!* He picked up a slice of toast and bit into it. 'I suppose you get good meals in the mess?'

'Well, you suppose wrong! On offer for this mornings was porridge, so thick you could have plastered the walls with it, cold corned beef with bubble and squeak, toast and marmalade but no butter.' Emily recited the menu with a shudder.

'Three courses for breakfast. How the army live,' Tom mocked her.

Emily looked up as the door to the café opened. The runner

that Emily was expecting was there. He looked a bit like a telegram boy, except that he was older and his smart black uniform was adorned with quite a lot of gold braid.

Emily got to her feet and picked up her new cap that had a shiny peak. 'I have to go now, Tommy, love,' she said as she put her arms around his neck. 'I would like very much to come to tea with Daisy. I am off this Sunday if that is any good for you.'

'I'll make it good, don't you worry about that,' he told her, showing her that everlasting cheeky grin. 'I'll pick you up at Lyons Corner House, Marble Arch, at two o'clock. How will that suit?'

'Perfectly,' she said.

Then to the envy of all the other customers in the café, Tom kissed her gently on the cheek then drew her more tightly into his arms and held her close for a full minute.

'Bye, luv, see you Sunday, God bless.'

'You too, Tommy. Just watch what you're doing.'

Emily fastened the top button of her jacket, ran her hands over the back of her skirt that reached just below her knees, hoping that she hadn't creased it by sitting so long. Pulling her shoulders back and holding her head high she marched out of the café almost as if she were on the parade ground.

Tom half smiled as he watched. Before this war was half over he was afraid that Emily would lose a lot of the enthusiasm that she now had for military life.

It was the very next day that the Germans began their daylight raids over London. Everywhere the air was filled with the sound of screeching wailing air raid sirens. At first the Germans concentrated on British shipping in the English Channel but within hours they had switched to airfields in the South East where British defensive air strength was concentrated. England was at such a disadvantage. Many of our planes and young pilots had been lost in France whilst protecting the British withdrawal from Dunkirk. When the next raid began the Luftwaffe switched its targets yet again, this time making London their main objective. In spite of all the big guns and the endeavours of the soldiers that manned them on every common and in every park, together with efforts of the young British pilots, these attacks from the air had a catastrophic effect on the people. It had brought the war right into the major city of England and everyone single person knew without a doubt that this was just the beginning.

Tom's face was long and his voice low when he met up with Emily on Sunday afternoon. Their greeting was emotional and Tom swiftly assured her that Daisy was insisting that she came to visit them as long as she wouldn't mind the house being a bit mucky.

Emily laughed at his choice of words but quickly she asked, 'None of the family were caught up in the air raids, were they?' She didn't have to wait to hear his answer, the look on his face said it all. 'Oh, Tom, I am so sorry.'

He linked his arm through hers and pulled her close to his side before he answered. They had walked a few yards before he said, 'Daisy and Don's house only caught the blast, bad enough though there isn't a window that hasn't been broken, not one in the whole house and at least three doors were blown off their hinges.' Tom paused and gave Emily a wry smile. 'You'll never believe it but it is the dust that is worrying Daisy the most. Keeps on an' on that no matter how hard she tries she can't get rid of it.'

'How about her children? Mum told me that some of them rented houses in the same street as soon as they got married.'

'Yes, that's right, they did. Two of them lived right at the other end of the street and they copped it badly, not only have they lost their homes but most of their belongings as well.'

'Oh Tom, that is terrible! Were any of them hurt? And where are they all going to live now?'

'That is the most surprising thing, not a soul in the whole street was hurt, they've all got cuts and bruises from flying glass and everyone is coughing their hearts up, choking from all the old brick dust. Would have been a different story if the raid had been during the night. Wouldn't have been many survivors then!'

They finally reached the corner of Blackwell Street and Emily stood rooted to the ground. Tom tightened his hold on her because she was shaking from head to toe.

'Come on, luv, get a grip, this can't be the first bomb site you've set eyes on and it's a dead cert it won't be the last bloody one.' Tom's voice was loud and forceful and Emily couldn't make her mind up as to whether he was very angry or very sad. Probably a mixture of both.

There seemed to be an army of men all working together, boarding up the empty spaces where only days before starched white net curtains had hung at sparkling windows. Wherever possible doors were being put back. Rough voices were yelling, 'Sorry, missus, you'll 'ave t'use yer back door from now on, we gotta block this opening right up cos it ain't safe.'

Suddenly a small ragged boy with a mop of dark curly hair was tugging at Tommy's coat tails. ''Ello, Tommy, this mustn't 'alf 'ave bin a big bomb, don't yer think?'

Tom's voice was deadly serious as he answered. 'Young Charlie, I think yer dead right, it must have been a really whopping great bomb to 'ave done all this damage. Was you an' yer mum here during the air raid?' Tom had had a hard job to keep a straight face as he looked at Charlie's dirty face.

'Don't be so daft, Tom! Course we wasn't else we'd all be dead now, wouldn't we? We'd all gone up the market, a lot of us. Nanny Daisy took us but me mum came as well.'

'We're just about to go in an' see your nan,' Tom told him.

'Who's she?' Charlie was pointing towards Emily who was looking decidedly pale. 'Is she yer lady friend? I know you live 'ere all the time with me nan an' grandad but I ain't never seen 'er before.'

'Young Charlie, you know more than is good for you to know,' Tom said laughing but at the same time thinking what brave kids these were. They were playing in the rubble as if a bomb dropped on a factory just round the corner every day.

'Charlie's mother is one of Daisy's daughters,' Tom said by the way of an explanation. Turning to face Emily, he gasped. 'By the look of you, Emily, the quicker I get you inside the house the better.'

'Stop talking about it then, me lad, and act on it, or that young lady is going to fall at yer feet.' Daisy had just come out from the house and had heard what Tom had just said. Taking a good look at Emily she raised her voice and shouted, 'Don, get yerself out ' ere an' give our Tom a hand.'

The words were hardly out of her mouth when he came through the doorway. Despite the fact that Donald Gaskin had been a well known prizefighter in his younger days but was now carrying far more weight than was good for him, he was remarkably light on his feet.

Within minutes he and Tom had each taken an arm and were half-carrying Emily over the threshold of what was now Don and Daisy's war-torn home.

'Are you all right, Emily?' Daisy asked as the two men helped her to settle on the settee. 'I have given that couch a jolly good brushing an' as you can see I've covered it with a bedspread what was in the linen cupboard. I even ' ad to give that a damn good shaking cos the brick dust even got into there.'

'I'm fine now, Daisy, I'm sorry to have caused such a bother but I did think I was going to faint,' Emily said, smiling weakly.

'Well, we can't 'ave this,' Daisy told her firmly. 'As soon as you feel a bit better we'll see about getting the tea ready but how about you and me 'ave a cuppa to be going on with like?'

'That would be nice if you're sure you can spare the tea. I shouldn't want to feel that I was taking your rations an' Daisy, before you do get up, I want to thank you for inviting me.'

'I'm ever so pleased you could come, luv. Tomorrow I'm gonna write a letter to yer mum. I've got to let her know that none of us 'ave been really hurt in the air raids an' I'll also be able to tell her that you've been t'see us. Do you think she will be pleased?'

'Oh, Daisy, you know she will be. My dad will be too. They think a great deal of you an' your husband. They are so thankful that you've given Tom a home.'

'It works both ways, my luv, we love 'aving Tom 'ere. That reminds me, I'm gonna make us that brew an' you've no need to worry about it being our ration cos Tom brought me in two quarter-pound packets of the Co-op's ninety-nine tea only last night.' Daisy finished with a cheeky wink and a knowing smile but she added, 'With Tom it is a case of yer don't look a gift horse in the face, if yer get my meaning.'

Emily struggled to sit up, but she was smiling as she said, 'You sound like my mum does when Tom comes home. She always lets him know how grateful she is for what he brings home but she tells us her motto is ask no questions and you'll be told no lies.'

They both laughed knowingly. 'My kids all say thank the Lord for Tom. Now you lay back down again and I won't be two ticks.'

Daisy put the kettle on to boil and while she waited she walked up the passage. There was no front door now, or rather there was but it was leaning against the lamp post out in the street. She stepped out into what had been her lovely neat front garden with a hearth-stoned step at the top and bottom of the path which she'd been used to whitening every Saturday morning.

'Lost that job now,' she muttered, feeling bitter as she looked at the piles of debris scattered everywhere.

Half-turning she saw Tom and her Don were sitting side by side on the broken window sill. Don was smoking a roll-up and Tom was just holding a match to a tailor-made cigarette. He immediately held out the packet to Daisy; with a thankful sigh she took one, he struck another match and held it against her ciggie until the tip was glowing.

'You want any 'elp, gal?' Donald asked, twisting his bulk around so that he was facing his wife.

'No, yer all right, Don. I ain't started nothing yet, they'll be enough of them turning up before long an' I think I'll leave them to it. They can all muck in and get the tea. Meanwhile though me an' Emily are gonna 'ave a cup of tea on our own while we can still 'ear ourselves speak.'

'Do you think Emily is all right?' Tom asked Daisy showing how concerned he was.

'Tired I'd say. Late duties an' early morning calls, then the sight of our street. Just look at it! Sunday an' loads of men working, all the women in pinafores an' headscarves, with brooms in their hands, fighting a losing battle against the dust and rubble. Suppose it's brought it home to all of us that we really are at war. None of us are gonna like it, are we?'

'Yer right, Daisy. Everyone had been lulled into a false security an' these first daylight air raids have been a great shock. They've more or less brought the entire war on to our own doorsteps and it's been a rude awakening.'

'To each an' every one of us, Tommy mate. It's a bloody wake-up call an' we need no telling it'll get a damn sight worse before it's brought to an end.'

Emily looked over at Daisy and she was impressed. It

was amazing! Only three days ago German bombs had caused sheer devastation to the homes of people that lived only three streets away from the house in which they were now sitting. The devastation caused by the explosion had been widespread yet the indomitable spirit of Londoners still survived.

Daisy Gaskin was surely proof of that. This front room in which they were sitting was tidy even though the windows had been blown out and Daisy herself looked good. Her short fair hair had been washed three times (but Emily wasn't to know that) and her natural wavy hair was glossy. She was about five foot four, had a figure that many a young girl would be envious of and she was a smart dresser. She was wearing a navy blue skirt, a red jumper with beaded work running across one shoulder and a scarf of navy and red stripes hung loosely around her neck. These ordinary men and women were proving that aerial bombardment could destroy their buildings but not their courage.

By the time they had both drunk a cup of tea and Daisy had gone to great lengths to explain how many of her family would be turning up for their tea, Emily had visibly relaxed and was feeling that in Daisy she had found a really good friend.

Between three o'clock and five o'clock Emily had come to the conclusion that being here in Woolwich was like being in another world. The number of members of the Gaskin family that were constantly arriving seemed endless. Sons, daughters, in-laws, aunts and uncles and so many happy lovely children. She gave up trying to work out the individuals and trying to remember names was a nightmare. She sat there, letting the women wait on her, allowing the children to climb up to sit beside her and one pretty little blue-eyed pet to sit in her lap. Come teatime the food was everything that one could wish for, maybe not served as daintily as her mother would have managed but by God she felt privileged to be there. By the time Tom was ready to take her back to her makeshift barracks she felt she had made friendships that would last a lifetime. What she didn't know at that point in time was that during the dark days that were to follow she would be eternally grateful she had the Gaskin family to turn to.

Tom was standing out in the street waiting while Emily

was saying her goodbyes. 'God almighty, this will take for-flipping-ever,' Tom muttered as he watched Emily pick up yet another little girl to give her a kiss and a cuddle.

'Oi, Tom, before you go, will you tell me where you slept last night?' Young Charlie had forced his way to the front and was staring up at Tom, waiting for an answer.

'In my room upstairs,' Tom answered without stopping to think.

'Well, you are blooming lucky,' Charlie told him, sounding really serious.

Tom was baffled. 'Why d'you think I'm lucky? Is it because your nan's house only caught the blast and wasn't wiped out like some people's homes have been?'

'Something like that,' Charlie said, sounding doubtful. 'Our house wasn't damaged that much more than me nan's was, but me mum said the bedrooms weren't safe no more so she made our dad take us all down the tube station to sleep on the platform.'

There wasn't much that frightened Tom Yates but hearing what Charlie had just told him scared the living daylights out of him. Already he had heard tales of hundreds of Londoners taking their bedding down the underground stations to spend the night sleeping on the platform. Fancy being that deep down! Like being in the bowels of the earth. Supposing a bomb was to be dropped and it went straight down the tube. However would folk get out? Imagine that during an air raid a water main was hit and the underground station flooded. God Almighty, everyone down there would drown. It didn't bear thinking about. The thought not only frightened him, it positively terrified him.

Daisy Gaskin gently took hold of Emily's arm and turned her until she was facing her. 'Emily, I want you to think of this 'ouse as yer 'ome. Don't know if we'll be allowed t'stay 'ere, it depends on whether the landlord thinks the 'ouses are safe or not, but wherever we land up you'll always be welcome. Yer own family is miles away so if you don't think we are too rough an' ready you come 'ere whenever you ain't on duty. You'll always be welcome, you don't 'ave to wait for Tom to bring you. One of me boys will always see you get back safely, don't matter what time of the day or night it is, we'll be 'ere for you.'

Emily was choked. She had to swallow deeply before she was able to say, 'Thank you, Daisy'. Then looking around at all the grinning faces in the street she managed to smile and thank all of them.

'No thanks necessary, Emily,' Donald Gaskin said warmly. 'If you can't get over t'see us drop a card in the post t'tell us yer all right, it would set our minds at rest.'

'I will do that,' Emily promised as she stood on tip-toe to plant a kiss on the cheek of this gentle giant.

'Now can we finally go?' Tom asked. 'You've said goodbye t'half the population of Woolwich.' Yet it was Tom who turned and blew the final kisses to the group that had gathered outside the Gaskins's house.

Emily was exhausted, today had been something of an experience in so many ways but she wouldn't have missed it for the world.

Thirty-One

B ack at North Waltham, Emma still grew her vegetables and kept her poultry while Sam had more work than he could cope with on his own at the forge, yet he still did his fair share with the Home Guard.

However, things had changed in this quiet rural village. Despite the abundance of local produce it had become a time of austerity and shortages. An orange, banana, or a lemon had not been seen for almost two years.

Mr and Mrs Trenfield had moved out of the Big House and were now settled in a cottage that stood within the vast grounds that belonged to the house.

Servicemen of all nationalities, mostly officers, were now billeted within the grounds of their house. English, Canadian, American, and Australians. Two soldiers from the Royal Catering Corp, Jimmy Thomas and Mick Meade, were installed as chefs.

Nobody knew what went on up there. It was amazing how quickly makeshift quarters had been erected on the edge of the woods. Quite a large number of huts, a building with a corrugated roof, presumably for use as a dining hall, plus a block of toilets and washing facilities. No sooner were all the buildings up than a battalion from the Royal Engineers moved in.

There were not great numbers of military personnel billeted in the neighbourhood but enough to make the social life a bit more lively, at least for the few youngsters who were still living at home. Of course the extra Land Army girls who had been drafted in were glad of the company.

The Sun, which was the only other public house in the area, was glad of the extra trade, though the Fox remained the favourite meeting place for the locals. Nothing really exciting was provided in the way of entertainment, best-loved diversions were darts, dominoes and sing-songs.

Ted Andrews had brought his gramophone down from upstairs and one of the first records that he added to his collection had to be that of the forces' sweetheart, Vera Lynn singing 'We'll Meet Again'.

The British people had suffered two years of bombing raids from the Germans. One thing had been proved Arial bombardment may destroy buildings but it can't destroy people's courage.

On a Friday afternoon Emily had finished her tour of duty early and was driving the car back to a motor pool on the far side of Wimbledon Common when the air-raid siren had started to wail. It was unusual for a raid at this time of the day, but beside the everlasting night raids the Luftwaffe had also taken to coming over London at about eight o'clock in the morning, their targets being factories, just as all the employees were commencing their day's work. The results had been devastating.

Now it seemed the German's were once again changing their tactics. As the warning wail of the siren died down, Emily decided as she was out of the centre of London her first thought was to keep driving. She could get the car signed in and then take herself into the nearest air-raid shelter.

Stockwell was behind her, a straight run through Clapham, Balham and Tooting. Another fifteen minutes, twenty at the most and she would be home and dry.

It was as she drove passed Colliers Wood underground station that she felt the whoosh, then she heard an almighty bang followed by a terrific thud. The car seemed to rock from side to side and she lost control.

The next thing she heard was a voice urging her to open her eyes.

'Come on, love, open yer eyes an' tell us yer name.'

Much later when Emily had come to from the effects of the drug that a doctor had injected into her arm, the only thing she could remember was the ambulance men, one on each side of her, both being so kind and caring but she'd wondered at the time how come they both had such dirty faces.

Perhaps it was just as well that she hadn't been able to look in a mirror at the time. From the top of her head down to her feet she was covered in red-brick dust.

A bomb had fallen approximately two hundred yards in front of the car she had been driving, a tram had narrowly missed being a direct hit yet had still suffered the nearness of the terrific blast. Blown completely off the line, most of the long tram had lain on its side, the front two carriages buckled and twisted, hanging precariously over the edge of the huge crater where the bomb had hit the ground.

The vehicles that had been between Emily's car and the point where the bomb had fallen had all suffered damage, the drivers and passengers had terrible injuries, and it was into this pile of wrecked transport that Emily's car had been blown by the force of the blast. Surprisingly, amongst all the carnage there had been only one death, that of an elderly gentleman.

Emily had broken her left leg and badly sprained her right wrist. At first they had feared she might have suffered head injuries, across her forehead was a very deep gash and she had a lump the size of an egg behind her ear. Her face was so badly bruised the ambulance men had rightly said that she looked a bloody mess.

Within hours of Emily being taken to hospital Tom had been made aware of what had happened. Over a period of time, Tom had become known to her friends and colleagues as her step-brother. He was often around. They went dancing at Rainbow Corner in Piccadilly, the Lacarno in Streatham, and the Palais de Danse in Hammersmith. They didn't automatically arrive together but Tom claimed her for many dances and he kept a beady eye on her. It was well known that he did not like Captain Clive Beaumont, Emily's current boyfriend. "A chinless wonder" was how Tom described him.

Within hours of Emily being taken to hospital, Tom had been made aware of what had happened to her. During the days that followed he put in an appearance as often as he could and within the week he had borrowed a car, begged, bought or stolen enough petrol to get him down to North Waltham in order to let their mum and dad know that Emily had been hurt but that she was going to be all right.

Two members of the Big Brass Brigade had visited Emily informing her that she would be moved out of London as soon as arrangements could be made for her to be transferred to a

Military Hospital and later she would be allowed a period of convalescence.

Every member of the staff that had nursed Emily was sorry to see her leave. She was a lovely young lady was the general opinion. They did have another reason for not wanting her to go. It meant that they would no longer get to see her brother whom they had named 'the cheeky chappie'.

'He could make a dying man laugh,' the staff nurse had been heard to remark.

Whenever he'd visited Emily he had never arrived empty-handed. Packets of tea for the staff room, digestive biscuits and to the surprise of the two main nurses who were in charge of Emily he had handed each of them a flat packet with the instructions not to open it until they were at home.

Each had received a pair of nylon stockings! Never even heard of before this war had started, and even then it might have been years before English women had experienced the delight of wearing them if the Americans had not entered the war. The yanks were over here and they had brought delights such as nylons, spam and candy bars.

Emily was propped up in a bath chair, waiting for her transport. She was well wrapped up, a blanket over her legs which were stretched out in front of her, a pile of pillows behind her head and shoulders. She was pondering as to why this contraption should carry the name of bath chair and then she smiled to herself. It was made of wicker but its shape certainly resembled a bath which was just as well because her leg was still in plaster and her two crutches were lying beside her.

She heard the noisy laughter and knew Tom had arrived. It was five days since he had put in an appearance and she had begun to think that she wouldn't get to see him before she was moved.

The moment she clapped eyes on him she felt better. As usual he was nattily dressed. He was wearing a dark navy-blue suit, with a white polo neck jersey and well polished black shoes. His dark hair seemed thicker and even more wavy than ever, he was smiling but the smile did not reach his deep brown eyes. To look into them was to see that he had seen sights that he would rather forget but what worried her most was the fact that his skin had a yellowish tinge which was mainly due to working in munitions.

'So, my lady is off then, pity they couldn't find you a better carriage,' he teased before bending down to kiss her tenderly. 'I've got a couple of things to tell you,' he said, passing his hand wearily through his hair.

'Well, pull that chair up an' sit down, you might not have long before the ambulance arrives for me.'

'Daisy and Donald have been told their house is no longer safe to live in, the whole street has been condemned. Suppose we were lucky, they've been given a flat, quite a big one, two bedrooms so I was able to go with them.'

'You make it sound as those it's all done and dusted already,' Emily said, her voice holding a hint of suspicion.

'That's what I'm trying t'tell you, it has been over a month now. Seeing as how I was only a lodger the landlord didn't have to count me in when he was re-housing his tenants. We all think it could have been a whole lot worse. I gave yer mum an' dad Daisy's new address when I went down to tell them about you.'

'So am I going to be given the address?' Emily quickly asked.

'Of course you are, here . . .' He put his hand in the inside pocket of his jacket and withdrew two envelopes and gave them to Emily. 'Both envelopes are stamped an' addressed, you can write to Daisy as soon as you get settled. Now I've got some better news.'

'Hey, hang on a minute, you haven't told me where you, Daisy and Donald are living now.'

Tom looked at her in amazement. 'I know you got a bang t'yer head but I thought the doctor said there was no lasting damage, seems t'me he was wrong. I've just given you two stamped addressed envelopes and you're now asking me where we are living!'

Emily picked up one of the envelopes that were lying on her chest and read aloud. 'Garden flat, number 4, Manor Street, Clapham, London.'

'Yeah, we've had to move t'other side of the water. Bit further for me to get to work but that's the least of our problems.'

'Oh, Tom, I feel so helpless, I haven't even managed to use these crutches properly.'

'Emily, you've never been a moaner so don't start now. I've

been told it's a great place near Hythe where yer going, that's only four miles from Folkestone an' I will be able to visit you once in a while.'

'How come you get to know so much?'

'Cos I use me charm.' Tom grinned and lightly touched her cheek. 'The first time you are pronounced fit an' well you and me are going racing at Epsom, so be a good girl an' practice with those crutches every day.'

'Tom, are you really telling me that horse racing is still carrying on despite the fact that this country is at war?'

'You've got it in one, gal. Racing is a hobby of the rich and money talks all languages. Not every race course is still up and running but Epsom certainly is. So, shall we set a date now for our day at the races?'

Before Emily had a chance to answer Nurse Walker called from the doorway, 'Emily, your transport is here. Are you ready? Shall I tell the two men they can come through?'

Tom looked at Emily, and he called out, 'Please, can you give us just a couple more minutes?'

'Yes, that will be fine, one of the nurses has just given them a cup of tea, so take your time.' Nurse Walker smiled winningly at Tom.

Tom reached out and squeezed a tearful Emily's hand.

'Now don't get upset, Emily,' he pleaded. 'I will be in touch. The sister here is going to do her best to get me the telephone number of the home where you will be staying an' I've promised to let yer mum and dad have it. Meanwhile, luv, there was something else I wanted to say t'you but I've never got around to it.'

'So say it now,' Emily said, her voice breaking. 'I really don't want to be buried down in Kent. I did ask my commanding officer if I could be given a desk job. But no luck. I have been told I shall be given leave as soon as I am able to walk a bit better.'

Emily, you are not going t'prison for Christ's sake! Yer going to be well looked after but what I badly need to say t'you is about this Captain Beaumont you've been knocking about with.'

As best as she could Emily pulled herself up into a sitting position. 'What's Clive got to do with you?'

'In the ordinary run of things I'd say nothing. But Emily,

you and all your family mean the world to me. It was the biggest tragedy of our lives when John died, he meant so much to each an' every one of us. In different ways I'll grant you, but we all felt that you and John were made for each other. Tell me off for interfering if yer want, but don't get in over yer head with that clown.'

Emily found that she was smiling in spite of the fact that tears were trickling down her cheeks. 'We'll talk some more another time, meanwhile stop your worrying I won't get in over my head,' she quietly promised.

'You'll have different company where you're going, make a nice change, so make new friends, go to a lively pub with them, have a few drinks. There might even be fellas around who would be thrilled to have yer company, the sort that are already married who don't want any commitments. If yer do decide to have a bit of fun, just promise me you'll play it safe for a while.'

Emily felt she had never loved Tom more than she did at this minute. He was the absolute tops. No one could ask for better.

'Why is it, Tom, that you play it like you are cock-of-the-walk? Yet when I need you, you're are always there and sometimes – ' she paused and gave him a sweet smile – 'just sometimes you talk sense and let me know that there is a brain inside that scheming head of yours.'

Tom threw his head back and chuckled loudly.

'Well, my old luv, if you do decide to have a bit on the side, just make sure there's no involvement, an' for Christ sake if that chinless wonder does turn up just tell him where t'go. Who in heaven's name wants t'be seen with a bloke called Clive!'

At that moment two burly doctors and one young lady clad in a Red Cross uniform walked into the ward and cheerily told Emily it was time to go.

The nurse fussed around making sure the blanket was covering Emily's legs and checked her locker to see that she hadn't left anything behind.

Tom leant across the bath chair and held Emily very tenderly as he kissed the top of her head, but as he straightened up he looked at the three medical staff and back again to Emily. The roguish grin on Tom's face should have warned her that his parting words were going to be outrageous.

'Two males, two females, fair do's, long journey down to Kent.'

Emily punched his arm and heard him giggling as he walked the few yards to the corridor.

'Goodbye, Tom,' she called out in a soft voice.

He lifted his hand in a wave. 'Bye for now, Emily love, God bless you,' he replied.

Thirty-Two

The news that air raids over London had got worse was a blow to Emma. Much as it had been expected it was a hard truth to have to face. Even as Sam held her close her thoughts were of Emily and Tom, she knew she was being daft to keep tormenting herself but she couldn't help it. Over and over again she prayed that God would keep them both safe but she had enough sense to realize that parents everywhere were praying for their children's safety. Now that this terrible war was well under way there were countless tragedies every single day and it wouldn't only be faceless members of our armed forces who would be fighting the enemy.

It was three weeks now, since Tom had driven down from London to let them know that Emily was in a military hospital having been injured during an air raid, and the heartache that Emma was still feeling was written all over her face. She broke free from Sam's arms, lifted her head and looked at her dear husband. Her small homely features crumpled.

'Why haven't we heard from either of them? I just wish there was some way we could find out if they are safe; it is even worse because we are not allowed to visit Emily,' she said brokenly. Then the tears came and wouldn't stop.

'Emma, love, both Tom and I have explained that our Emily is not a civilian but in the army, a member of His Majesty's forces.' Sam lowered her down into an armchair wishing there was something he could say or do that would comfort her. Relief flooded through his veins when the sound of the letter box rattling could be plainly heard.

'Let's hope to God the postman had brought good news,' he said to himself as he went out of the room and up the passage to the front door. Within minutes Sam was back holding up two letters and a postcard. For a fleeting second

Emma allowed herself to smile although her eyes were red from weeping.

'Tell me quickly,' she pleaded.

Sam let out a long shuddering sigh. 'See for yourself. One card is from Emily but her writing is so bad I shall have to find my glasses before I can read it.'

'Give it here, Sam, I'll read it out.'

Dear Mum and Dad,

You are not to worry. I was caught up in a blast during an air raid and have sprained my wrist hence the bad writing. I also broke my leg but it is well on the mend.

This card is just to let you know that I really am all right. Some time ago Tom took me to tea with Daisy and Don, had a great time. What a big family!

I miss you both and Bella, love you all,
Emily

'Oh my dear God,' Emma muttered. 'She hasn't told us hardly anything we didn't already know. Where is she? I'd give anything to be allowed to visit her.'

'Come on now, Emma, try and think straight. Even if our Emily was in an ordinary hospital she certainly wouldn't be allowed to write the details on an open postcard and she has said her wrist is hurt which accounts for her scrawling writing.' Sam spoke bluntly because he didn't want Emma to go to pieces. 'Just be grateful that she has managed to send us a card, surely that fact alone is reassuring. You feel a bit better now, don't you?'

'I suppose so,' Emma agreed but the words were said without conviction.

Sam sighed, bewildered as what to do for the best. 'I can see this letter is from Tom so I'll open that one, shall I?' he asked, doing his best to sound cheerful as he pulled out just a single sheet of notepaper.

'He says he is fine, fit and as well and when he last saw Emily she was doing all right, learning to walk with crutches. He hopes we are well and promises to see us again soon. Sends his love to Bella and to both of us. There are loads of kisses on the bottom of the page.'

Emma took a clean handkerchief from her pocket and wiped it round her face before asking, 'What about the other letter?'

'I'm not sure who it's from,' Sam answered, turning the envelope over and over in his hands.

'Only one way to find out. Here, let me open it,' Emma said quickly.

Sam's breathing was laboured as he watched his wife tear open the flap of the letter and take out a couple of sheets of notepaper, glancing quickly at the bottom line she happily exclaimed, 'Why it's from Daisy, isn't that kind of her to take the trouble to write to us?'

Sam had to bite his tongue. He was sorely tempted to say, read it first before you decide what about her intentions. However, minutes later he let out a long deep breath, his Emma was smiling and for that fact alone he was deeply grateful as he watched her stand by the window and begin to read the letter out loud to him.

Dear Emma and Sam,

You will have heard by now that the German planes have been over London lately and I have to say that most of us were taken by surprise. As you know there are three streets grouped together where we live and the bloody Germans flattened one of them to piles of rubble. The other two, which included ours, suffered a load of damage mainly from the blast but thank the good Lord nobody was killed or even seriously hurt every one of us is safe and well. So there is no need for you to go worrying yourself about us.

My Don says the Germans weren't very good at hitting their targets cos the docklands weren't badly damaged, at least not this time.

Tom brought your Emily to tea with us a few Sundays back. Lovely gal she is, no wonder you are so proud of her. I think every member of our mob turned up and I was afraid it might have all been a bit too much of a good thing for Emily but no she took to the little uns like a duck does to water and as for the grown ups they thought she was the bees knees especially our lads when they found out she drives a flash car.

Charlie my grandson, he's eight, he eats his tea wearing Emily's chauffeur cap. Cheeky little sod, he is, but downright adorable with it, bit like your Tom.

Now, Em, I don't want you to take no offence but I've told your Emily that as you and her dad are a long way away she is to think of our house as her home. Will be somewhere for her to come when she is off-duty when she gets out of that hospital and we will see she is all right and make her welcome if that is OK by you.

Got to go now. Mouths to feed. Will write again soon. You write to us, tell us what's going on in your sleepy village.

Bye for now, God bless, love from Daisy, Don and family xxx

Sam took the letter from Emily's hands and laid it down on the table before taking her into his arms and holding her close. As always she felt the depth of his love for her, and she was deeply moved. Sam was such a good man, a good husband and a wonderful father and she had loved him for all these years. He was still a big, burly, good-looking man, well over six foot still, with a good head of hair that only recently had begun to show a few grey hairs at his temples. He never seemed to change, he only seemed to get better as he got older. Sometimes she found herself worrying about the fact that it was only she that was looking old, shrinking in height and putting on more weight as the years passed.

'Sam, I am sorry, I just can't help worrying about our Emily and Tom being up there in London, not safe at all. I love you an' our children so much,' she said, her voice breaking. 'I know I should be grateful that our Bella is safe here an' we see her every day.'

Sam could feel the tension in her body, and he was shocked. 'Hey! You mustn't worry so much. Come on I'm going to take you back upstairs an' we'll have a lie down together.'

'Sam, it is only mid-morning and I have loads of jobs I should be getting on with,' Emma protested, but only feebly.

Sam guided her ahead of him and when they reached their bedroom he half-pushed Emily down to sit on the edge of the bed. Then he knelt down and took her slippers off before pushing her skirt well up beyond her knees. He slowly rolled each stocking down until he was able to remove them both. Next he slid his brawny arms beneath her knees and lifted her up in to his arms. Looking down into her face he began to talk. 'The luckiest day of my life was when I met you, Emma. If we both died tomorrow I'd say we'd had a wonderful life together.'

'You shouldn't talk about either of us dying.' Emma was really shocked, but Sam silenced her by gently covering her lips with his own. At the same time he laid her down on their big wide bed. Slowly and carefully he began to undress her.

'Your turn.' He smiled as she sat up. He held his arms up in the air like a young school boy as she pulled his jersey up and over his head. For both of them it was as if time stood still. Sam explored his wife's body as if he were rediscovering it, which indeed he was. When he stopped Emma drew his arm around her shoulders and nestled up against his brawny bare chest. It was some time before they began to make love and when they did there was nothing hurried about it. They made love tenderly, softly, lovingly, as had always been their way, and then they lay side by side, talking in the safety of the warmth of their bedroom. Sunlight, reflecting through the trees outside in the garden, shone on to Emma's grey hair and she sighed happily as Sam put out a finger to trace the outline of her chubby face, down her cheek, on to the lips of that dear soft mouth.

'Umm,' she murmured, enjoying his touch. 'You always make me feel so special when you do that.'

'You are special, very special, my darling, always have been, always will be. Do you feel better now?'

'Yes, yes of course I do,' she said smiling.

'Well, Emma, I want you to try an' remember we have each other. God willing, this war won't last too much longer an' we'll get our family back together again, then we'll all be happy for many years to come.'

'Do you promise?'

Sam looked down and saw there were still tears in her eyes and was deeply moved when one watery tear trickled down over her cheek. 'I can't promise,' he softly answered, wiping away the tear with the tip of a finger.

'Why not?'

'You know why not,' he chided gently. 'We none of us can see what the future holds, but what you need to keep hold of is the fact that we do have each other, three wonderful children and so many good friends in our lives.'

'In other words I should count my blessings.'

'Yes, my love, but I think you nearly always do, it is just that hearing of the air raids upset you and our Emily being hurt and us not able to visit her, but we've sorted things out now, haven't we?'

'Yes, thanks to you Sam, I'm all right now.'

Content now to be silent, they lay awhile together. It was a time of quietness in a love that had survived the years and was still deep and fulfilling. One of those rare moments that each of them would relish to the end of their days.

After a while Emma raised herself up on her elbows and as she looked out of the window she caught a glimpse of sunshine breaking through the clouds. Good gracious, she thought smiling, it seemed to signify what Sam had been trying to say to her. He's right, she told herself. We *are* so lucky, we do have each other and three wonderful children who mean the world to us. She turned her head and looked down at her husband, and her heart lifted. His eyes were closed, his breathing quiet and regular. 'Bless him,' she murmured as once more she snuggled down beside him and began to daydream.

In spite of all the horrors this war will bring it surely must come to an end one day. Then there would be so much to look forward to. Both their girls and Tom would almost certainly get married. She knew how heartbroken Emily had been when John had died and at that time she had held her in her arms as Emily had declared that there would never be another man for her. She had gently chided her never to say never. Thoughts of the children getting married had her heart singing, there would be grandchildren. Grandchildren who would most certainly feature largely in her and Sam's lives as they grew older. Oh, if only! She sighed longingly.

Emma was well aware that there would be many more heartaches before this war did come to an end, but end it undoubtedly would and then all the good things that she and Sam longed for would start to happen.

Suddenly she felt better than she had for days and she made a resolution to find the courage that would enable her to hang on to these wonderful thoughts and to believe with all her heart that sometime in the future they would eventually start to happen because she and even Sam wanted it all so badly.

Sam stirred and opened his eyes. Reaching out he took hold

of her hand and to his delight she lowered her head and kissed him full on the lips. 'I've been wondering how many grand-children you and me might possibly end up with. Got any idea, have you?'

Thrilled to wake up and find Emily in such a light-hearted mood, his answer was to lean towards her and gently pat her rosy cheeks.

'You haven't answered me, Sam.' Her voice was soft in his ear.

'Don't you think you are putting the cart before the horse, neither one of our brood has brought anyone home or even asked our approval yet.'

Turning her head she looked down at him. 'Give them time, I'm thinking of the future of the next phase in our life which is to come. You do want grandchildren, don't you, Sam?'

'Nothing would give me greater pleasure, but aren't you jumping the gun?'

'I suppose I am a bit, but it will happen.'

Sam watched her smile broaden and knew that for the first time in days she was happy and content. They kissed again and there was tenderness in their embrace.

'Whatever comes we'll face it together,' Sam promised. 'Get back under the covers an' we'll have another half an hour.'

More easy in her mind now, Emma snuggled back under the bed covers. For a while she let her mind roll back to when John and Tom had first stayed with her and Sam in 1930. It was amazing how they and the girls had immediately taken to those two undernourished ragged looking boys. What were her feelings now? If she had given birth to each one of them she couldn't feel more close to them or love them more. God had seen fit to take John but the years that he had been one of her children was a phase in her life that she wouldn't have missed. To have been loved by John as a mother and to love him as one of her own had been a priceless experience.

It had been an amazing episode in her life.

For now, though, it was as if life was on hold. It was a time to be brave and pray that as soon as this war did come to an end, families could move on, begin to live their lives once again for if any lesson had been learnt it was that family love and family ties were worth so much.

Thirty-Three

Having spent six weeks in a military convalescent home Emily had now been granted fourteen days leave. She had received travel warrants and had intended to go straight home to stay with her parents.

Tom had had other ideas. 'There is no way you are travelling down to North Waltham by train. You may have discarded those crutches but you're not much better walking with a stick, you are more than likely to end up breaking the other leg. I shall drive you home but not before I have kept a promise I made to you some time ago.'

Arguing with Tom had been useless and at this moment as she stood by his side she decided she hadn't felt so happy in a very long time.

'You'd never believe there was a war on,' Emily remarked to Tom as she gazed across the wonderful green turf. Then pointing with her forefinger she asked, 'Is this where the famous Derby is run?'

'Yes, it is, and the Oaks, but most of all I'd love to bring you and Bella here when it's Ladies Day. Now, that is a sight worth watching,' Tom told her with a wicked glint in his eye.

'The sight you're referring to, would that be the horses running or the ladies?'

'The ladies don't run,' Tom said, deliberately being contrary. 'They grace the turf, the Royal Enclosure, the licensed bars an' allow the general public to view their beautiful clothes and in particular the hats that they wear.'

'I have read about this event that takes place once a year on Epsom Race Course but not for a moment did I think it would still be going on,' Emily said thoughtfully.

'My dear Emily, when will you learn that there is one law for the rich and another one for the poor? Horse racing is a sport of kings, the little man likes his flutter but that counts for nothing, it's money all the way along the line that keeps horse racing on the go.'

Without warning Emily started to laugh and within seconds Tom thought she was hysterical. 'Emily, give over love, everyone is beginning to look at you.'

Emily withdrew a lace-edged handkerchief from the pocket of her linen suit and did her best to stifle her mirth by holding it across her mouth.

Tom took hold of her arm and turned her until she was facing him. He didn't say a word, just raised his eyebrows and looked at her dubiously.

It was still minutes before Emily could compose herself and by then Tom had led her towards a very large tent from which refreshments were being served.

He looked around, the place was pretty full but he spied a vacant table and using a bit of force he edged Emily towards it, making sure she was sitting down he propped her stick up against the wall before he asked, 'Is it safe to leave you?'

She looked up at him and for one awful moment he thought she was going to start laughing all over again. 'What would you like? Tea, coffee or a fruit squash, I don't think you had better have any of the hard stuff . . . not yet anyway.'

'Coffee, please, Tom. With cream if it is available.'

Tom didn't answer her but as he walked to the serving counter and saw the amount of food that was on offer and also the varied choice, he thought again how anything was available if you had the money.

He came back to Emily bearing a tray set for two with a silver coffee pot and a silver jug that contained really thick fresh cream. And wonder upon wonder there was also a plate of savoury pastries!

The silence, born out of wonderment of all that was going on around them, was not broken until Emily had poured the coffee, passed a plate and a serviette to Tom and helped herself to the unexpected treats.

They ate and drank without talking until they were on their second cup of coffee and the entire plate full of savouries had been eaten.

'Isn't it about time you told me what brought on that fit of hysterics?' Tom asked sounding much more stern than he had meant to.

Emily did her best to look composed. 'I guess it was the events of yesterday leading up to today, I'm sorry Tom but even you have to agree that I am entitled to be utterly amazed.'

'Why, what's so out of the ordinary that I should bring you to Epsom Race Course?'

'Well, let's start at the beginning, you turned up in Hythe yesterday afternoon about four o'clock, your friend drove you down in his van an' you introduced him to me as Bert Fisher. I hadn't a clue as to how you knew him or where he got petrol from to be driving a van.'

Tom went to speak but Emily held up her hand. ' Please Tom, let me get this sorted out in my head otherwise I'm likely to have another fit of giggles.'

'Bit more than the giggles,' he murmured, 'but carry on.'

'Bert took us to the flat that Daisy and Donald have been compelled to move into, Donald immediately told me I was to stay two nights with them. Daisy had dinner all ready and about half past eight to nine o'clock we all walked up Manor Street, God knows how many of Daisy's family turned up. Anyway we all spent the rest of the evening in the pub. Great night. Singing all the old London songs with a few Irish ones thrown in for luck, old women getting up to dance. For a while I think we all forgot that there was a war on.

'I don't know where Donald slept but I slept with Daisy in their big double bed. Hardly had we got to sleep, at least that is how it seemed to me, than you were hollering that we had to catch a bus outside Clapham Common Station in forty minutes. We made it and I bet the people that had to go upstairs on the bus must have been very grateful that the weather has turned out so well because the bus didn't have a roof to it.'

By now it was Tom that was grinning from ear to ear. 'It's an open-top bus, you silly cow, ain't you never seen one before?'

'Tom! I hear you swear often enough but never at me.' Emily was laughing again.

'Calling you a cow ain't swearing, Christ knows you've got enough of them roaming the fields back home, beautiful creatures they are.'

'Tom, don't change the subject, I haven't finished recalling the events that preceded my arrival here at Epsom Race Course.'

'Well, Emily, you sit an' do all the recalling you like but I'm going to get a bet on with Joey Brown, the most honest bookie on the course.'

Emily looked horrified. 'Are you saying that every other bookmaker here today is a scoundrel?'

Tom had just lit a cigarette, something he rarely did when in Emily's company, but he was nearly on his way to place a bet when she had dropped her bombshell. He almost choked. Coughed a few times to clear his throat and then he glared at her.

'Will you keep your voice down if you're going to make accusations like that. In all probability Joey Brown is not even his real name, he trades under it an' saying that he is the most honest bookie on the course is in no way damaging to his fellow bookies. It is a joke. When yer walking about later on, try reading some of the placards the bookies have put out. Each and everyone needs a trading license to set up a pitch at any race course, not any old Tom, Dick or Harry can call himself a bookmaker and take bets.'

'Different world here, isn't it?' Emily sounded as if she was out of her depth.

Immediately Tom was sorry he had scolded her, holding out his hand to her, he said, 'Come with me, I'll put my bets on an' then I'll show you where the tote is and tell you how it works. You can bet as little as two bob on the tote.'

Emily almost asked how much money did you need to bet with a bookmaker, but she decided she had shown her ignorance of the racing fraternity quite enough already.

Two hours later Emily had forgotten that she was a new girl at this lark and was thoroughly enjoying herself. She had had a two-way bet on four races, losing on two, winning on two and was richer by four pounds and six shillings.

She kept losing sight of Tom and when she did catch a glimpse of him he was always surrounded by half a dozen men, all of whom were engrossed in their racing catalogue. Although he had kept an eye on her, appearing at her side from time to time, it wasn't until mid-afternoon that she saw him making his way through the crowds.

While she waited she took off her close-fitting hat and ran her fingers through her thick long chestnut hair. It had been piled up under her hat and clipped in place on top of her head, but a few strands had come adrift. Emily pulled them up and used two side combs which she took out of her handbag to secure them. She saw that Tom was within yards of her now and she gave him a big smile.

Tom was well turned out today. He was certainly a good-looking young man. Tall and broad shouldered, his dark brown suit fitted him well, it certainly hadn't been brought from a fifty-bob tailor! No, this suit had been tailor-made for Tom and she wondered how he had come by a length of such good quality cloth. His dark hair always tended to be wavy but today it was smoothed down and parted in the middle. He smiled back at her, exposing a row of even white teeth. Only one thing was wrong and it made her sad to admit it. Tom had just turned twenty-two, but he looked closer to thirty and his skin did not have a healthy glow. It was a problem which stemmed from him working with munitions.

'Drink?' he asked.

Emily nodded. 'What time is the bus due to leave?'

Tom looked at his watch. 'Within the next hour, which is unfortunate because I wanted to buy you dinner in the Spread Eagle. It is a great pub but a few miles from here and if we don't go home on the bus we came on we are going to have one hell of a job to get home tonight. We can have a snack with our drink an' we should be home soon after eight. If Daisy hasn't saved us any dinner I could always go an' fetch us fish an' chips. What d'you think?'

'That we would be mad to let the bus go an' leave us behind, public transport being what it is.' She shrugged her shoulders.

'Good, we'll agree on the bus then,' Tom said as she held on to his arm and hobbled to the refreshment marquee. He saw her seated comfortably and took himself off to the bar. He hadn't asked what she would like to eat or drink but it wasn't long before Tom was back, he had a pint of Guinness for himself and a tall glass of sparkling wine for her. 'I've ordered fresh salmon sandwiches with salad for both of us. Is that all right?'

'Absolutely fine.' She smiled her thanks.

'How did you do overall on the tote?' Tom asked, grinning broadly.

'I lost an' I won.'

'Don't we all!' Tom wisely declared.

Emily couldn't hold out. 'I'm better off by four pounds an' six shillings though,' she told him cautiously.

'There's another two races yet, though. I think they've just closed the betting on one of them while we've been sitting here.'

Emily had heard an announcement but not exactly what was being said. 'Tom, if you want to go an' place a bet I'll be fine sitting here. Are they going to bring our sandwiches or do I have to go an' fetch them?'

'It's all right, Emily, I was going to skip this race anyway, but I am debating whether I should risk all on the last race or not. And, no, you haven't to go an' fetch our food, they will bring it to us.'

'Would you really risk everything you've won today on the last race?' she asked, letting her curiosity get the better of her.

'How do you know that I have won anything?'

'Because you said you were debating whether or not to risk it all on the last race an' if you had been losing the whole time there wouldn't be anything to risk. So have you counted your winnings?'

Tom shook his head, feeling thoroughly bewildered. Emily had soon cottoned on to this racing lark. 'That, Emily Pearson, is not something for you to worry about. Just wait an' see. If tonight I go for fish an' chips an' I come back with one piece of fish between the two of us, you'll know I made the wrong decision.'

'That's me told,' Emily said beneath her breath, but she was thankful that at that moment a young tall lad, dressed in black from head to toe and wearing a white bibbed-apron, laid a tray bearing their food in the centre of the table.

Tom gave him a ten bob note saying, 'Here, son, have a drink on me.'

'Thank you, sir.' The young lad beamed.

'My pleasure, lad,' Tom said

Emily was again telling herself Tom must have had a good day.

Tom was the first to finish eating. He smiled at Emily. 'If you want to go an' have a wash an' brush up an' then make yer way to the bus I'll meet you there. I'm going to place a last bet so don't hurry, take yer time.'

A lot of the passengers on the bus must have been Tom's workmates because on seeing Emily arrive at the bus on her own, several of the females, both young and old, called out to her.

'Tom in trouble, is he?'

'Caught passing dodgy fivers, and now he's down the cop-shop.'

'Not our Tom. He'd fall down a ruddy sewer an' he'd come up smelling of roses.'

'No, more than likely he's won a hefty bundle an' 'ad it away on his toes. Woolwich Arsenal won't be seeing his arse for dust if he 'as.'

It was all good-hearted fun and she thought how friendly they all were as two very pretty young girls stepped one each side of her and helped her up on to the high step of the coach.

However Emily gave a hefty sigh of relief when Tom did finally appear because the bus driver had already switched on the engine ready to leave.

Seated side by side on the bus, Emily was feeling very tired. Her head drooped and Tom twisted her round so that her head could rest on his shoulder.

As soon as he thought she was comfortable he put his hand into his inside pocket and pulled out some black and white five-pound notes which were folded in half.

Lowering his voice to little more than a whisper, he said, 'I had been given a tip for that last race, it was a rank outsider, the odds were fantastic, so I put a fiver on the tote for you. Here buy yerself something nice.'

Emily didn't want to move. Her bad leg was aching like hell yet she felt really comfortable leaning against Tom. She raised her eyes to meet him, and softly she said, 'What have I ever done to deserve you?'

'Here . . .' He slipped the notes into her jacket pocket. 'Close yer eyes now, luv, I'll wake you up when we arrive at Clapham Common.'

Tom could tell by her regular breathing that Emily was asleep, and it was only then that he answered her question.

'You and yours took John an' me in when no one else wanted t'know. You gave us both a home an' a family that loved an' cared for us. And that, Emily, my love, is some-thing that all the money in the world couldn't buy. When this war finally comes to an end it will be pay-back time an' then I fully intend to do my best to care for Mum and Dad an' you an' Bella. To make sure that none of you ever wants for anything.'

His vow had been said in such earnest that Emily would have needed no telling that he meant every single word.